A Matter of WORDS

Published by Scout Media
Copyright 2015
ISBN: 978-09913091-84

Cover: **Brendon Gazzard**

Visit: **www.ScoutMediaBooksMusic.com**
for more information on each author and future anthologies

Table of Contents

1. Brian Paone – *Outside of Heaven* … 1

2. S.M. – *The Face* … 39

3. Randy Blazak – *Elvis is My Rider* … 45

4. Chuck Mosley – *Mark Bowen* … 81

5. Kim Loraine – *Hungry: The Memoir of Abby Snow* … 87

6. Leah Lederman – *Lithium Sandwich* … 109

7. Douglas Esper – *My Wife's Favorite* … 115

8. Travis West – *The Most Beautiful Boy* … 137

9. Michelle Jillian Bailey – *Roadkill* … 147

10. Richard Lopez Salgado – *The World From Below* … 157

11. Stephanie Rogish – *Saturday Night* … 165

12. Lee Diogeneia – *Consumed* … 181

13. Jacob Prytherch – *The Uncanny Mr. Bones* … 185

14. A Lee Ajang – *Twin Lanes* … 209

15. Steven Hartov – *Dead Drop* … 213

16. Faith Cooper – *Aurora* … 241

17. Alfred Balcon – *L'ultima Raccolta Dei Rifuti: The Ultimate Garbage Collection* … 249

18. Cynthia Paone – *If This Color Could Tell a Story* … 263

19. Stephen Rhodes – *Just Another Day in Hell* … 267

20. Dan Golden – *It's Yours* … 291

21. Alex Lonchiadis – *Vampire Coyote* … 299

Outside of Heaven

Brian Paone

As Cecil subconsciously rubbed his bandaged left hand, he could feel the low throb of pain start again. This time it didn't appear that any blood was seeping through the gauze. He gripped the steering wheel a little tighter with his better hand and stole a glance at his wife.

"Everything okay?" Grace asked her husband.

"Everything's great."

The upstate New York sky was an explosion of orange, littered with wisps of gray clouds. The car's top was down; the air grew crisper by the minute.

Grace reached over and placed a hand on his thigh. Cecil tried to conjure a halfhearted smile.

"How's your hand?" she asked.

Cecil opened and closed his fist to prove that movement had not been compromised.

"Feels much better today."

"Do you need to check in with work while we're gone?"

"Nah. I took care of all the workman's comp paperwork when I left the hospital last night. I made sure that there's nothing hanging over our heads during our little getaway."

Grace smiled and removed her hand from Cecil's leg. "This trip will be good for us."

Cecil shot her a look out of the corner of his eye. He hadn't expected her to talk about it so soon after getting on the highway.

"I think so too," Cecil replied. "Everything will be different when we return."

"A clean slate. That's what I want," Grace added.

Cecil nodded. That's all he wanted too. This vacation was going to represent locking away forever the skeletons in their matrimonial closet. He just hoped that he was able to truly forget about Lucas What's-His-Name. Cecil had already proved to Grace that he had the ability to *forgive*, but he wasn't too sure about the *forgetting* part.

"We're about four hours from Toronto," Cecil said. "Any objection to stopping in Rochester for the night? We can leave first thing in the morning and be in Toronto before anyone stops serving breakfast."

"That's fine with me," Grace answered. "That'll give me a chance to rewrap your hand in some fresh bandages."

"Plus those clouds don't look promising."

Grace looked up and could see the orange and red sunset being consumed by sinister-looking clouds.

"You might want to pull over to put up the top before it starts raining," she suggested.

Cecil grunted. He knew she was right, but a piece of him wanted to defy her suggestion and keep driving with the top down just on principle. It came from a small place inside him that still hung on to some residual anger about Grace and Lucas What's-His-Name. Cecil was honestly trying to let go of the anger that reared its head whenever he thought about what his wife and her high school sweetheart had done together behind his back over the past few weeks.

He pretended that he hadn't heard his wife's suggestion and, instead, stepped on the gas pedal a little harder.

— · · —

Ninety minutes later, Cecil and Grace entered Rochester just as the skies opened up. Cecil caught Grace shooting him a glare as if to say, *Now will you listen to me?* Cecil knew she never would have said it aloud. Not with the frail balance that their marriage was in at the moment. Grace probably felt that she needed to walk on eggshells for a little bit longer, until their lives returned to normal, and this whole Lucas What's-His-Name mess was behind them.

Cecil's stubbornness cracked, and he slowly pulled the car to the highway's shoulder. When the car came to a stop, he pressed the button on the vehicle's console that controlled the convertible's top and reached back to help guide the roof down. After the top was locked and secured, Cecil carefully drove into the flow of traffic.

Cecil opened and closed his fist once more to alleviate the itchiness and discomfort that he felt. Grace noticed that he was in pain again.

"We can stop now," she said sympathetically.

Cecil didn't want to admit defeat or look like less of a man in front of his wife—especially when he believed that image of him may have attributed to Lucas What's-His-Name worming his way back into Grace's heart—but Cecil knew that stopping for the night was inevitable at this point.

"That might be a good idea," he answered.

Cecil steered the car onto the next exit ramp that boasted hotels and restaurants. He stopped the car at the bottom of the ramp, looking left and right.

"Which way do you think?"

"Umm … go left."

"Left it is," he said, forcing a smile.

Ahead of them were a multitude of gas stations and fast-food restaurants.

"There's a sign for a hotel," Grace said and pointed toward the right side of the road. "The Blue Leaf Motel."

"Really? Sounds seedy. There are no signs for a DoubleTree or a Marriott?" Cecil joked.

"I think it sounds quaint."

"*Quaint* is how I would describe someplace like Miss Sally's Bed-and-Breakfast. The Blue Leaf Motel sounds like our room will be sandwiched between a crack whore and a serial killer."

Grace playfully poked Cecil in the ribs.

"Where's your sense of adventure, Mr. Man?" she asked, mimicking Kathy Bates in Cecil's favorite Stephen King film.

"All right, all right. You know I'm a sucker for Annie Wilkes."

Cecil turned onto Yuka Street.

"Right there. Past the church," Grace said.

Cecil drove by the white church and churchyard that abutted the parking lot of the Blue Leaf Motel.

"Looks harmless enough," Grace said as they pulled into the parking lot. "I think it'll be—"

The sound of rain hitting the top of the car was so deafening that Cecil couldn't hear the rest of her comment. It sounded like bullets on tin. He frantically turned on the windshield wipers to their maximum speed.

"Can you see anything?" Grace asked.

"Barely," he answered, trying to navigate the car into the entrance of the parking lot.

"Just be careful please."

Cecil flexed his hand to relieve some of the pressure while he safely parked in the nearest empty spot.

"Should we wait it out?" Grace asked.

"We're only fifteen yards from the front door. Who's the one without a sense of adventure now?"

"Adventure is one thing. Getting my hair wet is another."

Cecil chuckled. Little moments like these were when he knew, down to his core, that Grace was the only woman for him. In these little moments, Cecil felt confident about not leaving Grace when she had come clean about Lucas What's-His-Name.

"All right, princess. We'll give it a few minutes."

Cecil shut off the engine, and the wipers came to a halt. The outline of the hotel's sign became increasingly fuzzier through the stream of water that continued to pour down the windshield.

"The sky must be broken," Grace said, looking at the clouds to find any sign of reprieve from the torrential downpour.

Cecil adjusted his bandage again and squinted through his side window at the cars sprawled out in the parking lot.

"Well, that's encouraging," he said with a hint of sarcasm.

"What's that?"

"There seems to be more broken-down cars here than working ones. You certainly have a knack for picking winners."

"Oh, get off my back," Grace said playfully.

Cecil studied the handful of cars that had been abandoned in the lot; some cars had flat tires; some cars looked so rusted that they might turn to dust the moment anyone tried to open its doors; and one car not only was propped up on cinder blocks but had a family of Triffids growing underneath the hood. Still the Blue Leaf Motel was a place to lay their heads for the night and would give him an opportunity to put a new dressing on his wound.

A gust of wind rocked the car back and forth.

"I don't think it's letting up," Cecil said. "I'm ready to make a run for it."

"Are you sure you're okay?"

"It's my hand that has the stitches, not my feet."

"Okay. I'll race ya. On four … Ready?"

"I was born ready."

Grace rolled her eyes, grabbed the door handle, and yelled, "Four!"

Cecil hadn't even realized he had been hoodwinked until Grace slammed her door shut, leaving him alone inside the car. He shook his head and jumped from the vehicle. He dug his heels into the pavement, trying to catch up to his wife. The rain doused them both with buckets of water, making it hard for him to see without wiping his eyes every few seconds. It was important for him to beat Grace to the lobby doors. It would be another check mark on his "man card." Any opportunity he might have to show her that he was just as testosterone-filled as Lucas What's-His-Name was a moment Cecil had to seize and conquer.

Grace was fast, but not fast enough.

As Cecil sped past her, he timed his footfalls accurately to make sure he landed square in a massive puddle, ejecting a perfectly aimed splash of water all over his wife. Grace pumped her fists in the air at him. Cecil was laughing so hard he almost tripped over his own feet.

When Cecil stopped at the front entrance, he smiled triumphantly at his wife. She still had to cover another few yards. As soon as they stumbled into the lobby together, there was an instant puddle under their feet before the door even closed behind them.

"Nasty out there," the man working the reception desk said.

Cecil shook his head like a dog. "You can say that again."

"What can I do you folks for?"

"We'd like a room," Grace answered.

"You're in luck. This is our slow season. How long will you be staying with us?"

"Just the night," Cecil answered.

"All righty. If you could sign in and pay, please. We only accept cash here."

The man slid a blue-colored piece of paper toward Cecil with today's date, *Sunday, May 4*, handwritten across the top.

Grace reached for a pen and jumped back when a cat landed on the man's desk and knocked an acrylic container of tiny rubber bands to the floor. Grace covered her chest with her hand.

"My God. That cat almost gave me a heart attack."

The man behind the counter chuckled. "Sorry about that, ma'am. Don't pay Lucy any mind. She's scared of her own shadow."

The cat scampered through a door into another room and disappeared. Grace reached for the pen again and signed the blue paper with their names.

"Alice!" the man yelled into the room behind him. "Could you grab the keys to eighteen, please?"

A moment later a young girl emerged from the back room with a key attached to a wooden board. Alice handed the key to Cecil.

"My name's Gabriel, and this is my daughter, Alice. Don't hesitate to ask for anything you need. My desk is extension 2570 from the phone in your room. We'll be here for a few more hours before heading home."

"Thank you so much, Gabriel. What time is check out?"

"Noon," Alice answered for her father.

Just as Cecil was preparing to thank Gabriel one more time, the lobby door flung open, and a thoroughly soaked man almost knocked Grace over.

"I am so sorry," the priest apologized. "I was just trying to get out of the rain as fast as possible. It's coming down like cats and demons out there!"

Grace's face immediately reddened.

Cecil knew she felt instantly embarrassed. She had never been comfortable around men-of-the-cloth—or anyone donning any kind of clerical attire for that matter.

"Everything okay, Father?" Gabriel asked.

"Better now that I'm out of the rain. I tried to call the extension but no one answered."

Gabriel shot his teenage daughter a stern look.

"I'm terribly sorry for your inconvenience. What was it you needed, Father?"

"There doesn't seem to be any shampoo or soap in my bathroom."

"Alice, could you get Father whatever amenities he is missing, please?"

Alice scoffed and mumbled something under her breath as she disappeared into the back room.

"We better get to our rooms," Cecil said.

"Again I'm so sorry about running into you, dear," the priest said to Grace.

"It's no problem, really," Grace replied.

"What is your name, child?" he asked.

Grace's hesitation and the look on her face told Cecil that she had gone from feeling uncomfortable straight into feeling claustrophobic in a split second. She could never explain why to Cecil, but police officers and priests had always intimidated her the most.

"I'm Cecil and this is my wife, Grace," Cecil interjected, extending his hand, and deflecting the priest's attention from Grace.

"Very nice to meet you. I'm Father Jackson."

"Nice to meet you too," Cecil said and touched the bandage around his hand.

"I hope you are on the mend?" Father Jackson asked.

"Yes, Father. It was a work accident. Fifteen stitches," Cecil replied, holding up his wounded hand. "Nothing a little tender loving care won't fix."

"Ah, the joys of marriage," Father Jackson said, smiling. "A very holy sacrament between a man and a woman. That's the only way God ever wanted it, you know."

Grace shot Cecil a look. She was certainly in no mood for a sermon about what defines a marriage in the eyes of God.

"It's been a pleasure, Father. Try to stay dry," Cecil said, hoping to cut short Father Jackson's opinion.

Father Jackson nodded, and Alice returned from the back room with a basket of shampoo, conditioner, and body wash.

Cecil and Grace exited the lobby to find Room 18. As soon as Cecil unlocked the door, he took Grace into his arms to carry her over the threshold. She always looked the prettiest when she tossed her head back like that.

Maybe this really was a new beginning.

—··—

"Shh!" Grace commanded, waving her hand and giggling. "I think they're all about to get it on."

Cecil stood at the only window in the room—a gaudy strand of lights hung around the window frame—looking at the parking lot of the Blue Leaf Motel. The rain had stopped and left behind the sound of residual droplets of water falling into puddles from telephone lines and gutters.

Grace was more interested in the muffled conversations coming through the walls of the adjoining hotel room.

"It's definitely two girls and one dude," she said, cupping her ear to the wall.

Cecil inspected the new dressing Grace had wrapped around his wounded hand. It felt tight and secure. The stitches didn't seem to bother him as much since she had changed out the bandages. The cut hadn't reopened in the past few hours either.

"I told you. Seedy motels."

"Oh, quit it," Grace scoffed. "You said we would be next to a crack whore or a serial killer. You should be aroused at the ménages à trois in the next room. I know I am!"

Cecil looked away from the window and his hand to stare sharply at his wife. Was that an obvious dig at what a typical man should be aroused by? Would Lucas What's-His-Name be turned on by listening to a threesome in the next room?

Grace pressed her ear against the wall again, ignoring the glare from her husband.

"What do you think Father Jackson would say if he knew what was going on down the hall from him?" Cecil asked, trying to lighten the mood.

"You gotta hear this," Grace said, ignoring Cecil's rhetorical question. "They are going at it!"

"I'm all set here. Plus it's an invasion of privacy."

"They are fucking in a hotel room! Three of them! And they are loud! What kind of privacy do you expect to retain in a setting like this?"

Cecil realized that she had made a good point, but that still didn't justify going out of his way to eavesdrop on the activities in the next room. Instead of entertaining her voyeurism, he pulled down the bedspread and turned on the television, hoping to drown out some of the sounds coming from the adjoining room. Cecil flipped through the generic cable channels until he came to one of his favorites movies: *Moby Dick*.

The dialogue of Gregory Peck transported Cecil from the Blue Leaf Motel to a simpler time. A time before he had to worry about things such as bills and jobs and dating and finances and mortgages and vows and tactfulness and politics and ass-kissing, and mortality and, most of all, Lucas What's-His-Name.

Cecil was dragged out of his happy place by Grace slithering toward him from the foot of the bed.

"Listening to them really did it for you, huh?" he asked.

She crawled closer to him, answering with a question. "Whose birthday is tomorrow?"

"Mine."

"How about I give you your birthday present a little early?" she said seductively.

Cecil closed his eyes and tried to let the sounds of the television drown out the moans and screams getting increasingly louder from the next room as his wife unzipped his pants.

Cecil couldn't help but think that she was only turned on by the debauchery in the next room and not because she wanted to please her husband on the eve of his birthday, when they were supposed to be reconciling a black stain that she had placed on their vows.

It made him feel dirty. But a "real man" would be selfish and wouldn't care about such menial things as *feelings*.

—·•·—

Cecil was jarred awake by a violent crash, the hotel room shaking. He sat upright and held his breath. Confusion kept him frozen in place, but only for a moment. Everything in the room bounced. Badly drawn art vibrated, clinging to the hooks that barely kept them secured to the walls. Loose items on the dresser fell and danced when they hit the worn-out carpet.

Panic crept in, and Cecil gripped Grace's arm harder than he had intended.

"Huh?" she asked sleepily, unaware of the room's tremors.

"Wake up!" he said with urgency. "We're in the middle of an earthquake."

Cecil wasn't completely sure though. He had never experienced an earthquake before.

"Earthquake? Are you kidding—" Grace's eyes widened. She sat up in the bed. "Holy fucking shit! Quick, stand in a door frame."

"A door frame?" Cecil replied, the volume of his voice rising. "Why not just go out to the parking lot?"

"I heard somewhere that a door frame is the safest place during an earthquake."

The earth continued to rattle. The complementary shampoo bottles rolled off the bathroom counter and crashed onto the porcelain floor.

Cecil thought he could feel the floor ripple underneath him. He grabbed his pants and tried to steady himself with the room's chair.

"Do earthquakes usually last this long?" Grace asked loudly as she hastily tied her sneakers.

"I don't think so."

Then another crash came. This time it sounded like a piece of the hotel itself had been destroyed. Cecil and Grace paused and stared at each other silently.

"What—"

Cecil quickly held up his hand to silence his wife's dialogue. He needed to concentrate, but all he could hear was everything shaking and banging.

"I can't imagine this is normal," he whispered.

"Should we go outside?" Grace asked quietly.

Cecil pulled back the curtains. The rain assaulted the glass so ferociously that he couldn't see past his own reflection in the pane. He was more nervous than he originally thought.

Then the hotel shook as if a bomb had exploded in their room. Cecil's forehead bounced off the window, and Grace was thrown backward with so much force that she was struggling to catch her own breath.

Screams erupted from the room next to theirs.

"We gotta go," Grace said matter-of-factly to Cecil, breathing easier now. "We gotta go now!"

The screaming from the next room became piercing, as if someone was being ripped apart.

"I'm right behind you."

Cecil gripped the doorknob at the same time that the ceiling of their room caved in. He closed his eyes and instinctively covered his head with his hands. After a few seconds passed when all the debris stopped falling, he looked around to make sure Grace hadn't been injured. She seemed okay, if still scared out of her mind.

A blanket of calmness consumed him when he decided that what he was seeing could in no way be possible or real.

The rain was falling through a hole in the ceiling of their hotel room. A large black insect leg, with the thickness of a tree trunk, stood planted in the middle of the room; the body that belonged to that leg was out of view, hovering somewhere over the hotel.

Cecil noticed the length of the hairs that randomly protruded from the massive leg, looking like obscene broom straws. The joint of the leg lined up just below the hole in the ceiling inside the hotel room. Whatever monstrosity was invading the hotel reminded him of something he would see in an old science fiction double feature, like *Them!* and *Tarantula*.

A second gargantuan insect leg crashed through the ceiling and impaled the middle of the bed—sending shards of wood spraying across the room. A piece of shrapnel struck Grace in the cheek, and Cecil lunged forward to grab his wife. He had to run around one of the spider legs to get to Grace. He noticed how the rain ran down the big insect legs and dripped from the long coarse pieces of hair that were as long as his arm. Just as he reached her, they heard a series of more crashes throughout the hotel that sounded like clumsy rudiments being played on a snare drum.

The room's combination fan and light finally let go of the damaged ceiling and crashed to the floor right where Cecil had been standing a few seconds earlier.

"What the fuck is going on?" Grace screamed.

"The sky must be broken, just like you said. I think it's the end of the world," Cecil replied as rain doused the back of his neck. When he extended his arm toward his wife to help her get up off the floor, he noticed that the wound on his hand had opened up again. The bandage was turning red as it absorbed the blood.

Grace reached for his hand and then stopped abruptly. The sound of giant legs crashing through the roof of the hotel had stopped but had been replaced by frantic, bloodcurdling screams from different guests throughout the hotel instead.

"We gotta get to the car and go. I don't even want to see what is—"

Cecil was thrown backward as a third leg crashed through the ceiling directly above his head and impaled Grace right through the chest. She lifted her head slightly; her eyeballs appeared as if they would pop out of her skull. A gurgling moan escaped her lips as blood splattered from her mouth and the gaping hole in her torso.

Cecil screamed with such force that his vocal cords quit working almost immediately. He lunged forward to grab his wife, even though he didn't know what he was going to do to help her. He wrapped his hands around the big hairy insect leg and tried to pull it upward. It didn't budge.

He let go of the leg and looked down at Grace. She was already dead. Her eyes were frozen open, and she was limp with the leg through her middle like a stake.

In a moment of panic and adrenaline, Cecil reached for the insect leg again. This time, just before his fingers could get a grip, the leg rocketed upward through the hole in the ceiling, taking Grace with it. Cecil stumbled backward as the body of his wife struck him on her upward journey through the hole.

Cecil watched his wife rise as lifeless as a rag doll. The insect leg had completely skewered her body. Then the leg and his wife were gone, disappearing through the hole.

The other two legs that had been motionless in the room also retracted through the holes they had created.

It must be walking, Cecil thought.

He bolted for the door and spilled out into the parking lot. He turned around and looked into the sky above the roof.

Walking on long legs that looked more like stilts were three colossal spiders.

With each step they took, another one of their eight legs crashed through the roof of the hotel. Even though their legs were black, their bodies were pale. Cecil noticed they were walking as a group—the church was the next building in their path.

He turned to run around the side of the hotel to follow the spiders. He didn't quite know why, but he felt the need to see where Grace was being taken. As he rounded the next corner, he smacked straight into Alice.

"They killed my dad!" she screamed. "What the hell are they?"

Alice wiped a flood of tears and rainwater from her face with the sleeve of her sweatshirt.

"I don't know. They got Grace too."

"Where are you going?"

"To see where they are taking them," he yelled and continued to make chase.

Alice swallowed, blinked the raindrops out of her eyes, and stood in a sort of limbo.

"Hey! Wait up," she yelled.

Cecil slowed down. "I'm not responsible for you, you know."

"I can take care of myself," she grumbled.

Cecil and Alice made it to the end of the building just as the spiders took their last steps before entering the patch of grass behind the hotel, leaving the Blue Leaf Motel looking like Swiss cheese. The three monstrous arachnids were now in full view.

Alice shrieked when she saw her dad still impaled on a spider leg, rising and falling with each step. Her scream was loud enough where it should have attracted the attention of the monsters. None of the spiders reacted as though they had heard Alice at all, nor did they seem to pay attention to any of the guests scampering around the parking lot.

Cecil thought that maybe the spiders didn't care about the people, and the deaths of Grace and Gabriel were accidental. Maybe they were just stepped on as the spiders made their journey forward. Perhaps the hotel was just an inconvenient barrier for the spiders and not the epicenter of an attack.

Cecil grabbed Alice's arm just as the spiders reached the churchyard—all walking in unison.

"Look," he said, pointing.

"What?"

"There is a third body on the last spider's leg. Can you make out who it is?"

Alice squinted through the rain and tried to focus through the mist that had rolled in from the churchyard.

"Not really, no. Where do you think they're carrying them?"

Cecil shook his head. "I really can't say. I know as much as you do."

The spiders continued traipsing toward the church without faltering in their stride or momentum.

"Should we keep following them?" Alice asked.

Cecil was about to ask her what she thought following them would accomplish, when they both heard a cry for help from inside the hotel. Alice glanced backward at the hotel.

Cecil gasped. "What the …?"

Alice spun around to face the churchyard again. The spiders were gone.

"Where the hell did they go?" she asked, bewildered. "Those things were huge. They vanished, just like that? We'd be able to see them if they were hiding behind the church, wouldn't we?"

"Yes. I don't think they are hiding."

"So where the fuck did they go with my dad?" Alice squealed.

Cecil swallowed hard and felt the tips of his fingers go numb. The muscles in his legs and arms trembled involuntarily. He couldn't answer her. He felt like everything in his body was paralyzed. His brain was shutting down. Shock had set in.

"Is anybody still out there?" a voice from inside the hotel room bellowed.

The cry for help snapped Cecil out of his catatonic state. He turned around and ran as fast as he could toward a broken hotel window.

Alice watched him go, looked back at the churchyard one last time for any sign of the absconding spiders, and then quickly ran toward the hotel to catch up with Cecil.

Cecil was already through the window and standing in one of the hotel rooms when he heard Alice approaching. "Be careful. There's broken glass everywhere."

They were halfway into the room when Alice thought she could see Father Jackson on the floor, the lower half of his body trapped underneath the dresser. Cecil lifted the dresser off Father Jackson's back.

"Thank you. Thank you. Thank you," he said as he got to his feet.

"Anything broken, Father?" Cecil asked.

"I don't think so."

Alice looked around the room in dismay.

Cecil followed her gaze. The ceiling had four large holes where the spider's legs had stepped through the roof. He was certain that every room in the Blue Leaf Motel mirrored the shambles of this room.

"I'm glad you were not one of the damned, child," Father Jackson said to Alice. "I see they didn't take you."

"What are you talking about?"

"The archfiends. They passed over you. Today was a day of reckoning, and only the pure were saved. The Earth has been finally cleansed again, this time not by a flood but a meticulous removal of the impure."

Initially Cecil thought Father Jackson's comment was preposterous. But then he remembered telling Grace that it was the end of the world. Maybe Father Jackson was on the right track.

"They took my dad," Alice snarled. "My dad was an amazing person. A *Christian*."

Cecil felt a pang of guilt that his own initial reaction wasn't like Alice's: to defend a loved one. He hadn't even thought to stand up for Grace.

"Did you get a good look at them?" Father Jackson asked.

"They were spiders. I'm not too sure if they were actually demons, like you proclaim, but I can tell you that they were abominations of some kind," Cecil said.

"How many were there?"

"Three. Each spider had taken one person. They disappeared when they reached the …" Cecil slowed down his words and never finished his sentence. The unspoken word hung like a piece of dust in the air. He hated to admit that Father Jackson's evaluation of the situation might very well be correct.

"The church?" Father Jackson finished.

"Yes. They disappeared there, just as suddenly as they had appeared."

"It doesn't make any sense," Alice sobbed. "If what's happening here really is some kind of biblical rapture, then why would the spiders—"

"Child, the good Lord's ways are not for us to make sense of. It's for us to accept," Father Jackson interrupted.

"Well, I want to get out of here before the next wave of whatever stomps through," Cecil said.

"I'm with ya on that. The faster the better. Let me just grab some supplies before we go," Alice said.

"You live here?" Cecil asked.

"Yeah. In the barn behind the hotel. My dad renovated it after Mom died."

"Now hold on a minute," Father Jackson boomed, his voice increasing in volume as he spoke. "We need to make sure there isn't anyone trapped in the rooms before we leave. We were spared the fire and brimstone because we are the pure and the righteous. If we don't take a few minutes to check the rooms for any survivors, we would be negating the reason why we were saved in the first place."

Cecil looked at his shoes and nervously touched his bandaged hand. The wound had stopped bleeding again, but the blood had crusted the gauze. He nodded in agreement.

"Fine," Alice said with a little more reluctance, "but I'm gonna grab my stuff first before I help look."

"We'll come with you. Who knows what else might have been unleashed and is lurking in the shadows," Father Jackson said and headed toward the door.

Cecil thought that Father Jackson eerily sounded like the clairvoyant Tangina from *Poltergeist* when he spoke like that. There was something unsettling about the priest.

Cecil and Father Jackson followed Alice around the back of the hotel to a large barn sprawled out in front of them. Alice unlocked the door, and they went inside. The interior of the barn had been meticulously renovated to mimic a penthouse suite. Astonishingly it remained completely untouched by any of the spiders.

"This place is amazing," Cecil said, looking around in wonderment.

"Thanks. I'll be right back," Alice replied and trotted up a banister-less staircase that was flush against the back wall.

When Alice was out of sight, Father Jackson opened one of the doors to his right and peered inside.

"What are you doing?" Cecil whispered forcefully.

"That girl's father was one of only three people taken away from here. Obviously he was a miscreant. I'm just interested in finding out what his sins were."

"That is an incredible invasion of that girl's privacy."

"Well, looky here," Father Jackson exclaimed and stepped farther into the room.

"I don't want to know," Cecil said sternly and looked away.

Father Jackson emerged from the room a moment later with a small mirror that sported a single line of white powder.

"Illicit drug use is a direct violation of God's design," Father Jackson stated, and then tilted the mirror, dumping the powder to the barn floor like snow. "It's purposefully destroying the vessel that God created for us. That, to me, is like a proverbial middle finger to Him and His divine love for us. No wonder that girl's father was taken away. God punishes the heathens."

"How do you know that isn't Alice's?" Cecil said, trying to play devil's advocate.

"Because she is still here, and he is—"

"What are you doing?" Alice demanded fiercely, coming down the staircase. "Who told you that you could snoop around in here?"

The mirror fell from Father Jackson's hands.

"Child, your father has already been judged. All of his dirty little secrets have been exposed. He joins the ranks with the abortionists, gays, atheists, adulterers, cheaters, liars, and whores."

Was that why Grace was taken away? Because of the affair? Cecil asked himself.

"You know what?" Alice said to Cecil. "I'll help him look for any survivors in the hotel, but if you choose to keep company with him when we leave, I'll be going my own way."

"I believe there is safety in numbers," Cecil rebutted. "We don't know what the state of the rest of the world is in."

"I guarantee only peace and harmony," Father Jackson interrupted. "Anyone still remaining shouldn't have any more deviant thoughts. We were chosen because we are the virtuous."

Alice darted toward the barn door but stopped to address the priest. "Everything you say condemns my father's drug use. Even as illegal the act may have been, I don't believe my father to be immoral."

Father Jackson and Cecil silently followed Alice back toward the Blue Leaf Motel. They entered the building through a side office door and inspected the damage.

"This place will never be the same again," she said.

"I don't think anywhere on Earth will ever be the same again," Cecil added.

"This isn't Earth anymore. God has brought Heaven down to us as a final gift to mankind. Now that the spiders have removed the filth and slime from the planet, Heaven can permanently reside right here."

"You're a fucking loon," Alice spat and jogged toward the hallway of the hotel. A moment after turning the corner, she noticed a man walking away from her. "Hey! Hey, you!"

The man stopped and turned his head. The fluorescent hallway lights that hung from the ceiling flickered and buzzed.

"Man, am I happy to see you folks," the man said and walked toward Alice. "Is there anyone else still alive in here?"

"That's what we are trying to find out."

"Did your hand get hurt in the attack?" the man asked Cecil.

"Work-related injury," Cecil replied, touching the bandage.

"What's your name, brother?" Father Jackson asked the stranger.

"Mel."

"We're about to give the hotel a once-over before heading out. We could certainly use your help. I'm Father Jackson."

"Absolutely. I'm just happy that I'm not the only one left here."

"Do you need to get anything from your room first?"

Mel looked at his hotel door suspiciously. "Nah. I think I have everything."

Cecil glanced at Alice to see if she had picked up on the same creepy vibe he was getting about Mel. Alice scrunched her shoulders and opened her eyes wide as if to say, *This guy seems weird.*

"What the hell happened here? What were those things?" Mel asked.

Alice just rolled her eyes as Father Jackson started spewing his biblical hogwash from his mouth again.

———— • • ————

Cecil was the first one to hear the screams.

"Help! Oh, God, will somebody please help us!"

"That sounds like it's coming from my room," Cecil said, and they all broke out into a full sprint.

As Cecil got closer to the cries for help, he realized that they were coming from the room next to his and Grace's—where the ménage à trois had taken place. When they reached the room, they found the door locked.

"Unlock the door!"

"We can't. We're trapped," a female voice replied.

"Are you far enough from the door for us to kick it in without you getting hurt?" Mel asked.

"Yes," a different female voice answered.

Mel and Cecil took a step backward and counted to three in unison. On *three*, they kicked the door as hard as they could. Wood splintered around the door frame, but the door held fast. Cecil and Mel kicked again. This time the door cracked right in half.

Two women were pinned under a large piece of the ceiling that had fallen when a spider leg had penetrated the roof. Mel, Cecil, Alice, and Father Jackson were able to remove enough of the debris for the women to shimmy out from the rubble. Both women got to their feet on their own accord and shook the plaster dust from their clothes.

Cecil was embarrassed to ask the women where the male was. He didn't want them to know that he and Grace could hear them during their sexual tryst.

"Does anything feel broken?" Father Jackson asked.

Without answering, one of the women immediately broke down and began to cry.

"They took him. Those … things took him!"

The mystery of the third victim has been solved, Cecil thought.

"Took who? Who was he?" Cecil asked, the urge to find the answer to at least one conundrum was too great for him to control his emotions.

"He was a DJ at Overland's," the other woman stated. "His name was Michael. That's all we know."

"I saw the spiders take him away," Cecil said. "There

were three of them. My wife, Grace, is also gone. Alice's dad, Gabriel, too. We followed the spiders to the churchyard, but then they disappeared."

"Oh, God," one of the women said and clasped her hand over her mouth. "What is happening here?"

"That is still up for debate," Alice responded quickly, hijacking any nonsense Father Jackson might offer up as an explanation.

"What were you two young ladies doing in this room with a man that you hardly knew?" Father Jackson asked.

Cecil shot Alice a look. *If he only knew what Grace and I had heard last night.*

"We came back here after the club closed. He wanted to play us some songs he wrote himself."

Father Jackson eyed them suspiciously. The silence became heavy and uncomfortable.

"My name's Lilly, and this is my wife, Victoria," she blurted out, attempting to eradicate any accusatory ideas Father Jackson might have about the women's intentions with Michael.

Cecil found it amusing that Lilly would rather give a member of the clergy the impression that she was homosexual instead of him thinking they were having a threesome.

"Father," Alice snickered. "Based on your theory, why weren't Lilly and Victoria taken away also?"

"What's this? What theory?" Victoria questioned.

"Father Jackson believes that the spiders were sent as a cleansing of Earth—a Day of Judgment and reckoning, if you will," Cecil said. "He lumped all people of homosexual orientation into the same category of the other evildoers in the world. The murderers. The rapists. The—"

"Enough!" Father Jackson commanded. "I will not sit by idly while you mock me. There is a reason why Lilly and Victoria were chosen to remain here in paradise. It's not my place to question the motives and decisions of the good Lord."

"But, according to your cockamamie theory, there absolutely *is* a reason why they *should have* been taken away," Alice snarled.

"I believe that the idea of Heaven," Mel spoke up, "is a gateway to hope—hope that something is better out there than this life. Hope that someone up there is willing to embrace us with open arms, no matter how we have lived our lives down here."

"Some people attend church just to sit in the fire," Father Jackson retorted. "The guilt from their own iniquities drives them to enter God's house, when, deep down, what they really want to feel is the weight of penance and a smidgen of His wrath in order to sleep at night. Sometimes, when you have fallen out of His good graces, it hurts to pray—and it should."

"Wow. I thought I was pretty fucked up with some of my opinions on the sanctity of prayer, but you take the cake," Alice grumbled. "I've never met anyone like you before, that's for sure."

"If things were perfect, there wouldn't be room for opinions—only truths," Father Jackson replied.

"If things were perfect, gigantic fucking spiders wouldn't have taken away my dad. Everything is wrong. I can feel it."

"On the contrary, child. Because spiders came and took away people like your father, things are now finally perfect."

Alice lunged at the priest. She tightened her fingers into claws, preparing to dig her fingernails into his face and gouge out his eyes. Cecil and Mel grabbed Alice around the waist just before she was able to reach him.

"That's enough!" Cecil yelled. "We have plenty to figure out without you guys at each other's throats. Father, I understand your convictions are unwavering, but, please, until we can clear the hotel and come up with a plan for what to do next, keep your tongue in check. This girl just lost her father in a very violent and nightmarish manner to a bunch of very real monsters. Just because you believe in your theory, it doesn't mean everyone else has to."

Father Jackson swallowed hard and took a deep breath.

"Is that really what they were? Spiders?" Victoria asked.

"That's what they looked like, at least," Cecil said.

"We're going to finish checking the rest of the hotel for anyone else injured," Mel said to Lilly and Victoria. "You're welcome to join us."

"What are your plans after the hotel is searched?" Lilly asked, stepping over a large pile of broken glass and plaster.

"We haven't thought that far ahead," Cecil answered. "One step at a time here. Once we get the hotel figured out, I assume we'll have to see what shape the rest of the world is in."

"Does anyone know how long it's been since they attacked us?" Victoria asked.

"About thirty-five minutes," Cecil answered, looking at the watch his wife had given him for an early birthday gift a few weeks ago. That was the day before he found out about Lucas What's-His-Name—when everything in his life changed.

Cecil reached out to help Victoria step over a pile of rubble. She grabbed his uninjured hand tightly as he guided her away from the debris. Cecil could feel the stitches in his other hand itch again.

"Do you think the people who were taken away were

chosen or was it random?" Victoria asked as she let go of Cecil's hand.

"I'm not sure."

Just then the lights went out, and the hotel was covered in a shroud of darkness. Outside was deathly quiet.

"Oh, shit. Are the spiders coming back?" Lilly squealed.

"Everyone stay calm. I don't think so. Last time they appeared, the ground was shaking like an earthquake. Yet it's totally silent out there," Cecil stated.

"I think it's a blackout," Mel said, looking out a window. "All the street lights are out too."

"Is this really the beginning of the end?" Victoria exclaimed. "Is this really how the world ends?"

"The world has already ended. The spiders took care of that. This is the beginning of a new Heaven," Father Jackson answered.

Alice shook her head, glaring at the priest for a moment. "There's a generator in the utility closet," Alice said to Cecil. "It'll give us maybe an hour of power so we can check the rest of the hotel."

"Lead the way."

Slowly shuffling their feet so they wouldn't trip on any debris, and gingerly touching the walls for guidance, they made it safely to the office. Alice felt for the doorknob and went in. A few moments later she returned.

"The office is destroyed. There's a pile of shit covering the door to the closet."

"Is there another way in?" Cecil asked.

"The closet's wall is butted up against Room 7. These walls are pretty thin. I'm sure we could break through the adjoining wall and get into the closet."

"That's my room," Mel spoke up.

"Finally a stroke of luck," Lilly said.

"Are you sure there's no other way?" Mel asked nervously.

"There's no way inside the closet from the office. Huge pieces of the wall, ceiling, and roof are stacked up in front of it. It would take us much longer to clean it away than it would to just put a hole in the wall small enough for me to crawl through. Trust me."

"What are we going to use to smash through a wall? Our hands?" Mel asked with a twinge of sarcasm in his voice.

Alice disappeared again into the office. Her eyes must have adapted a little bit more to the darkness in there. Cecil heard the squeak of a metal cabinet opening and some thuds afterward.

She exited the office carrying two sledgehammers.

"With these," she replied and handed one to Mel.

"I don't know. I just think it'll be easier to move stuff away from the door. There would be six of us working together. If we go through the wall in my room, there'd only be two of us making the hole."

"Yes, but sledgehammers can do much more damage in a short amount of time," Cecil retorted and grabbed the second sledgehammer from Alice's hands.

Cecil walked down the hallway toward Room 7, and Mel followed closely behind.

"Aren't you afraid of hurting your hand more by swinging the sledgehammer?" Mel asked, keeping up with Cecil's strides.

"I watched my wife be impaled by the leg of a spider taller than this building less than an hour ago. Do you think I'm concerned about something like the stitches in my hand? We need to get the power back on. We need to finish combing the building for survivors, and then we need to figure out what the fuck is going on out there." Cecil pointed toward a window, implying he meant the rest of the world. "Why are you so hell-bent about us not going through your room anyway?"

"I'm not hell-bent on anything."

"You sure as shit are hell-bent on us getting into the closet through the office. What are you hiding?"

Mel immediately dropped the sledgehammer to the floor and turned to run in the opposite direction.

"Grab him!" was the only thing Cecil could think to yell.

Instinctively Lilly threw all her weight at Mel, knocking him off his stride. He stumbled over a discarded chair and fell against the hallway wall.

Cecil walked over, handing off his sledgehammer to Father Jackson. With Cecil's injured hand, he grabbed Mel under his forearm, lifting him to his feet, while grabbing Mel's sledgehammer with his good hand.

"You're not going anywhere until we see what's in that room," Cecil said. "Could you do the honors, Father? I don't trust this one anymore."

"It is God's will that we are together. I would be happy to help in any way you need me to."

Cecil escorted Mel to Room 7 with the rest of the group in tow.

"Open it," Cecil told Mel.

Mel didn't move. Cecil gripped Mel's arm tighter.

"Open it," Cecil repeated, through clenched teeth.

"I can get the spare key," Alice suggested.

"Yes, please. It doesn't look like Mel is going to cooperate. He must be hiding something really good."

Alice went back to the office, retrieved the spare key, and was back at Room 7 within moments. Cecil stepped out of the way and held Mel a good distance from Alice, in case Mel tried to attack her. Alice unlocked the door and pushed it open.

"I'll go in first," Father Jackson suggested. "You stay out here to be safe."

Father Jackson entered the room and disappeared into the darkness.

"There's somebody in here!" he yelled to everyone in the hallway. Just then Father Jackson's shoe kicked an object that skidded away and clinked against the wall.

Cecil stepped inside, dragging along Mel, and focused on the room. Cecil could just barely see a person on the bed. He watched Father Jackson touch the body.

He told Cecil, "His shirt is wet and bloody. I feel a large incision. My fingertips can almost enter the abdominal cavity of this man. Oh, and I kicked something on my way in here."

He walked to the wall and picked up something. Father Jackson turned, holding a machete in his hands, the victim's blood dripping down the back of his hand.

Mel tried to snatch his arm from Cecil's grip but it was futile.

"Did you kill someone in here?" Cecil asked Mel sharply.

"It couldn't have been him. He is innocent and pure. The spiders would've taken him too if he had committed murder. Instead they spared him," Father Jackson said, defending Mel.

"Oh, would you shut up about the rapture," Alice barked. "You're the only one buying that bullshit."

With the priest's mention of *murder*, images of the past

few weeks—starting with Grace confessing about Luke-What's-His-Name and finishing with Grace being speared by the spider's leg—flashed through Cecil's mind. He felt his eyes begin to tear up as the epiphany became clear.

"No, Alice. I think Father Jackson is correct about the spiders and their purpose, only he's wrong about their intent."

"What are you talking about?" Victoria asked.

Cecil slowly loosened his grasp on Mel's arm. He felt like he couldn't breathe as the truth slowly emerged in his head.

When Mel felt Cecil's hand relax, he immediately seized the opportunity to escape. He bolted toward the office, through the lobby door of the hotel, and into the parking lot.

Cecil leaned against the hallway wall with a far off and vacant look in his eyes.

"Are you okay?" Father Jackson asked.

Cecil didn't say anything. His gaze met Father Jackson's. Cecil raised his wounded hand and, with his other hand, slowly unwrapped the bandage. Around and around the blood-stained gauze went, the dressing swaying down by his knees. When the last piece of the bandage fell away, Cecil held up his hand to show everyone his stitched wound.

"I believe now that Father Jackson is correct about the spiders, except for one detail. The spiders came to take away the pure and innocent and deliver them to Heaven. We, all of us remaining on Earth, are the forsaken and vile. My wife admitted that she had been having an affair a few weeks earlier. Two days ago, I made a poor decision. I paid the man a visit. I just wanted to confront him, to let him know what I knew. I brought my revolver with me. I only wanted to scare him. I wanted to prove to myself that I was a big man, that I wasn't a coward. I was someone who would fight for my wife. He attacked me with a knife. I protected my face with my hand, and the knife went through it. That's when I reached for my gun, and I shot him in the back of the head. I told Grace my injury was work-related. I told Grace that we needed to take a vacation to help right our marriage again. Yet I didn't tell Grace …"

Cecil couldn't finish speaking. He was overcome with tears.

"That your vacation was really you skipping town because you murdered someone," Alice finished.

"Exactly. Judgment Day is upon us, and I mucked it all up for myself." Cecil bawled in agony. "So tell me, what … what is it you've done? What dark sins are you all hiding that prevented the spiders from taking you to salvation?" Cecil turned to face Lilly and Victoria. "Grace and I heard you two fucking that dude in your room, but I can't imagine that act, along with your sexual preference, would be enough to condemn you. Just like I don't believe that Grace's infidelity or Gabriel's addiction were enough to deny them a spot at God's side."

Lilly wiped her own tears from her cheek.

"We travel throughout the northeast looking for men who are drunk and flashing their money around in bars and clubs," Victoria said, her voice cracking. "We bring them back to the room, rob them, and move on to the next city. Sometimes we indulge in some extracurricular activity to help them sleep, making it easier for us to get what we want. It's not just cash either. We've gotten away with cars, jewelry, and laptops, among other things."

"What about you, Alice? What have you done to seal your fate with God?"

Alice was reluctant to answer at first, but, after what Victoria had said, coupled with Cecil's own revelations of the skeletons in his closet, it was hard to dispute his theory.

"It does appear that something divine has occurred on Earth tonight, only we were on the wrong end of the outcome," Cecil said, prodding Alice to speak.

"I … um …" Alice began.

"It's okay to say it. We're all in this together now."

Alice lightly kicked a piece of a lamp against the wall and swallowed. "Let's just say, my dad still thought what happened to Mom was only an accident."

"And that leaves you, Father Jackson," Cecil said with intensity. "What wretched acts have you partaken in that would cast you out of our Lord's good graces? What vile and repugnant things have you done that were so atrocious that God, Himself, would reject you—a man of the cloth—on the day of reckoning?"

Father Jackson took a few steps backward and bumped into the hallway wall. He couldn't get his hands under control; they were shaking violently.

He fought with every fiber of his being to rebuff Cecil's new theory; however, the facts were hard to ignore if everyone else here had something in their past that would most likely prevent them from being saved.

"I don't have to answer to you or anyone else, other than God," he snarled.

"Looks like God already sent his calling card, and you were on the naughty list," Cecil said.

Father Jackson panicked. "God didn't abandon me, He must have just accidentally skipped me," the priest argued. "There has to be another explanation why I wasn't taken with the others. I have been forgiven for my sins. I have made my reconciliation. I have served my penance. God is merciful."

Cecil spoke, using an adage that Father Jackson had used himself a short while ago when talking about Alice's father.

"God punishes."

Father Jackson quickly turned and sprinted down the hallway toward the parking lot. When he made it outside, he noticed Mel in the distance, jogging away from the Blue Leaf Motel. Mel was just a small silhouette in the foggy mist.

"Don't leave me here all by myself!" Father Jackson cried.

Mel faintly heard Father Jackson's words over the hush of the night. Mel stopped and turned around, thinking that Father Jackson was addressing him. He realized that Father Jackson wasn't talking to him when he saw the priest facing the churchyard where the spiders had supposedly disappeared.

"Why did you leave?" Father Jackson screamed in the direction of the church. "Won't you come back to us? Won't you come back and save us again?"

Mel held his breath as he waited to see if there would be a reply. Mel held his breath as he waited to see if one of those spiders would reappear. Mel held his breath as he waited for something, anything, to give a sign that this wasn't the end of time.

Eventually he had to exhale.

Brian Paone was born and raised in the Salem, Massachusetts area. His love of writing began through the medium of short stories at the young age of twelve. After almost twenty years of consistently writing short stories for only his friends and family to read, Brian's first full-length novel, a personal memoir about his friendship with a rock-star drug addict entitled, *Dreams Are Unfinished Thoughts*, was published in 2007. Brian's second novel, *Welcome to Parkview*, was published in 2010 and is a macabre journey through a cerebral-horror landscape. Brian's latest novel, *Yours Truly, 2095*, was published in 2015 and follows a man who wakes up one morning, trapped in the future, to discover he's been the victim of a time-travel conspiracy. Brian is married and has three children. He is also police officer and has been working in law enforcement since 2002. Brian has enough ideas for future novels that he should be able to continue publishing books well past retirement. When Brian isn't writing, he is writing or playing music. He is also a self-proclaimed roller coaster junkie, and his favorite color is burnt-orange. For more information on all his books and music, visit www.BrianPaone.com.

The Face
S.M.

I fixate on the pavement beneath my feet. Focusing on gravity and the weight of my body, I perform the rhythmic cadence of the run. I concentrate on my breath and keep myself from floating away. I question my own thoughts. *Which is it? Trying to keep myself from checking-out and floating away? Or trying to keep myself afloat?* I finally break a sweat now in the southern humidity that arrives as early as April. I know the runner's high is not far behind and the endorphins will follow. By then I won't sense my feet pounding the pavement that so centers me once they hit, but my body will feel strong, and temporarily indestructible and tireless. It's an even trade.

I round the corner of Third Street for the eighth time this morning, peering into the centralized park that the neighborhood wraps around. It's a beautiful addition to the subdivision, but it seems to have been added as an afterthought, with insufficient funds to complete it. In the five days I've spent in this town, I have never observed a child, ball, or picnic under the sanctuary of the trees along its perimeter or in the openness of the interior field provided. To be fair, there is not even a playground or swings for children. Nor is there currently a garden or any landscaping—impressive or common. Yet the plot has found its niche as an unofficial dog park for the residential community. I scan the area again, looking for the unmistakable and rare Great Dane that I know belongs to *her*.

Today will be the day.

The air is humid but not as heavy as yesterday. The sun is shining, and my feet are steady. My body feels strong, and I know my voice and words will be clear. I came here for a reason, and I will not lose it in the blur of my thoughts concerning consequences. These are the lies I tell myself, because today has to be the day.

I let the fear creep in my heart as I finish deceiving myself. *Do I even know why I'm here? What will be the results of my actions, and what kind of absurd expectations do I have that it might relieve my suffering—or hers for that matter?* I am searching in vain, grasping at straws. I know this but see no other solutions than to watch myself fail and fall into the last pit of despair before I reach rock bottom.

I desperately scan the park but find no sign of her and the enormous pup. Through my unintentional stalking, I have come to know she will faithfully bring him here about this time each day. Observing her from afar, she has looked as lost in her quest to handle her life while exercising the Great Dane as I am while gathering the courage to confront her during my morning runs.

Stopping my current momentum is not an option. The images will come, and the words will be lost if I rest stationary while I anticipate her arrival. I have no choice but to take another round through the neighborhood.

A mile later, my feet aren't tired but have become numb when I spot the Great Dane and its owner through the trees lining the park's edge. Today's the day, and it's *her . . . her* face.

I force myself through the park gate without allowing myself to break stride or slow down, for fear I will turn the other way and put off what is the inevitable. Everything else is frozen, and I remind myself that, if I allow the fear to overtake me again, it will mean being frozen in my own life forever.

I maintain my pace, rushing to what is surely my own undoing and humiliation. But anything, ANYTHING has to be better than being static, overcome with white noise, lost in the images in my mind, and going through the motions of life.

I've been told, "Fake it until you make it," but it's been a year, and I haven't made it anywhere. I remind myself that a downfall has to be better than eternal suspension. I am selfish in my motives. I may be fulfilling a request, a promise, but I have not allowed myself that lie. For I am here, I have made it this far, for no other reason but to be able to feel something again. *Who am I to cause this person potential pain and suffering? Will I be able to provide any comfort to her or will I be as toxic as a ship that drags up objects from the ocean floor which are meant to stay there?*

All the doubts I have surface, but it's too late now. The dog sees my approach and positions itself for play, or maybe for defense. It's difficult to tell, but the Great Dane surely has taken notice of me, and it has caused *her* to turn as I continue toward them. Her face . . . It's all I need to see to allow the gates of my mind to open and to feel my heart recoil back in pain. We have never met, and yet I know her face.

"Mrs. Johnston?" I manage to get out through my drawn-in lips and shaky voice.

"Yes . . .?" she says, with curiosity, but with little surprise or concern.

I recognize the hint of vacancy and the effort to show emotion in her face.

I have spoken. I have arrived at her feet. There are no more excuses. I pause, panting from my exercise, and cannot recall one word I meant to say. Then it comes, the words. I hope they are words at least, because they flow out of my mouth faster than I can recognize their meaning. The sound comes from me, I know, but without thought or reflection before what I pray are rational sentences. The words start slow and quiver and begin to move faster as I submit to the panic and delirium.

"I . . . I . . . I'm sorry to bother you, but I'm a nurse. In the military. I met your son. I . . . held his hand. I told him that I would take care of him as he cried for you. I locked my eyes on his face and held his gaze until he fell under anesthesia so we could operate. I told him everything would be okay. But it wasn't. I cleaned him. I ran for equipment. I gave them everything they asked for, but it was everywhere . . . There was too much . . . I . . . We . . . kept working, but he was gone and behind him were more. It went on for hours . . . days, and then months. It just went on forever . . . I came back stateside, but still it seems like it never stopped!"

I am in shock and removed from all as I speak. I am completely unaware of the passing of information, as well as everything and anyone around me. I am a third party but with the sound muted.

"But . . . he cried for you . . . He said to tell you that he loved you . . . I saw it! I saw it in his face as he fell asleep. I wanted to . . . I had to tell you. I know this can't be easy for you, but I had to tell you. Because, maybe if I tell you, then maybe when I look at my own son, I will see something else besides your son's face. Maybe I can allow myself to love my own child again, because every night I go through the motions of tucking him into his bed and think about how your son deserved to see YOUR face. But it was me! I am so sorry. It was my face! I was the last face he ever saw, and I couldn't help him. I'm so sorry that it was my face."

I stop speaking and crumble to the ground with hot tears streaming down my face. I openly sob into the grass, feeling desperate and not any freer than when I began my quest for freedom. I have purged myself and will now wait to take the steps to allow myself to be filled again.

Elvis is My Rider

Randy Blazak

He was a hulking figure, maybe 250 pounds with bloodshot eyes. You expect to see discombobulated homeless people in LA; but on Hollywood Boulevard, not in posh Beverly Hills. This prize-winner was wearing a silk bathrobe, gold pajamas as he hovered in front of a small mansion on Summit Drive. He seemed confused, watching cars pass from each direction like he was in the middle of a psychotic breakdown.

I knew immediately who he could not be.

I was lost in LA in my own way. On a summer break I had driven down from Portland to, once again, push my novel in front of any interested Hollywood types. *Let's have a meeting* became *Just have your agent email me.* Without a literary agent I had taken to leaving copies in West Hollywood coffeehouse restrooms where I thought producers and A-list actors might find them. There are probably a lot of cleaning staffers in Los Angeles who own copies of my Great American Novel.

On a random sunny August day I took a drive into the Hollywood Hills to dream of the *Californication* life that I never really wanted. I went through Bel Air to see the Beverly Hillbillies' mansion and the house where Brian Wilson wrote the fabled *Smile* album by the Beach Boys. East to Brentwood, past the Nicole Brown-Simpson murder scene, and then toward Laurel Canyon where all my favorite 70's music stars produced works that somehow survived through the ages.

On Summit Drive I looked for Charlie Chaplin's famous house using the Celebrity Homes app on my smartphone. Chaplin had always been my hero. He used his craft to take a stand against the rise of fascism in Europe. On the way to Los Angeles I had to stop to see Diego Rivera's massive 1940 mural, *Pan-American Unity*, at City College of San Francisco. It featured a panel of Chaplin vanquishing Hitler—both with similar mustaches—into the fire.

It was there on Summit Drive that I saw him.

As I loaded the address into the app, it told me it was the home of Priscilla Presley, the ex-wife of the long dead king of rock and roll. The weird thing was this guy in a robe sort of looked like Elvis. The fat one, not the skinny one on the stamp. LA has plenty Elvis imitators harassing tourists in front of Grauman's Chinese Theatre, along with Transformers, Marvel superheroes, and yes, occasionally, Charlie Chaplin. But Elvis died of a drug-induced heart attack in 1977. My mom was convinced it was a hoax and somewhere there was a 70-something Elvis hiding from the cameras like a Sasquatch. But this guy was in his early forties and looked nothing like the skinny-stamp Elvises on Hollywood Boulevard.

With really nothing to lose I rolled down the window on my Prius and stopped hoping this wouldn't end up like a 21st century version of *Helter Skelter*. I had read a few Elvis biographies, so I thought I might be able to have a fun conversation with a schizophrenic before heading back to my hotel.

"E?" (That's what people close to the King called him.)

He looked at me and then at my Toyota and pulled the

sash on his bathrobe tighter. His face was bloated and he looked like he had been crying.

He gave his head a shake and said, "Man, do you know me?"

"I'm going to pretend like I do. Look, can I help you? Dressed like that up here you are going to get arrested." I noticed a tinge of white around his hairline like he had recently stopped dying his hair.

"I, I must be in some crazy dream. I was getting ready for bed and then I'm here in front of my wife's house, but everything is different. They told me to go away, like I'm nobody. Can you get me out of here?"

So I opened the passenger door and let this madman into my vehicle.

"I told my daddy that they were trying to drive me crazy. Maybe they finally did it. But thanks, I could use a hand. I gotta find Lisa. What's your name?"

"Andy. And I'm guessing yours is Elvis."

"I guess it's no use in me tryin' to hide who I am. I always want to grow a beard when I'm not on tour but they won't let me, say it will make me look like a drug addict. Ain't that funny? Kris Kristofferson looks pretty good with a beard and he's doin' my parts now, so I should get to have a beard, right? Don't you think I'd look alright with a goddamn beard?"

"You looked pretty good in *Charro!*"

Charro! was a 1969 western that was a break from Elvis's endless goofy 60's romance comedies. He didn't sing a single song in the flick. Instead he tamed a wild stallion with his bare hands. It was one of his last movies before he returned to the stage. He looked great with a beard.

"I'm really out of my head," he said. "I could use some

medication. But, I tell ya, first I really gotta go, you know. Do you live around here?"

I could see the sweat on his forehead. It was either a panic attack, drug withdrawal, or he *really* had to take a shit.

"No. I live in Portland, Oregon. I'm staying in a hotel on Sunset. Let's head down there and see if we can figure out how to help you."

As we drove down the winding hill he stared at the cars. Then looked around the inside of my car. It was a bit messy from the 1,000 mile road trip.

"Man! What kind of crazy car is this? It looks like a spaceship. Is it from a movie?"

"It's a 2004 Toyota Prius. I'm due for a new one next year. I've really stacked the miles on this one."

"Two thousand and what? Now I KNOW I'm in a damn dream. All these cars look like they are from a science fiction movie. The place has gone all *Star Wars* crazy."

I looked at this man, who seemed a few years younger than me, just a few, but had the weight of a hard life on his barreled chest. Okay, let's indulge this guy. What could be the harm?

"Yeah, I gotta ask you what year you think it is," I asked.

"Man, my head has been in a fog for years. But I feel sorta okay right now. Weird."

"Who is the president?"

"Don't ask me about politics. They won't let me talk about politics. Politics and God, I can't talk about them. It's that peanut farmer. The guy hung up on me when I called him. I was happy when a southern boy won. They gave Nixon a bum deal, but you didn't hear that from me."

"Carter? What if I were to tell you the president was a black guy from Chicago?"

He snorted and looked at me with a disbelieving stare and then shook his head again.

"Man, this is some crazy dream," he muttered as his fat body sunk into the passenger seat.

———————

He didn't say much as we made our way to Sunset. He just kept muttering, "Man." I tried to suss out what his angle was. He did smell a bit like hobo vomit but he had just the right bloat for 1977-era Elvis. Maybe this was one impersonator who just went off the deep end. Took his King right up to the end.

At a red light I opened up my YouTube app and quietly typed, *Elvis Unchained Melody*. It was a famous film clip of Elvis on stage six weeks before his death struggling to play the old chestnut. The video loaded and I held it up to my rider to compare.

"What the hell is that?" he shouted as he heard the singing coming from the tiny speaker. "What are you doing to me?"

"It's just my phone. Don't worry."

"That ain't no phone. Is that me singing? Turn your radio off. It sounds like shit."

"It's not a radio." I handed him my phone so he could see the video and his mouth fell open.

"What kind of Dick Tracy shit is this? Are you with the government? Why are you spying on me? I've always been loyal, man. I served my country."

"It's just a little film of you, I mean Elvis, in 1977."

I had to admit that he looked just like the guy in the YouTube. Right down to his triple chin. I began to wonder.

"Yeah, okay. Just get me to a toilet."

We pulled into the Rodeway Inn across the street from Hollywood High School, and I snuck the King of Rock and Roll, in his bathrobe, into my second floor room—surely not the strangest scene to transpire in this dump.

Other than the flat screen TV, this place looked pretty 1977 and he seemed to feel a bit more comfortable. The big guy sat at the end of the bed with his head in his hands.

"Dr. Nick told me something like this might happen. I'm on so many pills these days I must be hallucinating. He gave me some extra codeine for my tooth and that must have been what did it. Do I seem like I'm a guy on drugs to you?"

"Not really. You do know it's 2014 and not 1977, right?"

"Man, that don't make any sense. I gotta call my daddy and find Lisa." He fixated on his image in the hotel room mirror.

"Well, I'm pretty sure Vernon is long gone and Lisa Marie is grown up with kids of her own," I said as he laid back on the bed.

"I need to wake up in Graceland. I don't belong here."

He closed his eyes and began to mumble something that sounded like, *There's no place like home, there's no place like home.*

"Why don't you take a nap, Elvis. I'm going to go find you some clothes."

I waited for the signature, *Thank you very much*, but the sad fellow was already asleep.

— · · —

I hopped back in the car and jotted over to the Target on Santa Monica to pick up an outfit for a large-sized dead icon.

On the way I tried to figure out what the hell was going on. With me!

Was this some psychosis that had emerged out of my own failures as a creative person?

The scary truth was that my parents took me to see Elvis Presley perform when I was only nine years old. He was my first concert, allowing me to win the First Concert Game on most drunken nights (losing only to one person whose first concert was The Beatles at Shea Stadium). Maybe this apparition was my apparently severely fucked up subconscious trying to tell me something, but what? Probably to give up writing and get a job in elder care.

Wandering the blastingly bright aisles of the Target, I wondered what to buy an expired king.

I had no idea of his sizes so I stuck to the basics. Jeans and shoes that might fit, cheap packages of large socks, t-shirts, and underwear and an extra-large black and gold Beverly Hills University sweatshirt. I didn't really know what do after that.

I didn't actually know Priscilla Presley, who was now sixty-nine, or Lisa Marie, now forty-six, but I don't think either of them would appreciate me delivering this crazy man to their door. Maybe this was some personal vision quest for me. What does Elvis mean to me on some weird existential level? It seemed like there was only one real option here.

Get Elvis back to Memphis.

I mean, why not? There was nothing in Portland for me other than a blank screen waiting for another proudly self-published novel that my mom could review on Amazon. What's a week out of my life to drive across the country with a schizophrenic fat man? And if E was gone when I got back to the Rodeway Inn, I would at least have a funny story to tell. I should have taken a selfie with him in front of Priscilla's house.

Since no other name was suggested, I'm just going to call him Elvis in this story. There are plenty of people named Elvis out there: Elvis Costello, figure skater Elvis Stojko, Chinese actor Elvis Tsui Kam-kong. So let's just call him Elvis.

Elvis hadn't left the building when I got back to the hotel. By the smell, I don't think he left the bathroom.

He was sitting on the end of the bed with a remote in his hand and *The Rockford Files* on TV.

"Great show, but I didn't know it came on this early in LA," he said after a quick glance up.

Now I should point out that in 2012, I had to hire a PhD candidate from MIT to explain to me how to turn on my new flat screen television, but Elvis managed to find the On button on the remote without much problem.

"Look at the picture on this weird TV! I don't know where the tubes are but the picture is incredible. I gotta get some of these for Graceland."

"It's digital, Elvis. No more antennae. It's all the cable."

"They got cable in a crummy hotel like this? They don't even have cable at the Hilton."

I wondered if he did any channel surfing of life in 2014. Slaughter in Syria, Honey Boo Boo, TMZ. I imagined that news stories of floods, fires, and war in the middle-east could've been on the screen in the 1970s. Just now it was in HD.

"I got you some clothes so you can get out of those pajamas. We can get more later, if you like. If you are serious about who you are, we need to get you back to Memphis. Do you have anybody there you can call?"

"Yeah, that was the last place I saw Lisa, and Ginger, my little girlfriend."

As creepy as that sounded, that must've been Ginger Alden, the twenty-year-old model who had been living with Elvis at Graceland when he died.

"Yeah, all my boys are in Memphis. I should call Joe, or Jerry. Maybe the Colonel can get me a plane ticket."

I imagined that most of these people were dead.

"Problem is I don't know any of their phone numbers. My people keep track of all that stuff for me. My mind can't hold numbers."

"Well, that's a common problem these days." I thought about how once I enter a phone number into my Contacts, I have no reason to know it. Don't ask me what my mother's or girlfriend's phone number is.

"Let me ask the operator." Elvis hit 0 on the hotel room phone and was connected to the front desk clerk who told him to hang up and dial 9 and then 411. He did with more skill than a guy who was supposedly crazed by all the drugs and when 411 stopped ringing he said, "Operator, can you connect me to Graceland in Memphis, Tennessee." He paused with a confused look, one of many to come. "What the hell? Press what? Operator!"

Welcome to the 21st Century. There are no more operators who look like Lily Tomlin. There are only robots who look like my phone. All the old operators were laid off and had to resort to phone sex work. Then they were replaced by phone sex robots. *Press Two if you would like me to talk dirty with a Russian accent.*

I knew it was pointless to try to connect Elvis to Graceland, which since his death, had become a sort of Mecca for Elvis fans. For only $33 fans and the curious could tour the bottom two floors seeing Elvis' kitchen and Jungle Room, but not go upstairs where family sometime stayed. A quick check on Wikipedia revealed that the fiendish Elvis manager, Col. Tom Parker, had died in 1997 at age eighty-seven and his real name was Andreas Cornelis van Kuijk. He would've been the only one to buy into this fantasy since he never missed an opportunity to make a buck of off Elvis, including dead Elvis. But it didn't matter. I needed this crazy road trip to clear my own cobwebs. I needed to move so I was ready to kidnap the King.

Fortunately, Elvis was up for the idea. He seemed completely disoriented by LA. It was too much to take in. Unfortunately, he hated the shitty clothes I bought for him at Target and gave me the names of a couple of clothing shops that I couldn't find on Google. Well, except for Giorgio on Rodeo Drive which was a little bit out of my crazy-person outfitting budget.

"It looks like all those stores are closed, E. I guess it's back to Target."

"What is that *Star Trek* thing anyway?"

"I told you, it's my phone."

"It looks more like a damn tricorder to me."

"Yeah, it sort of is."

"Science fiction, man. I woke up in science fiction."

I packed my bag and took a good look in the mirror to see if I was the one that was dreaming before we left on our little adventure. When I look in the mirror in any dream, my teeth start to fall out one by one. Nope, not a dream. With all my teeth, I opened the door for his highness.

"I really want to thank you for helping me out here. I don't really get to make new friends," he said as he shook his head at the strange situation. "And sorry about the bathroom." Since it was a dump thirty-seven years in the making, I figured I could overlook the moment of humanness.

The real Elvis never had to go clothes shopping. He had his people bring him new outfits, which was really only loungewear. He had his crazy stage outfits and his pajamas but never really *went out* in the later years. Elvis never went to Studio 54 or even to a rodeo. He'd occasionally sneak into a movie theater for the middle of a film but no one saw him but his inner circle. The point is that to tell Elvis that Target was basically the same thing as K-Mart was pointless. Elvis never walked into a K-mart, and died before Wal-Mart erased the American landscape.

So in Target, this guy, whom I am now pretending is zombie Elvis, kept his head down for fear he'd be recognized in the ill-fitting outfit I bought him. He quickly realized his usual duds would not be found in the 21st century low-end store, so we got some black slacks, a few darkly colored dress shirts, a pair of fake leather boots, and a pair of aviator sunglasses and got the hell out of there for under $200. I joked that I was sorry we couldn't get a gun in the store as well.

"Can we pick one up on the way?" he asked as he headed into the Target bathroom to change.

But it wasn't the gun store my Elvis wanted to stop at before we left town. It was something called the Self-Realization Park. I Googled it and turns out it is an inter-faith temple that held some of Gandhi's ashes. It was west on Sunset (the opposite direction of Memphis) by the Pacific. It seemed like the kind of place this guy might need.

"Sure, Elvis. Let's go check it out."

I headed west down Sunset and once we passed the Beverly Hills Hotel, Elvis became more animated. I guess Beverly Hills hasn't changed much in all these years. There are still high walls with Mexican women getting off at bus stops to clean them. The time bubble was pierced by the pervasive technology that even the maids held in their hands.

"Oh brother, everybody's got those *Star Trek* phones. I mean, I can't figure what the hell is going on. I gotta get back to my people."

We finally made it to the Lake Shrine Temple. Most of the way he had his eyes closed and seemed to be praying, especially through the intense traffic around UCLA. Other times he pointed out familiar landmarks that were no longer there. I related to the out-of-time feeling every time I go back home to Atlanta. It's like a scene from *Dark City*. It's as if the city is constantly being rearranged. I can't turn left at the bank because the bank is now a Krispy Kreme.

There in the parking lot my new friend had a simple request. "Hey, do you think I could have a bit of time on my own? I won't be long, I promise. I just need to clear my head."

"Sure thing, Elvis. I'll just hang out here."

It didn't seem like the real Elvis ever went anywhere by himself but it I guess this was a meaningful place for him. After I watched him walk past the gates into the garden I read more about the park on my phone. Turns out that Elvis spent some time visiting this park on little spiritual retreats away from the disapproving eyes of Col. Parker and considered its director, Sri Daya Mata, an advisor. The park was also the location where George Harrison's funeral was held in 2001. I had mixed feelings about explaining that half of the Beatles were now dead. While he had often covered their songs (check out his version of George's "Something" on 1973's *Aloha from Hawaii via Satellite*), he also was known to blame them for the drug counterculture of the 1960s and the displacement of his kind of music from the charts.

I wondered if he was finding any answers around the tranquil lake. I wondered if I would find any answers by following this impulse to entertain this fantasy by hitting the road with a dead childhood idol. Would there be a moral to this story? The beauty of a road trip is you never know what will happen. We try to plan for every contingency in our lives. There are apps that will tell you when to turn left and look right at the scenic view. You can plan the whole trip before you ever leave your house. But, in reality, you can't plan shit. Chaos will come along and give you a flat tire, or put a dead hooker in your trunk, or will give you the sweetest piece of roadside café cherry pie you have ever had in your life. In that chaos there is creativity and answers. The road trip is the anecdote to overly planned modern living.

"Okay, man, let's get out of here," he said, startling me out of my Kerouacian daydream. The door was open and he climbed into the car.

"Find any answers?"

"Ever have a dream where everything's the same but different at the same time?"

"Yeah, I had a dream once that I was at my favorite Italian restaurant and they were serving human heads on plates of penne pasta."

"Okay, this isn't that bad. I just figure if we can get to Memphis and I can climb back into bed, I can finally wake up."

According to Google Maps it was 1822 miles to Graceland

and could be done in twenty-six hours if I trusted Elvis Presley to drive a Toyota Prius while I slept. I figured, in reality, four days with a bit of sightseeing. I just had to get on the Santa Monica freeway and head toward Barstow.

"Alright, my friend, let's head east. We can get supplies along the way. Let's just get the hell out of the LA. This traffic is too much for anyone, man or ghost."

Before I got on to the I-10, at the red light I tweeted, *Heading to Memphis with the King. As in Elvis. #noshit #wtf.*

Since I was only thirteen when Elvis died (yes, I remember the day), I only have vague memories of what the world looked like then. I'm pretty sure the highways are now a bit wider but not that different. I mention that because any time we were in a setting that seemed vaguely familiar, Elvis relaxed a bit. The Santa Monica Freeway, despite all the 2014 Mercedes Benzes on it, was pretty old school.

"So, what's your story, Andy? I should know something about you if I'm going to drive across the country with you in this car from the future."

"Yeah, it's from the past. The 2015s come out this fall. Sure, I'm a writer, mostly technical stuff, like teachers' manuals. But I have a novel out and I'm in LA trying to pitch it as a screenplay."

"I love to read, mostly spiritual stuff. What's your book about? You think I would like it?"

The thought of Elvis Presley reading my novel about Portland hipsters was a bit too much to process. "Maybe. It's kind of spiritual. It's about suicide and music. Maybe you could review it on GoodReads.com."

"Huh?"

Elvis began to recognize more landmarks outside of town

as we merged on to I-15 North and he saw the signs for Las Vegas. "Man, I've made this trip a thousand times." In the 1960s Elvis was bicoastal. While he made his movies, he stayed in his home in Bel Air and then he'd load Priscilla and his Memphis Mafia into the bus and head back to Graceland, often driving. "Look, maybe we should make a little detour to Vegas. I've got some friends there."

Once we hit the edge of the desert, I thought it was time that we had the talk. The *Elvis, do you know you are dead?* talk. I had found a classic country station on the satellite radio and had been enjoying him singing along to random lines so I hated to bring the mood down by killing him, but it had to happen at some point on the trip.

"So Elvis, I don't know if you have figured this out, but you don't actually exist in 2014."

"What the hell is that supposed to mean?"

"Well, um, you like died. A long time ago, back in the 70s."

"Well, then how the hell am I here if I'm dead? This sure ain't heaven." Then he paused to think if it might be. After all, there was commercial-free country music on the radio and *The Rockford Files* with no static on the TV.

"I wish I had a good answer for you. My answer is that you're not actually Elvis but a mentally ill dude, but my gut tells me otherwise. Maybe I just want you to be Elvis."

"I know who I am and I know this is a dream or something," he said, pushing the sunglasses tight to his face.

"What's the last thing you remember?"

"Well, I couldn't sleep. I have another damn tour starting up in Maine. You know, I want to put on a good show for my fans, but the press messes with me because of my weight and sometimes I forget a few words of all those damn songs. I told Ginger I was going to go to the bathroom and read. I don't know, I guess the last thing I remember is sitting on the damn toilet."

"Everyone knows that story. The story of how Elvis died." I pulled over to the side of the road and opened up the Elvis entry on my Wikipedia app. "Here, look." His eyes squinted at the 1957 shot of Elvis in *Jailhouse Rock*.

"I can't see that tiny print. The doctors say I have glaucoma. Read it to me."

"Elvis Aaron Presley, January 8, 1935 to August 16, 1977 was an American singer, musician, and actor. One of the most significant cultural icons of the twentieth-century. He is often referred to as 'the King of Rock and Roll,' or simply 'the King'."

"It says I died?"

I scrolled further down and read a bit about him being pronounced dead at Baptist Memorial Hospital in Memphis. I spared him the details about his enlarged colon.

"Well, I'll be goddamned."

We discussed the distinct possibility that either one of us might be dreaming and then the philosopher king pointed out that we might be the subject of someone else's dream, at which point I pulled out on the desert highway.

"Well, how's my Lisa Marie then? Is she okay?"

"I guess she's older than you now. Yeah, she's fine. She's been through a lot. I think her first husband was a Scientologist."

"What? That S.O.B. group tried to recruit me but they just wanted my money. I can't believe that's true. She musta known my feelings about that bunch."

"Well, she divorced that guy but had a couple of kids with

him. Then she married Michael Jackson, you know, of the Jackson 5." I waited for the reaction.

"Boy, now you are really fucking with me. That black kid?"

"Well, that was debatable. Yeah, after you died he pretty much became the biggest music star on the planet. He put out an album in 1982 that broke all the records. I'd love to play it for you."

"Lisa married Michael Jackson? ABC, 123?"

"Yep. It was a huge event. Lots of people said you would be rolling in your grave."

"Why, because he's black? I got no problem with that."

"No, because he was a weirdo and maybe a child molester."

"Sweet Jesus. What? Did she dump his black ass?"

"Yeah, and then he died years later in a situation similar to yours. No kids. Then she married this big actor you wouldn't have heard of, who was a huge Elvis fan. No kids. Now I think she's married to a guy in her band and they have a couple of kids. So about four Elvis grandchildren."

He seemed more interested in the word *band* than *grandchildren*, so I explained that she put out a few not entirely shitty albums in the 2000s and one really good song about Memphis and we could listen to them if he wanted.

"Maybe we can pick up some 8-tracks at a record store when we get to Vegas. I'm getting tired of this radio station. I've heard all these songs a million times." I kept the dial off the talk radio, but maybe hearing how bad the political discourse had gotten would be better than hearing how bad country music had gotten.

"Sorry, they don't have those anymore."

"8-track tapes?"

"Record stores."

We pulled in to Needles, California for a stop. I needed to pee and I'm sure E needed to do more than that, twisted colon and all. I noticed him squirming in his seat so we hit a truck stop on I-40. He took a little time in the john so I popped open a large Red Bull and leaned against the Prius waiting for a dead Michael Jackson to arrive to dance for the King. Since he didn't, I used the time to download *Thriller* on my iTunes app, and Lisa Marie Presley's 2003 album that had the "Lights Out" song that I had to admit loving.

When Elvis finally strolled out, he really looked like Elvis; all in black as the sun set, sunglasses framed by his massive sideburns. On top of that, he was singing a line from Hoyt Axton's "Never Been to Spain," a karaoke favorite of mine, the one about heading to Las Vegas and only making it to Needles.

I jumped in on the line about Oklahoma and carried it with him to the chorus.

"Son, you better keep your day job, whatever the hell it is," he said, shaking his head. Harshed by the king.

"I guess we're going through all those places on the way, right?"

"As long as you can get me to heaven, okay? But I'll settle for Vegas tonight." I tossed him a can of Red Bull and got in the car. "What kind of beer is this?"

As much as I could go through life not hearing *Thriller* again, I had a great time playing it for Elvis. I enjoyed explaining how I had downloaded the album from a cloud on to my phone and then jacked it into my car stereo. I enjoyed explaining how the album fit into Michael Jackson's musical chronology and his work with Quincy Jones (who apparently Elvis had met through former fling Peggy Lipton). I enjoyed relating how MJ was compared to Elvis as a complete performer and the father of a new medium; this time MTV (which we'd have to spend more time discussing). But most of all I just enjoyed just watching him listen to and process the music. This album was released only five years after his death but it opened up a whole new world of music and it sounded as new now as it did then.

"Damn," was all he said.

As the last track faded out, I let the silence fill the car. "I know, right?"

After a few more, now expected Elvis head shakes, the music lover in Elvis came alive. The next fifty miles was spent dissecting the music. He found everything from gospel to James Bond themes to 70s disco songs on the album. "There's really nothing new in music, but he sure found a new way of doing it. That boy's got some real talent, I'll tell you."

"Well, he's dead and it came out thirty-two years ago, but I have to agree with you. I'll show you the video for 'Beat It' and it will knock you out." I tried to imagine Elvis in the 1980s working his version of "Billie Jean" out on stage. Surely he would've come up with a better duet to do than Jacko's painful "The Girl Is Mine" duet with Paul McCartney. "Okay, let's play some Lisa Marie next."

His ears pricked up as he recognized his own voice in female form as the most famous daughter in America began to sing "S.O.B." Maybe he got a kick out of the fact the song was probably about him.

"Man, she's just my little girl. I don't get it. I don't get it."

I hoped he would sleep a bit but the Red Bull had Elvis counting the miles to Vegas. When we finally rolled in he was again in the state of confusion. 2010s Las Vegas is 1970s Las

Vegas on steroids. There was no Eiffel Tower on the Strip in the 1970s. The Flamingo and the Tropicana had been swallowed up by castles and pyramids.

"It looks like goddamn Disneyland!" he said. "Look at all these people! Where's Caesar's Palace?"

"It's there right past Bellagio."

"Bellagi-what? Just get me to the Hilton."

I imagined that Vegas looked more like *Blade Runner* to Elvis than the Vegas of the swinging Sinatra days. Sinatra's The Sands and many of those classic landmarks were long gone, replaced with massive casino infill. He seemed to finally accept that whatever world he was in, it was not 1977.

The Las Vegas Hilton didn't look that much different except for the monorail running through it. Elvis quickly pointed out the thirtieth floor that he regularly lived on in the 70s. "Man, this place looks like Scottie beamed it up into a *Star Trek* episode."

"That's kinda funny because there used to be a whole *Star Trek* section of the hotel where they could beam you up to the Enterprise, but the Next Generation version not the original series version."

"What?"

"Never mind. Let's get a room. It's been a long day."

"Don't worry. I have a penthouse suite that they keep for me. Where's the damn Hilton sign?" he asked.

"Oh, it's not the Hilton anymore. It's the LVH. Las Vegas Hilton. I think Paris Hilton sort of ruined the Hilton name so they just call it the LVH now."

"Who the hell is that?"

I guess I could have gone into a dissertation about how, in 2014, you don't have to be an artist like Elvis or Warhol to be a celebrity. You just had to be rich, have a sex tape, and reality show. And that there was a whole raft of celebrities that did nothing but be celebrities. They produced nothing of value but people were obsessed with them. I mean, really, how would you explain Kim Kardashian to Elvis Presley? But I had just driven 300 miles through the desert with a fat man who thinks it's 1977 and that he is the King of Rock and Roll, and I really needed a stiff drink, and to hit the hay. So I kept my mouth shut and parked the car.

"Hey, E? Just in case your contact isn't there, I'm going to book a room on Expedia before we go in."

"On your damn magic 'phone'? Get the penthouse suite. I have some clothes in it for when I wake up out of this mess."

A quick check online revealed that there was an Elvis Presley Suite on the thirtieth floor but it was $700 a night. As much fun as it would have been to slap it on the credit card, I would have regretted it later. Although the thought of walking up to the reservation desk with this guy and asking for the keys to that room made it tempting. But a double for $60 seemed like it might make more sense. Maybe I could gamble with the rest.

"Hey, will you look at that!" he shouted. I had forgotten about the Elvis statue by the front door. "Well, I put this place on the map, so I appreciate that very much." But when we walked into the casino his eyes glazed over.

Gone were the organized rows of one-arm bandits dropping quarters into metal drawers. They've been replaced by an infinite array of noisy beeping slot machines with pictures of Judge Judy and Desperate Housewives instead of lemons and cherries. Winners got tickets, not cash. But they were still mostly manned by blue-haired old ladies hypnotized by the lights.

"Goddamn."

"Let's just check in. I can pretty much bet that nobody you know is here anymore. So let me get us into a room and then maybe we can grab a drink." I have no doubt the woman at the front desk thought I was checking in with a piss-poor Elvis imitator who wore his sunglasses at night. Maybe he did a Fat Elvis bit singing "Hunka Hunka Burnin' Love" in the street down on Freemont. Regardless, she processed us in to a room on the tenth floor. I took my bag and my strange friend to the elevator, which happened to be playing the Elvis hit, "Good Luck Charm."

"Why didn't she even give you a key?"

"She did." I held up the plastic card.

"Part of me thinks all this science fiction shit is so cool I don't want to wake up yet. I want to go ride in a flying car or talk to a Martian."

"No flying cars yet. They totally lied to us about that one. There probably were Martians but they are all dead now." He looked disappointed as the elevator door opened and we made our way to the room.

"Well, it ain't my suite but it'll have to do since you're just a poor writer and all." He sat down on the bed, took off his sunglasses, and put his head back in his hands.

"You look pretty tired, my friend. Why don't you get some sleep. I'm going to go downstairs and have a drink and maybe gamble a bit. Do you need anything?"

"I think I'm going to take a shower. Yeah, can you turn on this weird TV for me, and call room service, and order me a fried chicken sandwich with fries and a Pepsi?"

Downstairs I sat at the bar and sipped my Fireball whiskey. If there were any lesson in this charade, it was a million (or at least 2000) miles away. I just found myself wanting to believe it was Elvis. That there *was* magic in the world, not just in movies. And that something like this *could* happen. That at one minute Elvis Aaron Presley was sitting on the toilet in Graceland in 1977 and then suddenly, the second before his heart stopped, he was in front of Priscilla's house in Beverly Hills in 2014.

My brain aspires to be a scientist. There is a logical explanation for everything. People who have near-death experiences and report going through a tunnel toward the light are probably just recalling the subconscious memory of their own birth and that tunnel is mom's vagina. It's just science, damnit!

But my heart wants to believe there is more. That in a universe ruled by chaos, all things are possible, including time traveling ghosts. Of course, my brain says that my heart's job is to pump blood and what I call my "heart" is just a fucked up part of my brain.

I moved to the roulette table because it's fun to pretend you are getting free drinks while you hand over mad stacks of cash to the casino. I put a $5 chip on black for Elvis and immediately doubled it. As is my rule, I put the original chip in my pocket ("at least break even") and put the winning chip on 35, for 1935, the year Elvis was born. As the host waved her hand and said, "No more bets," I watched the white ball spin around and around as I thought about my big gamble. When it hopped around, settling into the pocket of the 35, I took it as a sign.

I was hoping Elvis would be zonked out dreaming of

peanut butter pie, but when I got to the room he was sitting on the bed surfing through the infinite channels on the Hilton's cable system. His eyes were red again and he didn't look up to ask, "What the hell happened to the world?"

"Do you mean how stupid we've become or how idiotic we've become?"

"There's just so much. And none of it seems any good. If this was my TV, I would have shot it up hours ago." He was stopped on MTV's marathon of *Teen Mom* episodes and looked like he just had taken a bite of bad egg salad.

"Yeah, it's pretty pathetic. And that channel used to play only music. They would have loved you." He didn't flinch. "Hey, E, how about we get some sleep. I'd like to get at least 500 miles in tomorrow."

He pulled the covers up over his round shoulders. "Yeah, man, goodnight. And if I don't wake up in the future, thanks for the help."

I was up and showered by 9:00 and Elvis grabbed a clean pair of boxers out of the Target pack and threw the old ones in the trashcan. "Maybe I should burn these." I didn't know if that referred to their value on eBay or the King's colon issues.

As we gorged on the breakfast buffet, and elderly man stared at Elvis over his coffee. Finally he came over to the table. "I have to say I've seen a lot of bad Elvises in this town," he said, "but I knew the real one and you really look like he did at the end."

Elvis looked at the old man like he was the crypt keeper. "Tommy? Tommy, it's me. How did you get so goddamn old?"

Tommy Tayer worked in management at the Hilton in 1976 when Elvis had his last residence on the thirtieth floor. He was part of the staff that waited on the singer and his massive entourage. He had recently retired at the LVH but was given free buffet for life as part of his departure.

"Yeah, funny. You look pretty good for a fat corpse." The man was not amused.

"Remember when I asked you to bring up three banana cream pies just so I could throw them at Joe?" Elvis grabbed his arm like he was George Bailey, falling out of time.

The old fellow looked at me. "Friend, you've got one crazy Elvis here."

"I think we better hit the road, E." And we quietly vacated the LVH.

We got down to I-40 as quickly as possible without him saying a whole helluva lot. He seemed about as freaked out as anyone could be, giving a little more weight to the "this is the guy" theory bouncing around in my head. I switched on a Top 40 radio station out of Phoenix to subtly reassure him he was in the 21st century. He hated every song until Robin Thicke's "Blurred Lines" song started up.

"Marvin Gaye! I know this one!"

"No, it's this pro-rape song by this douchebag named Robin Thicke. But you're right, it's a total rip off of Marvin Gaye. More cowbell!"

"Wait, a pro-rape song? And it's got a black guy doing a poem in it. What the hell?"

"Yeah, he's saying that his dick is so big that it's going to tear her ass in two. And Thicke is singing, *You know you want it*. Kids love it."

"What the hell is wrong with you people?"

"That's a big question. Look, we're in a red state. How about I put on some Christian radio for a little bit?"

"A red what? Yeah, whatever. Thanks, man." But after three

minutes of Contemporary Christian music on KISS, Elvis blurted out, "What the hell is this shit?" Apparently modern Christian music sucks, according to the guy who sang, "How Great Thou Art." "How about some CCR?"

So we blasted east across America, listing to classic rock and oldies that were not really classic or old to him. The music opened him up, especially when "Suspicious Minds" or "Jailhouse Rock" came on. He told a hundred stories. Each song cued another memory; the day he met The Beatles, his untold rivalry with Tom Jones, how much he missed Priscilla and his mother. He seemed to have no idea about the legacy he'd left behind.

Somewhere in New Mexico I said, "You really don't have any idea about the impact you've had on the world, do you? I mean, there's absolutely no one on earth who doesn't have a favorite Elvis song. Buddhist monks in the fucking Himalayans are singing 'I Can't Help Falling In Love'! You really made your mark, not just in American history, but in the world."

He seemed to become quite emotional and that humble boy from Tupelo crept in. "Now boy, you're just messin' with me. My guys and my daddy say stuff like that sometimes, but they tell me all kinda things just to get me out of bed." It was clear that his Memphis Mafia had kept him in a small snow globe.

Around the top of Texas, I had to ask my one question I always wanted to ask Elvis if he were alive today. "Hey, can I ask you why you never made better movies in the 60s? You were so good in *King Creole*. Everyone thought you were the new James Dean."

"All those movies made a lot of money. I hated most of

them, but the goddamn Colonel kept signing me up for them. I guess he needed his gambling money. They wanted me for the lead in *West Side Story* and *A Star Is Born*. They even asked me to be in that X-rated movie, *Midnight Cowboy*, but the Colonel said no to all of them. So I did *Blue Hawaii* instead of *West Side Story*."

"Jesus, you would have made an amazing Tony. From what I've read, Tom Parker really got in the way of you being the great artist you should have been." Still feeling loyal to the old carny, Elvis just quieted down and stared out the window, nodding.

Approaching Amarillo, the discussion turned to Elvis' love of giving cars away. According to my rider, that was more of an urban legend than actual history. Although he did drop a few Fleetwood Cadillacs on deserving Memphis residents who were not part of his inner circle.

"I gave all my boys cars since the Colonel didn't pay them much. But then everybody started expecting me to give them a car. I'd get letters from ladies with sick kids asking for a Cadillac." He paused. "Now there's a car I like and it doesn't look like a damn spaceship."

A classic silver 1971 Mercedes-Benz 600 blew past us on the left.

"I had one of those. Do me a favor and see if you can catch up with it." Something had caught Elvis' eye and it was more than the vintage luxury car's out-of-placeness in 2014 North Texas. There was a young girl with long blonde hair in the passenger's seat staring at a smart phone.

I hit the gas on the Prius. My friends were always surprised by the pick-up on a hybrid, so after thirty seconds of going eighty-five we were side to side with the German machine.

"Oh, man, that's my Lisa Marie! That's her! And that's the car I gave Priscilla. Who the hell is driving it? We gotta stop them!"

"Oh, man. Seriously, that's not her. I told you she's like forty-five now and has a band and a bunch of kids. That just looks like she did a long time ago."

"Don't you think I know my own daughter? Look man, I'm sick of all this future shit. The game's over. I wish I had a gun. Just follow that car. Let's try to get this guy to pull over. He could be a damn kidnapper."

My head bounced with the image of my bloated Elvis trying out some rusty karate moves in the middle of I-40. Fortunately, the Benz veered off the next exit and pulled into a Love's truck stop. We glided in behind but before I could put the car in park, Elvis, suddenly limber and agile, jumped out and ran to the passenger side and pulled on the door.

"Lisa, it's me baby. It's Daddy! C'mon out." The little girl dropped the phone and screamed and the man driving stepped out of the car.

"Hey you, get the fuck away from my car. What the fuck do you think you are doing? You are scaring my fucking daughter!" He was a white guy about thirty, dressed like he was on vacation. It could have been his daughter or some kind of messed up Humbert Humbert scenario. Elvis crossed around and grabbed the guy by the neck and pinned him against the car.

"Who are the hell are you? Why do you have my baby? And stop all this cussin'!"

It was clear this was about to go south real quick. There was no way to explain the dead Elvis thing to this poor guy and his kid, who was screaming to high heaven. I had to step in.

"E, E, man, I promise you that's not Lisa. I promise you. She just looks like her." He loosened his grip on the guy who I tried to un-freak-out (if possible). "Man, I'm really sorry. My friend here has had a real shock recently and doesn't know where his daughter is. He had a car like this and thought it might be a kidnapping. It's just a big misunderstanding."

"Yeah, okay, I guess I might be in the same state if my Madison went missing. But your friend looks a little mental to me."

Elvis had stepped away and was looking in the window at the little girl who wasn't crying but was probably worried the big man would hurt her daddy.

"Uh, yeah, I guess I made a mistake," Elvis said, not completely believing his own words. "I didn't mean to upset your little girl. She just really looks like my Lisa. Do you think I could sing her a song?"

"Shit, that wouldn't be weird or anything," said the dad looking at the King like he was the King of Creepers.

"Seriously dude, you should let him. You will never forget it."

So the dad let his kid come out into the Love's parking lot and told her the scary man was sorry and wanted to make it up by singing a song. Elvis got down on one knee and began to sing "Puppet on a String" just like he did in the film *Girl Happy* and the little girl's eyes lit up.

"Holy fuck, the guy really sounds like Elvis Presley. Kind of looks a little like him too!"

We let the two go into the truck stop and got back into the Toyota. Elvis hung his head down. "Sorry about that, man. I really thought it was her."

"It's okay, my friend. Totally understandable."

"I'm never going to see my little girl again, am I?"

We covered more ground than I anticipated fueled by great old songs and stories about Red, Lamar, and the boys supposedly waiting back in Memphis. There were also spontaneous recreations of Monty Python skits, including Elvis riffing on dead parrots and singing about Spam (who the fuck knew?). He pointed out all the idiosyncrasies of modern life, like how every other person had white wires coming out of their ears. "To measure brain waves?" And I unsuccessfully tried to convince him to stop for a good haircut so he didn't look so much like Elvis.

Oklahoma City seemed like the best place to stop for the night. My head was spinning but I wasn't ready for my dream to end. I pulled in to where the Murrah Federal Building had been and explained how a lone anti-government racist had blown it up, killing 168 people including nineteen children. I pointed out the 171 chairs that were placed in the memorial to represent the victims.

"One hundred seventy one? I thought you said he killed 168 people."

"Well, three of them were pregnant women so the extra chairs are for their unborn babies."

Elvis pushed open the car door and leaned against the Prius, sinking down to his knees, tears dripping from his eyes. He clasped his hand in prayer. "Dear Lord, I don't belong in this world. It seems so cold and mean. I know mine ain't much better but please get me back to it. I wanna see my baby girl again."

We both slept in the next morning and woke up with each other in 2014. There was about half the distance to cover to Memphis so there was no rush, but I could tell he was anxious to get out of town. The city was stained with evil. So we got on I-40, headed toward Little Rock.

Through the Ozarks, Elvis began to get metaphysical. "You know, I've read about stuff like this. You think this might be a time travel thing, like I jumped thirty-seven years into the future for some crazy reason. But what if this is really a parallel universe and I traveled in space, not in time?"

I really had no response. Alien Elvis seemed as plausible as Time Machine Elvis. It seemed more like we were both in each other's disjointed dreams where things almost made sense. My scientist brain had no way to test these theories

We stopped in West Memphis and he finally agreed to get a haircut. He knew that driving up to Graceland looking like himself would create a stir to say the least, especially among the faithful who were camped out waiting for the arrival of their messiah. I let him know that, like everything else on our trip, not to expect Memphis, and especially Elvis Presley Boulevard, to look the same. "Okay, let's do it," he said, looking a bit more like a Toby Keith fan than the King.

As the sun started to set, we came through the cornfields of Arkansas to the Mississippi River. "Boy, I'd know that city in any century," he declared. Memphis certainly had grown. From the weary locale of MLK's assassination in the 60s and the intense racial poverty of the 70s, to a tourist hub and cultural center. (I think Elvis would have loved the civil rights museum at the Lorraine Motel.) But pictures of Elvis where everywhere, especially when we turned on to his street that, in the last thirty-seven years, had been transformed into Elvisland.

"Holy Moses."

"Yeah, I think Priscilla and Lisa Marie sold part of

Graceland to somebody—maybe the Japanese—and they developed it into a kind of amusement park. The good news is they are making shitloads of money off of Elvis-mania. There are people from all over the world here that just want to walk through your kitchen."

"Man, I don't know. I just gotta get inside."

Elvis seemed kind of stunned by the whole thing. We entered the complex across the street from Graceland to get tickets to go into his own home. There were images of him everywhere, his music playing through the PA, and old people with his face on their T-shirts. An obese man with slicked-back black hair had a tattoo of 50s Elvis on his neck. He just stared as I picked up two tickets at the window that would get us on a little shuttle bus that would get us to the door.

On the shuttle he kept quiet but seemed in distress. A teenage girl whispered to her mother, "That guy really looks like fat Elvis."

Young African-American tour guides with headsets ushered us through the front door that I imagine he had passed through thousands of times before. The distress gave way to recognition. The downstairs of Graceland had been frozen in amber. It was never a day after August 16, 1977 (except for the velvet ropes and security cameras). "They've turned my house into a damn museum." He instinctively moved toward the stairs to go up to his bedroom.

"Sir, you can't go up there! That's a private area."

Before the tour guide could get sucked into our little ripple in the time-space continuum, I grabbed his arm. "E, I think you should just come out to the garden."

We by-passed the tourists and went out to the Meditation Garden next to the pool on the side of the house. There were the graves of Elvis' mother and father, grandmother, and Elvis himself. He looked at the people staring at his grave, some in tears, most taking pictures with their phones. He sat on a bench, again with his face in his hands. "Boy, I guess you were right. I feel like Ebenezer Scrooge."

"You were a lot nicer than Scrooge. You made millions of people happy and you will continue to make people happy for a very long time."

"Well, I hope that counts for somethin'. I really don't know what happens next, but do you think it would be okay if I sit here for a bit and try to figure it out? I know I'm where I need to be but I don't have any idea where I need to go."

"Sure thing, my friend. I'll just hang out in front of the house."

I found a bench in the front yard and watched the busloads of tourists come and go; some were fans, some just wanted to look. Most were not even born when Elvis passed away. Some saw the trip as a Southern hajj, a religious trip to the most holy of shrines south of the Mason-Dixon Line. None really knew the man but all knew the myth.

It seemed like I knew the man and found him fragile and narcissistic at the same time. He spent his life walled off in a castle he didn't feel he deserved. As amusing as the twenty-first-century culture shock was (Why did so many girls have tattoos? Why did people put nails in their face? Why was everyone staring at their little *Star Trek* phones all the time? And on and on.), more than that was his need to know that his music still mattered. And it did.

As I sat there, I wondered if I could create something that people would still care about fifty years later. Maybe that was what I should focus on. I knew I had it in me, but was wracked with the feeling that my moment had passed. I should have written that book when I was twenty-one and knew fuck-all about anything but had the passion to actually sell it to the world. Maybe I should just keep driving until it came to me.

It had been nearly an hour and night had fully fallen. I worried that Elvis was barricaded in the Jungle Room, refusing to leave "his" home. But when I went inside, I couldn't find him. He wasn't in the stables or the racket ball court, which now displayed all his stage costumes. I asked the security guards if they had found a confused man upstairs, maybe locked in a bathroom, but they checked twice. He was nowhere. Maybe he was never there to begin with. I wasn't sure what to think.

I returned to my car and just sat there. The back seat had a few layers of Big Mac wrappers and Pepsi cans. That stuff is poison to me so there was physical evidence of my hefty hitchhiker. I was 3,000 miles from home with the weirdest ghost story ever. Or maybe he was right and he had returned to his parallel universe to die on a parallel Memphis bathroom floor. I missed him already and thought about the conversations we could have had, but didn't during those long stretches of silence. What did Elvis Presley think of dubstep music and the fact that Willie Nelson was America's number one pothead?

Maybe we should have tracked down Priscilla or Lisa Marie or some of the old gang that created a wall around him in his strange world. Or maybe I could have engineered a comeback career of a "new-found country singer" and gotten Rick Rubin to produce the album.

My mind spun at the possibilities now that he was gone. The hot August Memphis night seemed stickier than the day and the heavy air passed through the windows of the Prius.

The parking lot was emptying out as I saw a kid in a green sweater walking toward the car. Maybe he had seen my lost friend. He stuck his blonde shaggy head inside the passenger window and had that confused look on his face that I now knew.

"Hey man, cool car. I saw your Oregon plates. I'm, like, seriously lost. I really need to get back home to Seattle. Do you think you could give me a ride?"

❧

Randy Blazak is a sociology professor in Portland, Oregon. He usually writes about crime and gender, especially with regard to hate crimes and hate groups. Late at night, he secretly writes fiction. His first novel, *The Mission of the Sacred Heart: A Rock Novel,* was published in 2011 and has been optioned for a screenplay in Hollywood. It uses an Electric Light Orchestra album for inspiration. He is currently writing the follow-up, *The Dream Police,* which is inspired by a Cheap Trick album. Blazak also has a blog about feminist fatherhood called "Watching the Wheels," which chronicles the raising of his daughter in weird world we live in. Someday he'll take her on a pilgrimage to Graceland.

Mark Bowen
Chuck Mosley

(An excerpt of the forthcoming autobiography book)
with help from Douglas Esper

Standing onstage in San Francisco, out of my normal L.A. environment, smelling frankincense and other exotic fumes, I would look out and see the crowd's jaws drop and form stunned expressions like they were all saying, *Oh* at the same time. We, Faith No More, were playing "Mark Bowen"; one of the toughest songs I performed with them.

The song begins softly, slowly with a breakdown. Puffy's mellow jazzy beat gave me a few bars to croon like one of my earliest influences, David Bowie, but as soon as the mood is established, it kicks in: *But … you'll … never make the grade!*

The song explodes straight to an orgasmic climax and just keeps building in intensity. The vocals get more and more frenzied as the song progresses and the notes rise to the very tops of my range. The driving nonstop power of the song left me feeling like my balls, my head, or both would explode by song's end. A few times, after the song was done, I had to race offstage to throw up. Years later, while singing for Bad Brains, I had a similar relationship with the song "Soul Craft." There just wasn't any break to catch a breath.

Any audience member who wasn't sure if we were heavy enough, couldn't deny it as the song throttled their senses. Their hair was blown back and the shock escalated into hysterical excitement. After the climax there's a short breakdown. I dropped into a soft spoken tone and listed all these evils, the seven deadly sins, anything bad to show the dark side of the world to match the intensity and vibe of the song.

None of these things had to do with the man who the song is named after. In fact, he was like the polar opposite of them. Mark Bowen was the nicest guy in the world, a man's man. Someone I would aspire to be someday, if I ever grew up or matured mentally. If my mental maturity ever caught up with my physical side, which if that is to happen, I better do it soon because I'm already on the back nine. Mark was quiet, pleasant, humble, and funny.

Mark pre-dated me in the band and his song did as well. We played the song "Mark Bowen" a few times while Mark was still in the band, but I don't think I had the final lyrics developed at that point. Sometimes I procrastinate on writing lyrics and I think in this case, I actually waited until that last millisecond before we recorded to finish them off.

Even as I performed with Faith No More for the first time, Jim Martin was already on the band's radar via Cliff Burton and James Hetfield. I felt like Mark's days in the band were numbered because all of a sudden, I couldn't get straight answers about our next steps, and what was coming up. The guys from Metallica were pushing Jim to join us as he already knew Mike "Puffy" Bordin from other projects. Then, before long, Mark was out and Jim was in. Mark's song remained in our set, title intact. Again, lyrically it wasn't a reflection on Mark besides to say that he was none of the things listed.

Jim Martin and Mark had very different styles and sounds. Mark's sound was sound itself. He used effects pedals and his guitar to create noisy texture rather than straight chord progressions and riffs. Sure he was playing notes and all, but he built atmospheres like Brian Eno. Onstage, through the smoky haze, Mark would be playing with a cigarette in his mouth focused on his guitar, workman-like. He wasn't concerned about anything else going on. He just had laser focus on his guitar and the atmospheric sounds he was creating. Maybe there was more going through his head, but for me, on the outside looking in, it appeared nothing else mattered in those moments. He was so far down into himself making all these cool as shit sounds.

When I first came around, the band recorded practices and concerts, which was a huge help to assist writing lyrics and remembering vocal patterns. I'm a big improv guy and the first shows I played I was just singing and yelling by instinct. Playing by ear, you know what I mean. If we didn't have recordings, most of that stuff would've been lost to the wind. I can usually listen to a song a few times through and hear the melody I want to sing, though I'm much faster at that now than I was back then.

There's a demo of "Mark Bowen" that vocally sounds vastly different than the final version. My intention was to start quiet then build intensity with each and every line, but I ended up just yelling all of the lines until it was too much. It distracted from the music. Yelling was really all I knew how to do at that point. It had worked live. We had gotten a great response to the song during my first few shows, but listening to the demo it stuck out.

I remember listening to music in my girlfriend Diane's

room, back against the wall, sitting on a futon. David Bowie came on and I thought, *Hey, I can do that. Or at least try to.* After that I would constantly try to emulate actual singing, rather than just yelling or rapping, by vocalizing certain sounds without words to practice. After a while it started to sound pretty good and I thought, *Now, if I could just do that in tune …*

We recorded our first album, *We Care A Lot*, in about a week. The studio was in a barn, and I think we slept in the loft during the recording. "Mark Bowen" was a challenge live and it was the same in the studio. The only saving grace was using the magic of the studio. I could record a chunk of the song, take a breath, and then pick it back up right where I left off. I did record several takes all the way through the song, but some of the overdubs allowed me to identify variant melodies or harmonies that the taxing nature of the song didn't allow in one continuous track.

Matt Wallace, who engineered and produced the album, totally got me. He realized I wasn't a guy who was going to hit it on the mark and do it the same over and over and over. I like to experiment and play around. Of course, part of that was that at the time, I was just starting to sing. Previously I had been a keyboard player and a wannabe guitar player even though I couldn't play for shit. Hell, I was still afraid of the microphone and unsure of myself. Ever since I was thirteen years old singing in the shower, using my brush as a microphone, I knew I had emotion but no natural skills.

Matt kept the tape rolling and allowed me to find my way. He made the best of the situation and battled to bring me out of myself. I think he did get the best of me at the time. I'm sure recording Mike Patton was a lot easier for him because

Mike can sing everything and anything right on cue, and he can duplicate it the exact same way 50,000 times or however many times are needed.

It's been about thirty years since I performed "Mark Bowen" live, though I'm hoping to add that song to VUA's repertoire down the road. Looking back at the song, I'm proud of the lyrics, but also the vocal patterns. "Mark Bowen" provided a unique challenge and I like to think I managed to match the intensity of the music with my vocals. I like the journey the song takes the listener on.

It really is one of my favorite tunes and I hope Mark Bowen is happy to be associated with it.

Musician, chef, and dad, Chuck Mosley has crammed several lifetimes of experience into a few short decades. Chuck has been the lead vocalist for Faith No More, Cement, and Bad Brains. His latest music can be heard at www.chuckmosley. bandcamp.com, his experiences as a father can be read in his upcoming autobiography. The food, however, is already eaten, so don't even ask.

Hungry: The Memoir of Abby Snow

Kim Loraine

175

Okay, let's start this memoir off right. My name is Abigail Snow. I'm twenty-eight years old, and I am not fat. There, I said it. I didn't always feel this way. It has taken me a long time to be able to get the words to actually mean something to me. I write this without the intention of sharing it with anyone. It's my touchstone. It is here to ground me when I feel myself slipping. I've been a yo-yo dieter for a very long time, dropping thirty pounds and gaining it back over and over. Since early in my teens I've struggled with body issues, so has my mom. Like mother like daughter, or so I've heard.

I've always considered myself a smart person. My head is full of facts, some useful, some not. I am pretty. Not drop dead gorgeous or anything, but I'm not ugly. Then there's my job. I kick ass at my job. I'm a teacher and a damn good one. I teach first grade at Applewood Elementary. I love my kids. They are sweet, adorable, and even when they're little terrors, I always feel better after seeing them. They also love me and never make me feel ugly.

But let's backtrack a little. I'm in a good place right now. A year ago this was not the case. I was preparing for my first day at Applewood. My second teaching job ever, if you count student teaching as a job. Yes, yes, I know what you're thinking, *Why is she so* old *and yet so new to teaching?* Well, unlike most of my co-workers, I waited a few years before I was hit with that eureka moment and figured out what I wanted to do with my life. I worked the crappy retail jobs, did the high pressure sales thing, and finally figured out that I loved teaching people.

Of course, in order to follow my passion I had to go back to school. Do you know how hard it is to go to school full time while working to keep the lights on in your dinky little apartment? It's hard. With a capital *H.* I lived in the city, Seattle to be specific, while I attended school at the University of Washington. My tuition was expensive. In fact, I'm still drowning in crippling student loans, and my rent was astronomical. Yes, I could have lived on campus in the dorms, but I'm sorry, there was no way in hell I was going to live with an eighteen-year-old philosophy major or some other under water basket weaver. So, I took on a massive amount of debt to avoid teenaged angst.

But I digress. I was preparing for my first day at Applewood. With nerves standing en pointe and three cups of coffee in me, I checked myself out in the floor length mirror, and sighed. A few days before I'd bought my dress after falling in love with it at the store. A stylish fit and flare in navy blue with a cute bow detail at the waist and pockets. I love a dress with pockets! It fit like a glove and accented my hourglass shape. Now as I looked into the mirror, I saw a lot less Joan from *Mad Men* and a lot more Tracy Turnblad a'la *Hairspray.* All I saw was thick. I felt bloated, chubby, chunky, and every other adjective you can come up with. My pixie cut hair made me feel like my round face was on full display, accentuating my double chin and fat cheeks.

I stood there thinking, *God, what is wrong with me? Why*

did I get this ridiculous haircut? I looked at myself in the mirror again and felt the sting of desperation laced with panic, wishing for a different body. My phone buzzed in my pocket and I reached down to check it. A message from my boyfriend Alan.

Have a great first day, babe.

I smiled as I thought of him sitting at his boring accounting job, hating every minute of it. Alan was handsome, perhaps a little flabby around the middle, but who was I to judge? He'd been a jock in high school, popular, prom king and everything. When we started dating a few years ago now, I was floored by his interest in me. In high school he barely spoke to me, treated me like I was invisible. I really didn't know why he wanted me. He swore up and down that I was beautiful, that he liked me curvy and didn't want me to lose weight. I never believed him. I should also mention that he doesn't like it when I gain weight either. He'll let me know if I shouldn't indulge in that gorgeous cream puff on the counter or the pint of Ben & Jerry's in the freezer. A simple, "Are you sure you want that?" is all I need to hear from him to keep me from reaching for the spoon.

My life was a jumble of contradictions. The only constant that kept me focused was teaching. I knew I loved it. As I stepped out the door to my house and started my car, I forgot about being *fat*, and started to let the excitement build.

———

Teaching is hard! In case you've never wrangled twenty or so six-year-olds for six straight hours, I'm here to tell you something. It. Is. Hard. On my first day I was sneezed on in grand snot-rocket style, whined at, yelled at, and puked on. That was all before lunch. I was also hugged, told I was beautiful, and proposed to. So, it wasn't all bad. When I got home after my first day—after an hour long commute—all I wanted was to kick off my shoes, spend some time with a bottle of wine, and a romance novel. Instead, Alan was sitting on the couch playing video games online with his best friend, as usual.

"Hi," I called from the doorway as I removed my heels. "What are you doing here?"

Alan grunted at me while he tried to take down a herd of zombies from the safety of my couch. I don't know why I let him bring over his video games. I hated them. Alan and I hadn't made the leap into co-habitating waters quite yet but as I watched him stare mindlessly at the television, I didn't mind his fear of commitment so much.

"Nice to see you too. Why yes, I had a good first day. Thanks for asking."

I rolled my eyes in his general direction and headed to the kitchen in search of wine and chocolate.

"Goddammit! That's bullshit, dude!" Alan's voice made me jump as he accused the video game of cheating, yet again.

I sighed and poured myself a large glass of cabernet while I continued to rummage around the kitchen, looking for the stash of emergency chocolate.

"Babe? When did you get in?"

I emerged victorious from the back of the pantry beaming as I held the chocolate bar in my hand.

"I've been home about fifteen minutes." My feet ached from being squished into pointy-toed pumps all day.

Alan eyed my fingers as I slid one under the wrapper of my coveted chocolate. "You sure you want that, babe?"

That made me angry. I had worked all day at a really hard job. I earned this.

"Is there any dinner ready? I'm starving and this looks like the only thing ready at the moment."

Alan had the grace to look abashed. "No, I was gonna make dinner for you but I got caught up online with Max."

"Fine, whatever." I grabbed my wine glass and headed for the phone. "Pizza okay?"

Alan was already back at the couch saving the world from a zombie apocalypse. Amidst hoots and hollers from my idiot boyfriend, I ordered a pizza and sat down at my dining table with my wine and a book. All I really wanted was for him to go home so I could soak in a hot bubble bath. I couldn't remember why I was even with Alan in the first place.

Because he loves you. No man has ever stayed this long. And if you eat that whole chocolate bar, no one ever will. My inner voice was kind of a bitch sometimes.

A month after my first day at Applewood I was starting to feel at home. I knew the names of all my coworkers, had all my kids figured out, and hoped I was going to make friends soon. The teacher's lounge felt a little like Siberia, or a scene from *Mean Girls*. All the other teachers were Barbie-doll-pretty and super thin. They talked about their Pilates classes, meeting up for spin class, and their crazy cleanse diets. It's not that they were mean to me, I just felt out of place.

One particular morning I was enjoying my coffee during my classes' music time. This was the only time I had to myself during the day. I sat in the teacher's lounge sipping at my steaming cup and watching some of the kids play outside.

"Abby. Oh Abby, what are we going to do with you?"

I turned to see who'd joined me in the empty room. Lucinda Martin, fourth grade teacher and resident Queen Bee, walked toward me with a wide smile on her perfect face. She was arm in arm with the most gorgeous man I'd ever seen. Yes, I know, I have a boyfriend. Stop judging me.

"Hasn't anyone told you the vintage look is out?"

Lucinda was beautiful. She had the kind of body I'd only seen on TV. All smooth lines and lots of shimmer. Her hair was a flowing mass of buttery blonde. It cascaded off to the side in a tasteful ponytail.

I looked down at my green a-line skirt and cream cardigan. "I'm sorry?"

"Don't get me wrong," she said, eyes going wide with feigned innocence, "you're absolutely adorable. I just think we need to update you a bit. Get you into something a little more … classy."

Rage boiled up inside of me. "I'll pass thanks. I like my clothes fine."

The man looked at me, his cheeks pink with embarrassment. "I'm Brandon Baker." He held out his hand to shake mine.

I scrambled to my feet and took his hand, mortified he'd witnessed Lucinda's attack on me. "Abby Snow. Are you the new sixth grade teacher?"

Brandon nodded and smiled slightly. "Nice to meet you, Abby. I'm sure I'll see you around."

Lucinda fumed as she watched our exchange. "Anyway Brandon, this is the lounge. Let's get the rest of the tour over with."

She placed a hand on my arm and gave me a pitying look. "Abby, if you ever want to go shopping, I'll be happy to go with you. I know how hard it can be to find clothes in *your* size."

She turned on her heels and clacked down the hall. If steam could have escaped my ears it would've. She had some nerve talking to me that way. As the day wore on, her words seeped into my subconscious. I found myself tugging at my clothes uncomfortably and using my lunch hour to research power cleanses.

I avoided the teacher's lounge after school was over for the day and headed home, ready to change my life.

— · · —

165

After my humiliating experience with Lucinda in the teacher's lounge, I scoured Pinterest for cleanse recipes. I figured if those Barbie doll look-a-likes could stay thin that way, I could get thin the same way. I decided on a fourteen day detox cleanse that required me to only drink a special lemonade and water.

Ten days into the cleanse I felt exhausted, hungry, and surprisingly thinner. I'd told myself I was not going to set foot on the dreaded scale until after my fourteen days were up, but I couldn't wait. That morning I shed my clothes and stepped on the scale. I thought my eyes must've been playing tricks on me because according to my scale, I'd lost ten pounds in as many days!

I picked up the phone to call Alan with the exciting news.

"Hello? Abby are you okay?"

"Alan! Ten pounds Alan. I've lost ten pounds."

"Abby. It is five in the freaking morning. Why the hell are you calling me right now?" His voice was gruff and annoyed.

"I'm sorry. I'm just so excited."

He harrumphed into the phone. "A pound a day is too much. That's not healthy."

"Killjoy."

I was frustrated. This was a big deal for me. My clothes were getting too big. My face looked thinner, more angular. I was finally in control of my weight. My fingers itched to call someone, anyone, who would share in my excitement since Alan had let me down.

I found myself dialing a familiar number but heartache set in as I remembered with a pang that Kelli, my long time bestie, was halfway across the world with her new husband. Kelli had gotten married two months earlier to a gorgeous Navy man, but apparently the U.S. Navy didn't care that I needed her. They packed up and left for Japan without consulting me.

I hung up the phone without another word and dressed for the day. I chose a sheath dress from the back of my closet. I hadn't fit in it for years but didn't have the heart to get rid of it. I did a happy dance as the side-zip slid up easily and checked myself out in the mirror. My lumps and bulges were barely noticeable. I left the house with a spring in my step and a thermos full of lemonade.

People started commenting on my weight-loss. Lucinda smiled and cooed with the rest of them but I could see her jealousy. She stared daggers at me every time Brandon looked my way.

I didn't want this feeling to go away. After my fourteen days were up, I became obsessed with the stupid scale. I checked my weight each day, and if that red needle raised even a pound higher, I restricted my food intake. By the time Christmas break rolled around, I'd lost twenty-five pounds and had to buy a whole new wardrobe. That shopping trip did *not* include Lucinda.

I arrived at my parents' house feeling proud of my accomplishment. I just knew my mom would be excited to see my dramatic weight-loss.

"Abby! Oh my God, you look fantastic! Is this that amazing cleanse you told me about?" My mom beamed and took in my svelte form. She pinched at my belly and grabbed a little of the fat I was still so ashamed of. "Got a bit of work to do still, huh?"

I worked hard to restrict my calorie intake during my visit with my parents. My dad commented on how little I was eating but my mom, ever the calorie conscious, shushed him.

After the break I was surprised to find Lucinda's group of friends waiting for me to join them while we sipped our low calorie beverages and nibbled our leafy greens.

"Abby. You look so amazing. Have you tried spin class? It helps your body get rid of even more toxins through sweat." Magnolia Callahan, former beauty queen and resident kindergarten teacher, sipped her detox tea as she told me more about spin class.

"Where did you get this amazing vintage dress, Abby?" Clarissa Hogan asked me, her fingers reaching out to touch the lace detail at the hem.

I opened my mouth to tell her all about the vintage store I'd found while shopping in Old Town, but was silenced by Brandon Baker. He'd walked into the lounge looking delicious in a pair of dark jeans that hugged his muscular thighs. His forest green button down fit him just right and the charcoal grey vest he wore over the shirt accented his trim physique.

"What was that, Abby?" Clarissa laughed at me.

I shook my head and smiled in Brandon's direction. He rewarded me with a heart-stopping grin as he moved to join us.

"He's so hot," Magnolia sighed and twirled her wedding band.

"It's men like him that make me wish I wasn't married," Clarissa agreed.

"You know he likes you, right, Abby? He's always waiting around for you." Magnolia refilled her thermos with tea and gathered her lunch bag.

"He's my friend, Mags."

"Sure he is. If *friend* means someone who wants to bend you over a table and screw your brains out."

I nearly choked at her statement, and flushed so deeply I was sure my face was cherry red.

"Leave her alone, Magnolia." Clarissa came to my rescue.

"Thanks, Clarissa."

She grinned wickedly. "He's probably more of an up-against-the-wall type."

—••—

Brandon Baker was the best thing about my weight-loss. The man was hot, intelligent, had a great sense of humor, and he liked me. I remained very aware of Alan in my life, but honestly, since I had started losing weight, Alan and I were drifting from one another. Brandon was here, I saw him every day, and he was interested in me. Alan was a lazy ass who couldn't be bothered to put the toilet seat down in the middle of the night, routinely leading to me falling into the toilet when I got up to pee.

I sat in my classroom grading papers after my kids had all been ushered to the school busses or picked up by parents. My stomach grumbled in annoyance at its emptiness and I reached for the protein bar I'd been nibbling on all day. The packaging said it contained 200 calories and I'd eaten about half of it since this morning. I began totaling my intake for the day and realized if I finished it, I wouldn't have enough calories left in my 600 for the day to fit in dinner. I wrapped the bar back up and shoved it in my desk drawer for the next day.

"Um, Abby? You busy?" Brandon poked his head in my room and grinned.

My heart fluttered as I took him in. He'd been away all day on a field trip with his class and I realized how much I missed seeing him.

"No, come on in, Brandon. What's up?"

He came around my desk and leaned against it, facing me. God he smelled good, like clean linen and sandalwood.

"I just wanted to see you. I was heading home but saw your room light was on."

"Oh, yeah. I'm just finishing up some grading. I've got a spin class in about an hour so there's no real reason to go home." I rose from my chair and started wiping down the whiteboard.

"You look good, Abby. I don't know why you're always dieting."

"I'm not really dieting. Just watching what I eat," I lied.

I felt him before I turned around. His hand brushed against my neck and down my shoulder. "You're beautiful."

My hair stood on end, every part of me tense at his touch. "Thank you. So are you." I looked into his bright blue eyes.

His lips touched mine briefly—just a slight brush—as if testing the waters before diving in. I sucked in a breath and sighed as he took my face in his hands and crushed himself to me. Before I knew what was happening, I was laying across my desk with my skirt rucked up over my hips having the most amazing sex of my life with a man who was not my boyfriend.

He kissed me as he left, still tucking his shirt into his slacks. "Have a good spin class, Abby."

I sat on my desk, rumpled and breathless. "Well shit," I said to the empty room.

— • • —

I stepped on the scale and cheered for joy as the needle dropped another five pounds since I started my weight-loss journey. The girls and I completed yet another juice cleanse and I was the thinnest I'd ever been. I loved running my hands across my hip bones to feel their definition. I could even feel my ribs begin to stick out a little. Finally the woman I always wanted to see was appearing in the mirror. I ran some styling creme through my hair and sighed in disgust at all the hairs that were left on my hand. *Great, my hair is falling out. I finally start to get thin and now I'm going bald!*

Alan was so busy at work it was easy for me to keep seeing Brandon without any suspicion. Brandon and I were hot and heavy. We met up at school, at motels close by, or sometimes just in his car, as often as possible. I sort of felt guilty for cheating on Alan, but honestly, he was a pretty crappy boyfriend anyway. At least that's how I justified it. When Brandon looked at me and told me I was beautiful, I actually believed him. I was putting my detox thermos in my bag and heading home for the day when Magnolia came into my classroom.

"Oh. My. God. Did you hear about Lucinda?" Her cheeks flamed red with embarrassment.

"No. What?"

"Well, apparently she found her husband sleeping with her sister yesterday. She had a complete breakdown today during her planning period. They had to call her mother to come get her and take her away."

"Oh, God. That's awful."

Magnolia looked smug. "Well, now I guess she's not so much better than the rest of us."

My heart squeezed with anxiety. How could she be rejoicing in this woman's misery and expect the same of me? Was this really the person I was becoming?

"I've got to go Mag. Spin class tomorrow?"

"Yep. I've got a great new cleanse we can try too."

I nodded and headed home, guilt weighing heavily on me.

It was ironic that just a few months after I was the social pariah—the Ugly Betty of Applewood—I suddenly took the place of Lucinda, all because of a few pounds.

Alan was waiting for me when I got home. The house smelled heavenly, music played softly from my iPod speakers, and the house was immaculately clean.

"Hey, babe. You're just in time for dinner." Alan stood behind the counter in my small kitchen, a proud smile plastered on his face.

My eyes widened in shock at this unexpected gesture. "What is this for?"

"Abby." His face turned serious. "I know I've been a crappy boyfriend. I'm sorry. You've been working so hard lately and I wanted to show you how proud I am of you."

"It's our anniversary?" My heart lurched. How could I forget this? "I … I've been so busy. I didn't get you anything."

Alan walked around the counter to meet me in the dining room. "You already give me everything I need."

He took my face in his hands and kissed me. His lips were soft. The scent of his usual bar soap and shaving cream caused a jolt of guilt to run up my spine.

"Alan." I pushed him away, eyes unable to meet his questioning gaze.

"You ready to eat? You must be starved."

I smiled weakly. "I could eat."

I totaled up my calorie intake for the day and figured I could allow myself five bites of dinner. Five bites would be just enough to make it look like I'd really eaten.

We sat across from each other at my small dining table. I pushed my food around on my plate, trying to eat slowly and avoid Alan's eyes.

"You don't like it?"

"No, it's delicious Alan, thanks. I had a big snack before I left work today." I was such a liar. The only snack I'd had that day was Brandon.

"I need to ask you something." Alan reached across the table for my hand.

My palms started sweating as apprehension wormed its way into my head.

"I think we should move in together Abby."

"What?"

"Three years is a long time, I practically live here anyway.

We're both employed and have stable jobs. We could get a bigger place together."

My heart was threatening to beat its way out of my chest.

"Um, well. Let's think about it okay? I don't want to rush into anything. Living together is pretty serious."

I watched disappointment cloud his features. "Yeah. Okay. You done?"

He snatched my plate and shoveled the remaining food into the garbage. I rose and helped him clear the table. My heart broke for him at that moment. I knew I'd hurt him. I thought about all the reasons we couldn't live together. He was a slob, he snored, and I'd have to answer a lot of questions about my eating habits. I didn't want to share that part of me with anyone. I worked hard for this body and nobody was going to tell me I needed to change. We couldn't live together. *Especially not when you're screwing the sixth grade teacher after school every day.*

Did I mention my inner voice was a bitch?

—··—

130

Weeks after Alan made his grand gesture, I made plans to meet him for dinner after work. I planned to break it off with him. Brandon and I needed to be able to see each other in more settings than our usual half-dressed-and-rushed-to-screw style. I wanted to date him, to be seen in public and be able to beam with pride at the beautiful man who was with me. I was down to the skinniest I'd ever been and I felt fantastic, most of the time my hunger pangs not-withstanding. I thought I could take on the world.

I'd just said goodbye to my gaggle of little monsters for the day and waited seated on my desk for Brandon, top button popped, and skirt hiked up to flash a generous amount of thigh. Our typical routine went something like this: school ended, we screwed like bunnies, I slunk back home. Not today. Today was the day I freed myself of Alan and his less-than-glamorous life. So there I sat, expectant and more than a little horny. And I waited, and waited.

I fished my phone out of the depths of my bag and scanned for some message explaining Brandon's absence. Nothing. I wracked my brain trying to remember if we'd planned on meeting somewhere else. Finally I punched at the phone, dialing his number.

"Abby?" His voice was a tense whisper.

"Where are you? I've been waiting. I've got on the thigh highs and garter belt you like so much." I put on my most seductive voice, smiling as he cleared his throat.

"I can't."

I sat up, alarm bells clanging in my head. "What?"

"Abby, there's something …"

That's when I heard her calling to him in the background.

"Who the hell is that?"

"It's my … my wife."

A cold knot formed where my heart should've been. "You're married?"

"I'm sorry. I … I should've told you."

"Um, yeah. That's a pretty freaking big thing to leave out. Or were you just too busy screwing me to remember to mention her?"

"I can't do this anymore, Abby. It's been great, but Mel and I are trying to make it work. I can't see you again."

My tongue sat heavy in my mouth like lead.

"Abby?"

"Go to hell, Brandon." The shout reverberated through my cheerfully decorated classroom.

I hung up the phone with shaking fingers and slowly slid off the desk. Tears welled in my eyes, hot and insistent, but I willed them away. I would not cry over this asshole.

⸺ • • ⸺

After the debacle with he-who-shall-remain-nameless, my perspective changed. Having a man want me, albeit a gorgeous Greek god of a man, shouldn't be the driving reason for me to lose weight. I wanted to be thin enough that if I gained a few pounds back I'd still be below my ideal weight. I needed a safety net. I still hadn't broken it off with Alan or given him an answer about the whole moving in together scenario. He was circling. Anxious for an answer or for me to just do something.

"Abby? Abs? Wake up." Alan stared at me. A look of concern etched into his brow.

"What?"

"Abby, it's four in the afternoon. Why are you sleeping?"

I looked around my apartment confused. I'd come in from checking my mail and been so tired I'd needed to sit for a rest.

"I must've fallen asleep. I think I'm coming down with something. I'm so tired lately."

In fact, I felt like pure shit. I barely had the energy to walk up a flight of stairs. Most days at school I had to sit after each trip around the classroom just to catch my breath.

"Abby, I think you need to see a doctor."

I waved him away. "I'm fine. I'm sure it's just a cold."

Alan lowered his face to mine. He grabbed my wrist and held it in front of my face. "*This* is not fine Abby."

I looked at my tiny wrist, so proud to see how small it was. "I'm fine. You're just not used to seeing me at my ideal weight."

"No Abby. You barely eat, you exercise like crazy, and you do all these weird cleanses. Not to mention, since you lost all that weight, you've become a shadow of yourself. I don't think I really even know you anymore."

I had no words. He was accusing me of having an eating disorder, of that I was pretty sure. The nerve! Here I was, working so hard to be the beautifully thin and fit woman I'd always wanted to be, and he said I was sick.

"You're just jealous. Jealous that someone else is going to want me now."

"Abby, look at yourself. You need help."

"Get out. We're done."

His face went pale. "Abs …"

"Oh, and by the way. I've been cheating on you. I think we need to break up." My words were laced with venom, a far cry from the Abby I'd been.

He turned on his heel and walked away, slamming the door on his way out.

I stood, heart hammering in my chest, and went to the mirror. He was right. The girl in the mirror looked haggard. Her eyes were sunken, ringed by dark circles that no amount of concealer could hide. Stringy, lifeless hair framed her sallow complexion.

Who was this? Alan was right.

— · · —

I knew I had a problem, but for the life of me I couldn't stop. Every calorie I took in felt like a betrayal to my progress. The school year was coming to a close, only two days left, and I couldn't wait to be done with my first year of teaching. I needed a rest. Time to reevaluate my life and my choices. I was so terrified of gaining an ounce and going back to my old ways.

I'd lost a grand total of sixty-five pounds, bringing me down to a record weight of 110. I'd never been so thin, and yet I so desperately wanted to escape the prison I'd created for myself.

I'd finished for the day and was dreading dinner with my parents. My mom had been annoyingly persistent, so I relented. As I sat in my car, parked in the familiar driveway of my childhood home, I breathed deeply, trying to calm the erratic beat of my heart.

I woke to the wail of sirens and the flashing lights of an ambulance. My mom stood on the porch, eyes shining with tears and a look of terror on her usually jovial face. The first thing I thought was, *Oh God, who died?* until I realized the paramedics were prying my car door open and pulling me onto a stretcher. I faintly heard my mom crying my name as the doors were shut behind me, but things faded to grey and then black before I could tell her I was fine.

Technically I was dead for three minutes. That's not something most people can say happened to them. It's not something I'm too proud of either. I woke with a burning sensation on the skin of my chest. My head ached, my throat hurt, and my arms were connected to various tubes and monitors.

"I see you're awake, Ms. Snow." A gentle female voice at my ear coaxed me from the edges of unconsciousness.

It hurt to swallow and my voice came out cracked and harsh. "What happened?"

"I'm Doctor Sheffield. You have a cardiac arrhythmia which caused your body to go into cardiac arrest." Her soft features calmed me against the terrifying words. "We had to restart your heart twice. Your throat might be a little sore. That's from the tubes we had to put down your throat. You weren't breathing on your own for a while there."

Panic rose and I heard the beeping of my heart monitor speed up.

"I know it's scary. I've got to ask you some questions Abigail."

"Abby. Call me Abby please." I whispered.

She pulled out a clipboard and started scribbling. "Abby, have you ever heard of the condition Anorexia Nervosa?"

I nodded.

"Okay, do you understand that you are drastically underweight for your height?"

I nodded again.

"Abby, your body is shutting down. Just by looking at you I can tell you are suffering the symptoms of starvation. Do you understand me?"

Tears spilled down my cheeks as I nodded yet again.

"We've got a staff psychologist coming to see you shortly. I recommend you talk to him. Set up a treatment plan." Her eyes were sad, as if she thought I might be a lost cause. "You can get better, Abby. I've seen it. I've also seen it go the other way too many times. Be the success story, Abby."

"Thank you, doctor."

She left with a soft squeak of shoes on the shiny tile floor. I took a steadying breath and waited for the psychologist to walk through the door.

— · · —

110

Almost dying really gets to you. I say that in all seriousness. I spent three months in intense therapy after my near-death experience. My shrink says I'm on my way to recovery. I've gained a few pounds and am looking in the mirror less and less. My life isn't validated by a number on a scale or in a clothing tag. I lost a lot more than weight over the last year.

After missing the last two days of school due to a medical emergency, I'd gotten a lot of visitors. It was pretty clear to my *friends* what happened. Needless to say, they dropped me like damaged goods and moved on to the next sucker. Good riddance.

Alan and I are broken, and that's my fault. We're talking, but it will never be the way it used to. I'm okay with that. I have a lot of work to do to get healthy. Food and I still struggle to maintain a healthy relationship, and honestly, we probably always will.

I never realized a grown woman could develop an eating disorder. Maybe I saw the world through rose-colored glasses before. I thought those kinds of things only happened to neurotic and troubled teens. Silly me. I will always struggle with anorexia. I probably did lots of damage to my body that I will pay for in my later years. But at least I will have later years.

Every morning I wake up and say. "My name is Abigail Snow. I'm twenty-eight years old, and I am not fat."

Most days, I believe it.

❧

Kim Loraine is the author of the "Golden Beach" series, including *Restoration* (2015) and *Renovation* (2015). She started writing at a young age, scribbling down song lyrics, short stories, and poems she was too afraid to share with anyone. Busy working as a music teacher in her Pacific Northwest hometown, it wasn't until her family of four picked up everything and moved to beautiful Japan that she decided to finally take the plunge and send her characters out into the world. The central theme in Kim's books is self-discovery, whether that is found through taking risks, breaking down walls, or admitting mistakes. Kim likes to write characters that seem like someone you actually know, who find that life is a journey not without its challenges. When not writing Kim spends her time with her husband, chasing around their crazy kids, exploring Japan, and binge-watching *Doctor Who* on Netflix. Pick up Kim's books through amazon.com and Barnes & Nobles. You can follow Kim on Twitter @kimloraine2 or Facebook www.facebook.com/kimlorainewriter.

Lithium Sandwich
Leah Lederman

There were probably ten of us in the room. We were free to go, except for the fact that the door was locked.

And so we waited.

The orange jumpsuits they had us wear had a strange scent, like vomit mixed with tortilla. We filled them out differently, each one of us. It looked nice on the tanned-brown desert skin of a few of the girls, though it made the fat girl look like a Creamsicle. She seemed self-conscious about this, and covered what she could of herself with a wool blanket. It had the same vomit smell. She and another girl—practically an albino—sat on the metal bed, which was simply a block of metal built out from the wall.

Most of us tried to get as far away from the toilet as possible. None of us really wanted to look at it, though one girl pointed out bitterly, "There's not even toilet paper in here! How the fuck I'm s'posed to take a piss?"

"They lettin' us out soon." When this girl spoke I used it as an excuse to stare at the tattoo that trickled downward from her hairline, cut in front of her ear, then crept down her neck. She seemed comfortable, and was standing by the toilet using the crinkled aluminum foil mirror to finger-comb her stringy black hair. Strands of it drifted away from her hands and landed on an older woman sitting nearby, crumpled. I'd seen her when they brought her in. The blood on her face was cleaned away but the bruises were starting to show. She didn't move.

And we waited.

The biological imperatives arrived, and finally one of us, who just couldn't take it any longer, sat on the metal throne and stared into the middle distance while the stream rattled against the dented tin. I didn't want her to see me look at her, but I wanted to see the face of a woman who was pissing on a toilet surrounded by ten other women, ten strangers. She wobbled her hips over the rim, then leaned up onto the balls of her feet and bobbed her butt up and down like some nasty club dance.

Days like this I could see the benefit of being a man. Just piss anywhere. Shake it off. Resume normal duties.

Neck Tattoo got up and banged on the tiny window. "Hey! We need some mahfuggin toilet paper in here!"

Another girl threw her head back and shouted, "Let us out!" This one was painfully skinny, and I watched her knees knock against each other from the exertion of her scream. "I'm hungry, man." She snuffled and wiped her eyes. "About to get some nachos when I get out this bitch."

The albino sat with her legs crossed and her hands upturned on her knees. She lolled her head back with her eyes closed and looked like she was practicing drunken yoga. "Hungry," she breathed, then mouthed the word again and again. "Hungry. Hungry. Hungry."

A collective grimace. It had been at least twenty-four hours since any of us had eaten, and then it was just broth.

"Somebody tell her to shut up."

Knobby-knees sucked her teeth and glared. "She ain't even making noise. Leave her alone."

The pale girl kept rolling her head back, hitting the wall with a metallic *thud*. Her face sagged on its neck like an ill-fitting Halloween costume. Her mutters were barely-breathed whispers. "We hold these truths to be self-evident … no, no wait."

"Jesus, what's she saying?"

No one answered.

Neck Tattoo sighed loudly and stormed on the window again. "Why ain't you lettin' us out?"

The blonde girl was making us uncomfortable. Before, we'd all just hugged our knees and stared at the floor in front of us. Don't ever make eye contact; that one we all learned quickly. But it had been quiet.

We were just waiting.

Now our stomachs pulled at the corners of our thoughts, tearing off sentences and leaving the thoughts incomplete. We were hungry.

"It is a truth … acknowledged …" She rocked her head back and forth, slowly. Her hands pawed clumsily at the air, grabbing at words that eluded her.

Then she shot straight up and smiled, triumphant. "A woman in want of a sandwich will make a sandwich!"

I chuckled in spite of myself, but it caught short in my throat like a sob. Neck Tattoo glared at me, and the fat girl looked worried. Knobby knees giggled unashamedly and called, "Ooooh, that bitch is crazy!"

"That girl needs some help." It was the girl who had pissed on the toilet. Somehow nothing she said mattered, because I'd seen her bob up and down over the toilet, and it was all I could see when she spoke. "I think she needs some meds."

"I was here all weekend, and she was here before me. They haven't given her any of her lithium since she's been in here." Fat girl said.

"She ain't on no lithium. Bitch is straight-up crazy." Knobby knees peeled off the fake nail on her ring finger and chucked it at the poor, muttering girl. Then she threw back her head and shouted, "Let us out!"

The albino began to mime.

She made fists in the air in front of her face, bent her elbows, and then moved her fists outward. No, they weren't fists—what was she doing?

At first we tried to ignore her, but it wasn't long before all of us were watching her every movement. It passed the time, and we were transfixed.

"She's opening doors!" I said.

"Shut up," Knobby Knees spat.

Pasty-face peered into the doors—or was it a window? She was looking hard for something. Her face lit up—aha! She'd found it—some sort of jug, the way her hand closed around it. She brought it close to her stomach and hunched her shoulders while twisting her hands in mid-air. Whatever she'd taken out of the imaginary door was hard to open.

There were more doors opening, and items gathered. She set them carefully on the metal around her, politely moving the fat girl's wool blanket from her workspace. Closing her eyes and humming, she waved one hand rhythmically over the other, as if she were buttering bread.

The preparations continued and became more elaborate. She squeezed, she poured, she sliced. She stirred something in a pot with one hand.

We watched, spellbound. Our stomachs rumbled and we

glared at one another, daring anyone to say anything. Still, she did not open her eyes.

There were several invisible piles in front of her, and she took something from each one and laid it on the bread slices, now sitting invisibly on her lap. She'd piled everything on, added spices, and finally closed what could only be a sandwich. With both hands outstretched, barely containing the deli monstrosity, she inhaled with anticipation and offered a coy smile before unhinging her jaw for the first bite.

Her top teeth clicked on her bottom teeth, hard. Her eyes opened, and her bottom lip dropped.

It wasn't really a sandwich. There was nothing there.

Her eyes followed her hands, still in formation, down to her lap. Then everything crumbled. Her hands collapsed into her lap, and her chin fell to her chest.

Neck Tattoo stood up and moved around the small room like she owned it. She was laughing. "You tryin' to make a sandwich?" She stepped toward the albino and slapped at the curtain of hair in the girl's face. "Huh? You gonna share some of that Oscar Meyer shit up here?"

Knobby Knees joined the ridicule. "Her face look like mine done when I got my cherry popped!" She mimicked the phantom-sandwich and exaggerated the girl's shocked face. "Like, what the fuck was *that*?"

The albino didn't hear us. She rolled her shoulders and craned her neck at the walls and corners of the metal room, bewildered like a caged cat. The whites of her eyes rattled around. "I just want some food," she breathed.

The crumpled woman began to weep, though I don't know if she had been paying attention to any of us at all.

Neck Tattoo shook her head and pounded the knuckles of

her clenched fist on the thigh of her orange-pants. "Man, but I am fucking hungry."

And then the howl again. "LET US OUT!"

My Wife's Favorite

Douglas Esper

Trent used to frequent Gil and Jill's frame shop back in high school, but he hadn't ventured a single step in his old neighborhood since becoming a bona-fide rock star. Sure, you could argue that being a replacement drummer for the band currently featured on the cover of *Rolling Stone* didn't make you a rock god, but try telling that to the two girls tailing Trent's car in a brand new Benz.

Trent regarded the storefront with disappointment. "You're not seriously taking me in there, are you?"

Ever the wanna-be art snob, he'd had a few pieces framed here even when he could scarcely afford the work before his *big break* in the music biz. At the time, he hadn't been drawn to the shop by the high quality, but rather by the eye candy.

Jill.

Every boy, man, and curious woman knew about Jill. She was a total fox. When she was working, business doubled. The first time Trent entered the shop he had a firm budget of $150 to get a piece framed, but thirty minutes later he was the proud owner of a receipt for his $150 down payment for a $415 frame job. Having no idea how he would pay rent that month, Trent felt Jill's company had been worth every penny.

He had come back a few times, but only to interact and order from Jill.

Now, after a year of non-stop touring, along with his hired art dealer, Trent had returned to his hometown to pick out his first real fine art piece. He rolled his eyes and ran his fingers through his multi-colored Mohawk, which he had left productless for the day. "Dude, I'm paying you a nice chunk of change to expose me to some of the best art this city has to offer, and you bring me here?"

Though excited at the opportunity to see Jill and show off his recent success, Trent felt wary of being swindled. He leaned forward in the rental car's back seat to make sure the attitude in his voice was clear. He pointed toward the rustic red and brown brick building half-covered in ivy across the parking lot. "This is a frame shop. They don't even sell real art here."

Shaking his head, Trent pushed back into his seat just in time to observe a homeless man dumpster diving in the crisp Oregon rain.

In the front passenger seat, Joseph—the anorexicly-framed art dealer—turned just enough to let Trent know he was speaking to him. "Statements like that expose you as a nobody. You didn't hire me to whisk you to all the known dealers. The reason I'm here is to immerse you in a pool of art that most people have no idea exists. Inside this building are not only beautiful works of art, but you'll also be treated to things dark, dangerous, even illegal. Just like you requested."

Left with that bit of news to chew on, Trent watched Joseph—failed artist, failed dancer, failed chef, yet all too successful social pariah—exit the car, straighten his thick hipster glasses, tussle his long acid-trip-inducing scarf, and light an exotic Turkish cigarette that cost more than the scarf.

Trent slapped at his latest tattoo to calm the itching sensation in his calf, and then followed Joseph into the rain and across the parking lot.

A ding announced their arrival, but the heavy wooden door slamming closed behind them made for a better introduction. Inside the claustrophobic shop there were two walls full of famous framed art prints, one wall with a mind-blowing selection of glass and matte choices, and the last wall, behind the counter and work area, had shelves with tools and scraps of a wide range of colors.

Bent over a worktable was Gil, tracing on pink matte for his next job. He finished the line and rose, though he wasn't much taller standing straight than he was bent over. The only reason Gil measured over five feet tall was his thick, curly hair, which pushed up his hat a few inches.

Joseph sprang around the counter and embraced the shop owner in a bear hug. His high-pitched, excited tone filled the small the shop. "*Hell-oooo*."

Gil grunted as he was squeezed by the dealer, but found the breath to say, "It's good to have you back here, Joseph. Have you heard anything about the piece we discussed?"

Joseph scowled, answer enough.

Waving a dismissive hand, Gil said, "No worries. You know as well as I how these things happen. The buyer's patience is much deeper than Depp's pocketbook."

Gil turned to Trent, flashing a toothy grin from underneath a gray mustache that dropped down the man's cheeks and ended a few inches below his chin. Trent thought if Gil shaved his facial hair he'd get carded buying cigarettes.

Trent shook the shop owner's outstretched hand. "Hey Gil, it's nice to finally meet you."

Red-faced, Joseph stomped his foot. "His name is Gil. Gil!"

As he spoke the name, the *G* became a close cousin to a *J* so that it sounded as if the man and his wife had the same name.

Joseph crossed his arms. "Gil is short for Gillette. He is one of the most well respected art dealers in the world. Jesus, I'm sorry, Gil. I told you in advance he's a waste."

Taking a step back, but keeping his gaze on Trent, Gil grabbed a pack of smokes. "Joseph, it's not a big deal." His voice was nasally, and while some of his words were uttered quickly, others were drawn out. When Gil said "big" it came out "beeg."

Trent's band had played three festivals in France in the last eight months. In that time, the drummer had made the acquaintance of enough French women to pick up the flavor and rhythm of the language, but rock musicians live in a world that rarely requires them to apologize for anything. Trent mumbled, "Pardon," in a weak attempt at a French accent, and then added, "Thanks for showing me around. You … have a great shop here. I actually had Jill frame a few pieces for me back in the day."

Gil tilted his head in a polite bow. "We are well aware of who you are; the local boy making it big and all. My wife actually loved your last album, *Short Story Long*."

Trent felt his cheeks blush. The band's latest release was the only one Trent actually appeared on. Most of the reviews had been mixed, saying the band's older material had been fresher and more original, whereas this latest collection just rehashed the same old sound. Trent had taken the criticism personally since he had spearheaded the recording and writing because

Jeffrey, the band's vocalist, was dealing with drug abuse and a secret admirer that had morphed into a deadly stalker.

Gil continued, "If you earned a nickel for every time Jill watched the *Blink of an Eye* video alone, you'd have a fortune."

Trent tried to play it cool, saying, "Well, I'm just glad the guys added me to the lineup and trusted me enough to write that song." But his grin spreading ear to ear betrayed his excitement and pride.

Gil fixed his gaze over Trent's shoulder. "Joseph, if you will excuse me and my friend, we have some discovering to do." He opened the front door and ushered the perplexed art dealer out. Joseph tried to protest his expulsion, but Gil said, "Out into the rain with you, old friend. I'll take good care of your man."

Glad to be rid of Joseph, Trent sneered and held out his fist with a raised pinky and index finger; the symbol he had learned from Ronnie James Dio in South America. He watched the dealer slink back to the car, feeling Gil studying him from behind. He turned and confirmed it.

Trent had been checked out before, but not often by married men. Uncomfortable with the attention, Trent looked around the shop and realized there was no other doorway. "So, will Jill be watching the store while we … go?"

"No," Gil said, eyes dropping to the floor. "No, today is about exploring your psyche until we find the perfect piece of art. The store will stay closed until we're done."

He then flipped the *Open* sign to reveal, *Be Back Soon.*

When Trent saw the man focus on his chest area again, he said, "I know my shirt is hard to read. It says, *Esper Talaw.* They're a band we toured with in Asia."

When Gil's gaze dropped to the floor, Trent went from

feeling weirded out by the attention, to guilty for calling the man out. Just as quickly, though, Gil's gaze returned to Trent's chest. "It's not the shirt I'm curious about. It's the tattoo you have concealed underneath it."

"Oh, I have a lot of tats under here." Trent rubbed his belly and smiled.

"Yes, but Jill, she loved the one on your upper chest and shoulder there." Gil pointed, and continued, "In the video you play shirtless, and she always paused the TV to admire the 3D design of the woman falling into the black hole. She used to joke that it looked just like her."

At this, Trent couldn't even attempt to hide his embarrassment as he had tried earlier because the woman in the tattoo actually was meant to look like Jill. Trent thought the artist had nailed her features, and her hair was so life-like people had told him it looked like it was moving on windy days.

"I, uh, well," Trent stumbled.

Gil barked a laugh. "That's amazing. Please, do not be embarrassed. This isn't the first time my wife's beauty has been brought to my attention. No, you should be proud. Jill was a tattoo fanatic and saw thousands of them in person, and even more online or in magazines, and that one, that was my wife's favorite."

"Wow, really? I mean, that's awesome. In fact, she's sort of the person who got me into tattoos in the first place. She has that amazing chest ..." Trent trailed off, again feeling awkward about discussing his admiration for another man's wife's body, but he continued because stopping there would be worse. "Chest tattoo, that is."

Gil's face lit up in a wide grin. "It's a thing of beauty."

"Mine is actually by the same artist that did hers. Though

I had to track him down halfway around the world, and I paid a hefty price."

Gil nodded. "I had heard he retired years ago. Listen, I know the piece you'll want to buy. Let's get started."

Trent followed Gil over to a display full of generic prints. With two fingers, Gil felt along the wall between a row of abstract pieces. Dust sprung up revealing a large skeleton key underneath. Gil took off his smock and safety goggles revealing a lavender buttoned-down shirt and a shiny silver tie emblazoned with some sort of wavy design. Then he made his way behind his counter. "This way, please."—though it sounded more like *'Zis sway, please.*

The wall behind the counter was floor-to-ceiling shelves. Standing between two shelving units was a grandiose grandfather clock. Though it had seen better days, Trent thought its elaborate engravings were still as powerful as the day they were carved. Gil grabbed onto the grandfather clock, which was taller than him, and pulled it away from the wall with considerably less effort than Trent expected. Behind the clock was an equally extravagant mahogany doorframe, decorated with carved gargoyles. Trent followed Gil through the secret passage, closing the clock behind him.

The hall was well lit, and Trent realized that fact stood out to him because of the absence of any visual stimuli. Virtually every inch of the previous room had been covered with colorful prints and framing tools, so to see bare, bright walls was unexpected and disappointing.

The duo passed pairs of doors on each side. When they came to a T-shaped intersection, Trent followed Gil to the left. They then made a quick right. The instant they did, the air chilled as a gentle breeze met them.

Gil stopped two paces ahead and turned to face Trent. "This is the best place to start. Please do not take this assumption personally as I explain that there are twelve hallways like this one here. The doors all lead to rooms displaying different styles of art separated by style, era created, artist, price, and so on. So, we come to you; a young rock star, hometown boy comes to indulge in fine art. I admire your decision, but I also recognize the limits of your purchasing power. Right there that eliminates two of our hallways as they both carry price tags of $25,000 or more."

Gil's assessment did rub Trent the wrong way, even after being warned not to take them personally. Trent grabbed his wallet, which was chained to his pants. "Well, you may be right that I'm not the richest guy on the block, but that doesn't mean I came to waste your time. I have money to spend, and believe it when I say I'll drop $25,000 if I find the right piece."

The creaking of Trent's leather jacket echoed down the empty hallway.

"I believe you, Trent. I do. I'm not in the habit of insulting my patrons. What I am saying is the cost just to view the art behind those doors is $25,000. The hallway beyond that is $100,000."

Trent's eyebrows shot up as he began to realize just how high the stakes were.

Gil grinned. "You want to know what's down the $100,000 hallway?"

Trent nodded dumbly, jaw dropped.

"Ever wonder what the Devil truly looks like?" Gil's eyes glowed with mischievous excitement. "He was painted, you know, by an American Indian chief who had been brought to Italy on a slave ship in the 1600's. This chief told his captors of his encounter with Lucifer himself and how the Devil had tricked his people. Intrigued, they provided materials for the man to paint. It's said that the night the painting was completed, the local governor threw a party and displayed it in his foyer for everyone to view. By morning, all the patrons were dead and the captive chief had disappeared. I can't let you see it, but I can tell you that I get the creeps every time I peer into the Devil's eyes. Once Robert Plant and I watched as a bleeding scar was painted on the Devil's cheek right in front of us by some invisible hand. I know what you're thinking and I wouldn't believe me either, but I know what I saw."

Trent's eyes went wide. "You know Robert Plant?"

Gil nodded. "I gave him the same tour I'm giving you now, he just saw more corridors."

"What else is down that hall?"

"Da Vincis, Picassos, a map hand drawn by Ponce De Leon that supposedly leads to the fountain of youth, Aztec paintings proving the existence of aliens, *Broadway Boogie Woogie* by Piet Mondrian, a silk rug woven by Romani in the mountains of Turkey depicting Ali Baba and his forty thieves said to harness magic powers—and that's just the tip of the iceberg."

Trent held up his hand holding an unlit cigarette. "Hah, I'm calling bullshit on at least one of those. I know for a fact Mondrian's *Broadway Boogie Woogie* is on display at the New York Museum of Modern Art. I saw it in person when my band filmed a video there. My manager was fawning all over that piece. I guess little blue, red, and yellow squares get Fat Dave's rocks off. So you want to cut the crap and start shooting me straight?"

Trent readied himself to either leave or be forced out after his brash comments.

Gil just chuckled and then spoke in a tone so thick in sarcasm, it almost sounded sincere. "Sure, Piet Mondrian's masterpiece is wasting away in a gallery rather than for sale on the open market."

Gil patted Trent on the elbow. "Come on, Trent, you know true art isn't for public viewing and government grants and all that bullshit. You know this. Art is for the obsessive-compulsive assholes like you and me. The hapless collectors who once they see something they like, they have to own it."

Trent grinned. He wasn't sure if this guy was a nut-job or shooting him straight, but he thought Gil's truth was way cooler. "Well, okay then. I see six doors plus one at the far end of the hallway. Let's get the show on the road."

Trent followed Gil inside the first gallery, which boasted several large works of art hung from its walls. The room was voluminous, but just eight paintings were present. In the center of the space was a single black pillar as wide as a guitar body at its base. It rose just three feet off the ground before narrowing to an uneventful tip at its peak.

Trent took in the art and within the first thirty seconds of entering, dismissed all eight pieces as drivel. Yet, desperate to have something positive to say, Trent regarded each piece over and over. Each painting was dark-on-dark and they all showcased the same demon, silhouetted in various neon colors inflicting pain on horrified victims wearing clothing you'd expect to see in reruns of *Sherlock Holmes* episodes. Whether he clawed, bit, or stabbed his prey, the demon made sure their blood sprayed into the air. Trent moved to the center of the room and stood next to the pillar as he took in the entire collection. He followed the trails of red paint splattered around the room, some splashes even running right over the various paintings.

Feeling a wave of dizziness, Trent balanced himself by grabbing the pillar. The texture of it was rougher than he expected, and when Trent looked, he saw red paint on his hands.

Trent looked back at the entrance where Gil still stood, giving his customer space and time to study the art. Trent asked, "So the guy propped the can of paint here and just flung it all over the room?"

Gil asked, "Do you not approve of this technique?

"The technique creates a terrifying atmosphere, but these are awful."

Gil cocked his head in question.

Trent pointed at the paintings. "These are like some pubescent teen acting out his misplaced rage on the canvas just trying to get a rise out of people. These are like the Marilyn Manson of fine art. Look at that girl in the third painting to the right, there." Trent pointed to a large canvas featuring a pale-skinned woman with thin lips and green eyes. "The lines around her face are jagged and stern, as if she's the one in control even as the razor splits her neck. I could excuse the color of her skin spilling over the lines on her arm as a sign of the absolute chaos of the moment, but it looks like she has a third leg down there because this artist was too focused on shock and awe and not on the details. Now, the blood spatters are a great touch. I like how they hit the canvas randomly and hit the walls in here as well, but when the art is taken out of here, the buyer loses that."

Gil kept his expression neutral. "The artist approached me about three years ago, detailing their vision of this room and its paintings. I had shown and sold several other pieces by her, so the blood-spattering request didn't strike me as too left of center as we had collaborated on other weird ideas to showcase the art in the past. One day she came in here alone … and …"

His voice trailed off and under the bright lights Trent realized the man was getting pale. Gil stood with an arm wrapped around his belly as if it was the last thing holding in his intestines.

Trent regarded his own red-stained hand in a whole new light.

Gil said, "She came in here wearing these crazy robes and a tall, decorative hat like she was the pope or something. She impaled herself on this pillar here and … well, let her blood fly all over the room. By the time I heard the screams and came to check if everything was all right, it was too late. The artist was dead."

Astonished, Trent recoiled a bit and took in the room with a new appreciation. "Why don't you take these down and call the cops?"

"I started this place with the notion of making artists free to express themselves however they want, no matter what anyone, even me, thought. I'm not running scared at the first drop of blood in my establishment." His jaw jutted out proudly, and his chest puffed in a way that, for a man of his statute, was just sad, but Trent appreciated the man's courage.

"Plus you realized you could make a few bucks off these, right?"

As his chest deflated, Gil shrugged his shoulders. "As painful as it was, the artist was already dying of cancer and had done this as the ultimate expression of themselves. I sold two of these within a week of the incident."

Gil pointed up. On first glance it looked like the plain white ceiling had taken a few random shots of blood, but as his eyes adjusted, Trent noticed a large square area that seemed a bit lighter than the rest.

"There was another painting up there?"

"Two, actually. The first I sold almost before the blood was dry."

Shaking his head, Trent headed for the door. He was done with this room. "What kind of schmuck bought the first one?"

Without missing a beat, Gil said, "Jeffrey Paxton, the singer of your band."

Trent guffawed as he exited the room and walked down the hall. "Why am I not surprised? That dude has too much money for his own good."

"Oh, it didn't cost him any money."

Trent paused. "Seriously? I bet you can get 20k for something like that down in San Fran. Why would you just give it to him?"

Gil opened a door across the hall and chuckled. "I never said it was free. I just said he didn't pay for it with money."

Trent did not want to hear about any kinky stuff Jeffrey was involved in, so he changed the subject. "I'm surprised Jill lets you keep weird displays like that here. She always seemed like a normal person."

Gil arched an eyebrow. "Are you kidding? Jill's passion and spirit are what made this whole complex possible."

The room they entered was much smaller than the previous gallery, but just as well lit. The paintings in this room were hyper-realistic paintings so lifelike, Trent first thought they were photographs. One was a stunning B-52 dropping its load of bombs over a European city. Another depicted a jovial man standing before a corner pub in Prague, beckoning the viewer toward the establishment as if offering to buy the first round.

Trent marveled at the painter's disciplined line work. The stone facade of the pub looked like genuine limestone, and he was tempted to run his hands along the canvas to check. Prague has its own atmosphere and light, and the artist crafted the shadows in a way that perfectly mimicked the flames of torches along the building's side. Whether viewed from ten feet away or three inches from the canvas, the integrity of the piece remained intact, and Trent couldn't help but reflect on the night he had been jumped at a similar looking pub at the start of the last tour.

Absently Trent rubbed his left wrist over the bruise that was no longer there. The pain had ebbed months ago, and yet the night he was beat up for no reason remained fresh in his mind. Though he knew the man from this painting hadn't been involved in the fight, he wondered if he had seen him somewhere before. He shivered as déjà vu overcame him.

Trent backed away from the painting. "I've seen enough of this room."

Gil nodded and headed back toward the door without questioning his client.

Wondering if he had just offended one of Gil's artist friends, Trent added, "This artist is brilliant. I can't get over just how real it looks, but I feel like I enjoy art with an element of fantasy and oddity involved. You know, mix *Alice in Wonderland* with *Nightmare Before Christmas*, and a dash of

Pink Floyd for good measure. I get chills looking at this Scott Radke piece I have depicting his take on *The Little Engine That Could*."

Gil's eyebrows shot up. "You have a Radke?"

Trent was more than happy to brag. "Yeah, it's the one really nice thing my band has done for me. Radke designed their first CD booklet so they knew him from way before he blew up, and they asked him to do a piece for me after our first tour. He and I discussed some concepts and he picked my favorite story as a kid to recreate, but with his own twist. The train on the cover is frowning and all the animals and people on board are crying and depressed. The sky is dark grey and the train is passing dilapidated buildings and fields littered with trash. Real gloomy, real … awesome."

As he finished speaking, Trent reached for the third door's handle, but Gil said, "Eh, this room is not what you'll want to see. Again, the artist is very talented and I know you'd appreciate it, but, well, these are from their happy period."

Trent wrinkled his nose as if catching a whiff of week old garbage. "Happy period? Do artists really ever get those?"

Gil nodded. "Not everything has to be doom and gloom. Maybe one day you'll fall in love and write a warm ballad for her."

Walking further up the hall, Trent decided to not divulge his first attempt to write a song about a girl, as this was that girl's husband.

The fourth room was sculptures that, though Trent respected them, didn't qualify as the bedroom wall masterpiece he was looking for. The fifth room contained multimedia creations where photographs, paint, pencil work, scraps, poetry, and other mediums combined to make stark and vast landscapes, bustling cityscapes, nude studies, and more.

"Each one of these makes an amazing statement," Trent said as he paced around the room.

"But ..."

"Well," Trent explained, "Most of these are too busy for me. I like chaos as much as the next guy, but these are enough to make me anxious. There is certainly a difference between dark and moody, and dark and chaotic. I'm surprised Jeffrey didn't buy one of these—this is right up his alley."

Gil chuckled. "He never made it passed the first room. So, I take it this is a no-go?"

Trent nodded, though he lingered on one collage made of thousands of tiny bits of colored paper that had been put together to look like a gigantic tidal wave was about to crash over a beach and nearby city.

Trent pointed to it. "Now that is cool."

Gil came and stood next to Trent, also admiring the collage. "I agree. It was the last piece this artist ever did like this. If you look closely at the bits of paper, you'll see pen marks on some of them. Those are handwritten lyrics given to us by Jeffrey as part of his payment for his paintings."

Trent squinted and did see the markings now that they were pointed out to him. "What songs did he write out?"

Gil said, "They were brand new and never recorded."

"Why would he sacrifice lyrics that will never see the light of day?"

"Art isn't cheap. Besides, look at this beautiful piece they were turned into. Certainly more beautiful than any three-minute radio rock song I've ever heard." Gil tugged Trent by the forearm. "Come on."

Trent followed him out into the hallway.

"Remember in the shop when I told you I knew just the

piece for you?" Gil asked, his voice resigned. "It's at the end of the hall. I was hoping something else would catch your eye, but it's obvious no matter how many rooms we visit, it will be moot until we go to Jill's room."

If Jill had a room it meant she was an artist herself, and if her art was a tenth as beautiful as she was, Trent knew he would love it. "Lead on."

Gil produced the skeleton key he had procured from the dust cloud in the frame shop and led Trent through the last door. The room was pitch-black, save the blacklights highlighting neon colors from the canvases inside. The pigments glowed bright green, blue, orange, and yellow, but the reds used were dark shades.

The dozens of works on display ranged from very small, stapler-sized pieces, to larger pieces that Trent thought would fill up the wall behind his bed perfectly. The closest work to Trent depicted a dragon in fiery red and orange, wrapping itself around a black tower. While the image was powerful, Trent didn't feel the detail was to his liking. Large areas seemed to be filler, with very few elements to keep the eyes interested.

As he walked amongst the room, Trent thought that the canvas used on each piece must have been of low quality. They had all aged into an orange-brown tint, making it hard to see the painting from a distance.

Trent asked, "How old are these?"

"Some have been here for years, some for a short time. I know it's hard to see, but there is a good reason," Gil said from across the room. "The canvases are very sensitive."

"How so?"

"Well, these are tattoos."

Trent heard, but didn't fully understand.

Gil spelled it out for him. "These canvases are human skin."

Trent took a closer look as if expecting to see a freckle or nipple to give truth to the man's words. A deep chill took hold as he realized why the canvas was colored the way it was.

Trent made his way to the back of the room where Gil was standing behind a small counter and chair. The area reminded Trent of a dentist's office, except for the human flesh on the walls and the dance party lighting, of course. Trent wanted to ask what kind of weird freak hung inked skin at their place, but before he could get the words out, he saw the centerpiece he had been dreaming of.

It was a detailed canvas depicting a collage of weird creatures in the exact style Trent had loved for years. He watched a thousand-legged creature inching its way along rocky terrain; he smelled the burnt skin of a large blue elephant stuck on a small island. He felt the pinch of a peculiar porcupine attacking a frightened gargoyle, and tasted the neon green lipstick from a bulbous-headed, four-armed female alien emerging from a wormhole in the upper right hand corner.

Gil broke the silence. "Here, sit down and enjoy it for a few minutes."

Trent removed his jacket and sat. He studied the tattoo, noticing some other odd little detail every time he moved his gaze. It was like looking at Jim Henson's take on a Joseph Carl Close Jazz Piece. "At first it's an innocent band playing an old familiar tune, but as you look deeper you have to ask if that pair of eyes was peering through the smoke before."

Trent's chest tightened and he felt short of breath. He knew this tattoo, he had seen it before, but it didn't make any sense for it to be hanging here.

Gil sighed. "This's the one you want, right?"

"Yes."

"Thought so."

A jolt of excitement overpowered his sadness and confusion as he said yes. The truth was, Trent didn't care how much this tattoo cost, he was going to own it.

"I still remember the first time I saw this. Look at that three-eyed fish jumping through the water and shattering the surface like glass. Each shard has its own life and light, and the fish has an expression of curiosity mixed with confusion and joy—" Trent stopped as he realized Gil looked uncomfortable.

He fumbled for words to comfort the man, but in his state of euphoria from devouring the art he felt any consolation would ring hollow. "Are you sure Jill would want you to sell this?"

Through the darkness, Gil said, "Jill made me promise that I would make sure her body art lasted far beyond her life."

Hearing Gil admit that Jill was dead hit Trent like a punch to the gut. "I—I'm so sorry. I didn't know. How did she die?"

Gil looked up at the centerpiece tattoo. "You see that scarring in the lower right hand corner?"

Even in the dark light, the scar was easy to make out.

Gil continued, "Well, Jill fought a losing battle against cancer, but the actual cause of death was that spiked pillar in the first room we went in. That was her last project, when she had given up hope on surviving any longer."

Trent thought about the man's words. "Wow, I had guessed that the second room we were in might have been hers."

Gil nodded. "It was. In fact, each room in this hall was full of her art. She loved switching styles and mediums depending on her mood that day. I knew you'd fall in love with something from her collection, but I didn't want you to feel pressured to like it all just because she's the one who did them."

Trent thought back, wondering if he had said anything overtly negative.

Gil continued, "I knew this tat would catch your eye, but I wasn't sure if you were ready to sacrifice enough to purchase it."

Leaning the reclining chair back, Trent cocked his head and looked up at Gil. "Well, how much is it?"

Gil walked to a small counter, which appeared to hold more framing tools. "This piece isn't for sale, only for trade."

Trent was excited. He could own one of the most original pieces of art he had ever seen, created on one of the most beautiful canvases imaginable, and not even pay for it. "Sure thing. I have stage-used drum heads or gear, unreleased demos, dirt on each of the guys in the band, whatever you'd want."

Gil grabbed something from the counter and returned to stand next to Trent. He held up a small black box with several red buttons on it. He pressed one of the buttons.

Trent gasped as metal flaps flipped from the chair's arm to restrain his legs and hands. "What the hell?"

Gil put down the remote and extracted a syringe from his pocket. "Relax, Trent. You and I both know you'll give me what I want willingly. This is just to make the removal a bit easier on you."

"Removal?" Trent said, his voice cracking on the edge of hysteria.

Gil jammed the syringe into the left side of Trent's chest just below his collarbone. As Trent screamed, Gil emptied the needle of its contents.

"You're sick, man," Trent said, struggling against the restraints. "Get me out of here right now, asshole."

Sneering, Gil grabbed a scalpel. He came forward and sliced Trent's shirt in half. "No can do."

Trent's arm tingled and then went numb. He stopped struggling and allowed Gil to explore his tattoo as he himself had examined Jill's. "Take a good look 'cause when I get free, I'm going to smash you up so bad it'll be the last thing you see."

Gil nodded toward the dozens of tattoos hanging in the room. "I've actually gotten quite good at this. Besides the scarring and the immense pain, you'll be fine."

A cellphone in Gil's pocket rang, but the art dealer ignored it. "That would be your friend, Joseph."

"That piece of shit is no friend of mine. C'mon, you've had a good look, now let me free."

"Well, he got you a great deal on this centerpiece, did he not?"

Trent cocked his head.

"He and I arranged this sale. He even brought a buyer for your tattoo to the table. I'll bet he already has the agreed upon item in hand. Of course, it will take a few weeks to properly prepare your skin for safe hanging."

Trent's stomach turned as he pictured his flesh hung out for public viewing. "What if I made you one final offer? I'll clear out my account and promise you all of my ink after I'm dead. I won't be able to handle the pain, man. Please." His voice cracked and he struggled with his one working arm as he made his desperate plea.

Gil made a tsk-tsk gesture with the scalpel. "I won't just give away my wife's beautiful flesh for money. No, I want something Jill would love in return. And like I said, your tattoo, that was my wife's favorite."

Douglas Esper's debut novel, *A Life of Inches*, was released on May 26, 2015, via Limitless Publishing. His other publishing credits include short stories in anthologies from Frontier Tales and AITE Publishing, essays and interviews for Popdose. com, Domaincleveland.com, Faithnomoreblog.com, and Reputationshot.com. Douglas has self-published two picture books for kids featuring the artwork of Jeffrey Fernengel. When not writing, Douglas, a native of Cleveland, Ohio, can be found recording music and spending time with his family. Find out more about his writing, music, and charity work at www.douglasesper.com or @douglasesper.

The Most Beautiful Boy
Travis West

At first I didn't see her. I saw my friends. Everyone was gathered on the corner in front of the daycare center; laughing, playing with their Transformers or He-Man action figures, and using the juniper bushes on the corner as a makeshift fort.

It's difficult to remember the names of the neighborhood boys I ran around with in 1984, but I'm positive there were some Jason's and Jeremy's. Half of the guys from my generation are named Jason or Jeremy, so I'm sure there had to be at least one or two of each hanging outside of the daycare that day.

The daycare center had been a grade school from my parents' school days until I was a toddler, although I don't remember it being so. It took up half of the block and had a nice big playground the neighborhood kids would take advantage of after closing hours. During its hours of operation, if the weather was nice, all of the daycare kids would be outside— about fifty of them.

My friends and I would ride our bikes up and down the sidewalk in front of the playground flaunting our freedom, and teasing the kids beyond the fence. Especially thrilling to us were the ones (usually boys) who would come up and grip the fence like prison inmates longing for the outside world.

Some would even press their noses and lips through the links as if the air on the other side was somehow sweeter and richer than within.

The adult caretakers despised us and tried, to no avail, to shoo us away, telling us that we were being mean and unfair to their charges. A prison guard is not the same as a police officer, and has no jurisdiction over the actions of a free man.

— · · —

It was a Saturday, so the playground would be ours to rule. Morning cartoons were over and my mom was watching *American Bandstand*. Usually I'd be watching with her, but there must have been someone on the show that my young aural palate found boring or irritating. Billy Ocean, perhaps. Whatever the reason, I bailed on *American Bandstand* and lunch.

I was pleasantly surprised to find several other kids out and playing *Masters of the Universe* in our bush fort. Maybe their mothers were watching Billy Ocean as well.

I noticed her from the corner of my eye as I crossed the street. Out of place in our little suburban neighborhood, even for the edge of town, the sight of the girl astride her beast immediately drew my full attention.

"Who is she?" I asked Jason/Jeremy.

He looked up.

"I think her name is ____," he said. "I think she may be one of those foster kids that live over on Miller Lane. She's thirteen."

Five years older. Her name might have been Jennifer, it may have been Stacy. She was down the street talking to another girl and it was hard not to look at her. She wore the typical girls' western apparel of the day: bright plaid flannel of yellow and pink tucked into blue jeans, tucked into red leather cowgirl boots. She carried an air of sprightly intent that lived in her cheeks; soft, warm, and roseate. Her corn-silk hair was cut short and moussed into a multitude of fine spikes in a hairstyle made popular in a couple of years by such young actors as River Phoenix and Christian Slater.

She looked, to me, the most beautiful boy I had ever seen, and I was in complete awe of her.

Jason/Jeremy saw me staring at her.

"Why are you looking at her? Do you think she's pretty?"

I heard the teasing tone in his voice and chose to ignore it, although he had gained the attention of a few of the other Jason's and Jeremy's.

"She *is* pretty," I said.

"Even though she has boy hair?" he asked.

"She does kinda have boy hair, huh?"

He didn't answer.

"I have some men in the fort," he said. He pointed to the bushes.

I went in searching for the stash of action figures I knew would be hidden within its coniferous depths. I rifled through the pile of G.I. Joes, Transformers, He-Men, and wrestlers in search of my few good men. I was in luck. A Skeletor and Cobra Commander lay there for the taking. How lucky was I? The baddest of the bad!

Scooping them up, I exited our juniper fort.

"How come you didn't bring Optimus Prime with you?" one of the other boys asked.

The previous Christmas I had received a full-sized Optimus Prime and was seen as the luckiest kid in five blocks as all the other boys only had the smaller versions. Optimus Prime was leader of the AutoBots—the good guys of the Transformers. Everyone had been clamoring to play with it ever since.

"I didn't think of it," I said. "It's pretty early. I didn't think anyone would be down here yet."

The truth was that my mother had emphasized the expense such a toy had cost my parents, and that under no circumstances was I to have it out in the dirt. There was no need for all the Jason's and Jeremy's to know this, however. I was wise enough to not subject myself to that ridicule.

Jason/Jeremy opened his mouth to retort, then closed it again.

I heard it behind me. *Clop, clop. Clop, clop.* The two girls had come up the street and were now on the other side of our bush.

"Hey, Denise!" Jason/Jeremy called out.

"Hey there, kiddo," Denise replied.

Denise was tall and gangly with a red curly ponytail and a constant sneer. I'd seen her hanging with some older kids, but I didn't know her well. What I remember is her face, with its sneer, as she'd sic some teenaged meathead on any kid she felt to be deserving of a beat down. Which happened a lot.

Wary of Denise, I'd focused all my attention onto her, which is why I nearly missed seeing Jason/Jeremy giving another kid a *watch this* tap on the shoulder. I still don't understand why he did what he did next, but it would change our friendship forever.

"He thinks your friend is pretty!" he yelled.

My face grew hot, I was so mortified.

"D-d-don't," was all I could manage to squeak out.

My Betrayer was pointing at me, a mask of accomplishment pulled tight over his face.

"I didn't say that. I don't think that!"

Denise raised her eyebrows in apparent disbelief.

"You don't think she's pretty? So, are you calling her ugly?"

"What? No! I didn't say that."

"Well, if you don't think she's pretty, you must think she's ugly."

Denise was clearly enjoying herself.

"That's not what I meant!" I screamed.

"Oh yeah," said Judas/Jason/Jeremy. "He also said she'd be even prettier if her haircut didn't make her look like a *man*."

Denise glared at me. If she'd been teasing before, she wasn't now. What I saw in her eyes was pure hatred.

"Why, you little *shit*!"

"No!" I screamed. Pointing my finger at Judas/Jason/Jeremy, I made my own accusation. "He said it first! I never would've thought of it if he didn't say it first."

I was near tears and desperate. Why was this happening? Why was he doing this to me? Was this because I wouldn't bring my Optimus Prime to the playground? He was supposed to be my friend, but, alas, as children the first blood on our hands often comes from where we stab our friends in the back.

Either way, the girls weren't buying it. At least, Denise wasn't. "You can't just go around talking shit and not expect to face consequences, kid."

Surrounded by my accusers, I began to panic. Denise was still speaking, but I'd ceased hearing her words. My lungs started to hitch as I struggled to breathe. I looked from face to face. Denise, with her persecuting eyes, her words a droning buzz in my brain. Judas/Jason/Jeremy like an excited kid at a circus waiting for the next stupendous feat, an exploding clown car perhaps. Strangest of all, the girl at the center of the whole affair who sat upon her beast studying me. Expressionless, motionless, voiceless, and nameless.

Unable to take much more, I dropped the action figures I was holding and started walking away. Denise tried to stop me, grabbing at my jacket. Pulling away, I dodged in the other direction and came up against a wall of horse. The girl looked down at me, her eyes and mouth saying nothing. Hearing myself whimper, I tried going the other way and, once more, found the animal in front of me.

One step, two; edging slowly backwards, I scanned for an escape route. The girl urged the animal one step forward for each of my steps backward. My eight-year-old mind cracked in an internal voice screaming, *Run! Run now!*

Turning, I ran as fast as I could toward the daycare center doors. Gripping the handles, I pulled and struggled. Writhing against the doors, I heard little snarling sounds, like an angry rodent. Only later would I realize they had come from me.

Saturday. It was Saturday and the daycare was closed. No one was there to let me in.

Clop, clop. Behind me now. She was going to use the horse to trap me against the doors. In the door glass I watched her, the reflection resembling a ghostly rider on a phantom steed. Bolting to my left, I ran along the edge of the building. My shoulder scraped against the bricks but I dared not come further into the open lawn. A fence ran twenty feet from the end of the building to the sidewalk where it angled north down the length of the playground; half a block.

There was a hedgerow that grew along the twenty-foot stretch of fence and I kept myself between the two. The girl and her horse could not reach me in this neutral ground but I still had nowhere to go. I couldn't climb the fence, as it rose ten feet; its mesh too small to get a good toehold. My only option was to make a dash for the sidewalk then run as fast as I could to the gate at the end of the playground. Once inside, I could climb to the top of the jungle gym or a slide. I'd be trapped, but I couldn't be trampled to death.

Making up my mind to run for it, I made deliberate eye contact with her. Still she gave no sign of emotion; no smile, no frown, and no words. If anything, she looked bored. The variety of boredom you'd see on the face of a kid who, after depriving a fly of its wings, grows tired of watching the poor insect crawl around and uses his thumb to end it all in the corner of the window sill.

Prolonging the eye contact in a final act of defiance, I felt a little confidence creep back in. Maybe I wouldn't get away. Maybe I'd be run down and hoof-stomped into boy-jelly. Even so, I'd be damned if I was going to curl up into a little ball of coward and let it happen. I started to puff out my chest when the horse snorted and shook its head from side to side, breaking the spell. Taking the cue, I ran, crashing through the hedges and grating my elbow along the fence.

Reaching the sidewalk, I turn and sprint with every ounce of adrenaline powering me onward to the gate. Hot tears burn trenches through my cheeks as I run along the top of a concrete ledge that rises between the sidewalk and the fence separating me from the safe harbor of the playground.

The gate is so far away! Images of what I might look like if she runs me down fill my head. I think about how I don't want to die. I think about my mother answering the knock at the door to news that her little boy has been smooshed under horse hooves. I think—

The peach fuzz on the back of my neck is blown over

from hot horses' breath and I scream again. Running harder than ever, I finally reach the gate. It's already open, and I plow through a muddy puddle not caring about my shoes or clothing. I slam it shut and throw down the latch.

As I pass the swings, I finally dare to look back. My lungs are on fire and a painful stitch has seized upon my side below the ribs. Her eyes, at the ready, lock onto mine.

It's one of two things I've always held in my memories of her. She never broke eye contact; she was a hawk, predatory. The other was her cheeks. More so, perhaps, because it was this particular attribute that drew my attention to her in the first place; what made her so pretty and caused my eight-year-old heart to pitter-pat before the mirage came crumbling down. Because they contrasted so with her hunters' eyes, contradicting her whole being.

Her face was hardened and delicate, at once. Terrifying. And beautiful.

For a few eternal seconds, I was sure of my freedom. I had escaped! Then her eyes narrowed and the corner of her mouth raised in a cocked grin, mocking me. Emotion had made its debut performance and I was not a fan.

She reached down and opened the gate. I ran to a metal slide—the tallest piece of equipment in the schoolyard. Horses were capable of many things, I knew, but I'd never heard of one able to scale the rungs of a slippery slide. I began to climb as she led the horse through the gate and onto the playground.

I perched at the top of the slide, a prisoner with my feet and legs tucked beneath me. She drove the horse around the slide in slow circles, now and again giving me a casual consideration from the corner of her eye. Burying my face between my knees, I watch the tears and snot collect in a puddle between my muddy shoes, and I wait. For several minutes I listen to the animal make slow rings around me, it's breathing noisy and labored; and then . . . nothing.

Lifting my head, my eyes take a while to readjust to the sunlight. The girl and the horse are on the opposite end of the playground exiting through a driveway used as a delivery entrance.

I pull my legs from under my ass and let them stretch out before me, taking deep painful breaths, and calming down. My first decision is to never speak to Jason/Jeremy again. I wait at the top of the slide. Looking around, there's no one outside of their homes, no signs of life except for the songs of birds doing their days work. Did any of this happen? Did no one notice anything?

Seeming eons pass. Not fully convinced I am safe, I begin my descent. When my feet touch ground, I return to the gate by which I entered.

On the sidewalk I take slow cautious steps toward the direction of home. When I reach the edge of the daycare building, I peek around the corner. My pursuer is nowhere to be seen. Neither are Denise, Jason/Jeremy, or anyone.

Slowly I walk a little further. Reaching the juniper bush fort that I'll never play in again, my foot settles on something hard upon the ground. It is one of the action figures belonging to my 'friend'. Skeletor! Picking up the toy, I look into its face. Moist dirt is packed into the crease of the plastic where Skeletor's cloak and skull meet. Using my finger, I rub out the dirt.

He belongs to me now. Judas/Jason/Jeremy forfeited him

to me with his betrayal, and I have more than earned it. I place Skeletor into my back pocket and run home, glancing over my shoulder the entire way.

❧

Travis West lives in Lawrence, Kansas, with his wife, Angie, and their three children. "The Most Beautiful Boy" is his first published work. An avid fan of literature and music, he is currently writing the Next Great American Rock-n-Roll Novel. See more: travisjackflash.blogspot.com

Roadkill
Michelle Jillian Bailey

They crouched down in their normal spot. It was slightly lower than the two-lane highway in front of them. The drainage ditch sloped down and away from the road. Sometimes, during extremely heavy rains, the massive lake on the other side of the road would deluge, and water would flood their sanctuary. They had been doing this together for years. And yet. And yet, this time she was acutely aware of the heat radiating off his bare skin. She had noticed over the past several months that being around him jumped her heartrate and flushed her face. They had been best friends since birth, there wasn't a memory that didn't contain him in some way. And now, at thirteen, her palms began to sweat at the incidental contact of their arms.

He turned and smiled at her. At fourteen, he was a few months older than she was. His smile was dazzling. It reminded her of a movie star. Even without money for braces, his teeth had turned out naturally straight. His smile, however, wasn't just his Hollywood perfect teeth; it was also his dancing eyes, and the genuineness behind the action. His whole face lit up when he smiled. Just recently she had noticed other girls were taking note of him as well.

"I'll go first." His voice had a sweet southern drawl. She couldn't hear it, to her it simply sounded like the voice she knew better than her own. They had grown up neighbors in a small town in southern Louisiana. Their mothers were pregnant at the same time. Each woman spoke of hopes and dreams for their unborn babies. Sadly, things don't always go as planned.

Her mother had died when she was six. Her father's bereavement couldn't be alleviated and he searched for answers in a bottle of whiskey. He wasn't a particularly mean drunk, however, it was a stark contrast from two loving parents to none. She was forced to learn how to care for herself—eat, bathe, prepare for school. At six, unable to grieve the loss of her mother, she became fully self-supportive in her father's frequent absences.

His father, on the other hand, was a cruel, vicious drunk. As a young boy, he and his mother often wore badges of unprovoked, one-sided battles. His mother was a broken woman, in body and soul. If he couldn't save his mom, she would die at his father's hands. He swore someday he would stand up to his old man, and he felt that day was coming soon. Finally, he struck his large growth spurt and was feeling larger, stronger, and more confident than he ever had before.

It was late July, the air was heavy and sticky. Now and again, there was a distant blink of a firefly. Not the abundance of their childhood when they would catch them in jars, but only a small smattering. The slow disappearance had been disheartening, and now just a single flicker would bring her joy. There was only the slightest shift of the air now and again. Just strong enough to occasionally bring the wretched smell of a decomposing body; she assumed it was a dead nutria rat.

They were in their usual place. It was a place that had become all too familiar. Over the past five years, they had worn the long grass thin. Many hours had been passed right where they sat now. They talked about the horrors of the past, their dreams for the future, where they wanted to go, and just how far they were willing to run.

The first night she went out there she was eight. Her plan had been to end her life. She didn't fully understand the totality of suicide then, but she knew that the pain that suffocated her was too much to handle. He had sat there with her, willing to bear witness to her pain. Somehow, after talking with him, the pain subsided just enough for her to face another morning. For a year they met out there, day after day, her ready to die. Just his presence and friendship was enough to encourage her to try one more day.

Even when the vice grip on her heart finally released a fraction of an inch, they still continued to meet. They talked about everything. Sometimes they didn't talk at all, just watched the cars speed by. It was a long ribbon of two-lane highway. It wasn't traveled all that often, and they could see oncoming traffic for miles. They made up stories about the drivers in the cars. She liked to imagine her mother would stop, open the door, and take her home. He would fantasize about the college baseball recruiter that offered him a full ride to anywhere but here. Sometimes they were there so long they watched the sun crest the horizon. Finally, they would sneak back home, long before anyone would ever notice they were gone.

Two years ago they'd added a game to their meeting place. They began playing tricks on passing vehicles. The roads were flatter there than anywhere else on earth. There was nothing but pitch black around, the headlights were the only things to pierce the inky darkness. The first night she had been wearing all white; they joked that she could be a ghost. As a car neared, she stood on the side of the road, unmoving, with arms spread wide. The car swerved, obviously surprised by the vision. She dropped back down into hiding and they laughed so hard that her cheeks and sides still ached the next day.

For months they developed their game further, creating elaborate costumes: ghosts, devils, zombies. At first they only stood by the side of the road before dropping into hiding. As the game grew, they started dashing out in front of the cars. First it was only to scare the unsuspecting drivers. But then it became a contest to see who could wait until the car was the closest.

He held the record. He always held the record. In the years after her own desires to die, she realized that being with him gave her the greatest will to live. So she would cross the road close enough to thrill herself, but never close enough to kill herself. She had noticed the changes in him over the past year; his form growing taller, faster, and stronger. She knew he was testing the limits of his new body. He always returned from his sprint exhilarated, amped up on adrenaline. In his highest states of mania, he would talk about getting out of the oppressive homes in which they lived. Always his plans for the future included her.

It was only recently that she realized those plans were more than two best friends moving away. As she felt her subtle body changes around him, increased pulse, flushing of cheeks, and sweating of palms, she also noticed how he looked at her differently and sometimes even sat just a little closer.

His father had an extensive library of porn, and sometimes when nobody was home they would sneak one of the DVDs to the TV. The first time, she was horrified. The second time, she was still horrified but slightly aroused. Just a few weeks ago, for the first time, she envisioned the two of them together, moving in rhythm like the people on the screen.

For years, strange women would come to visit her father. Her father never introduced any of them, just went back to his bedroom—the same room he had once shared with her mother. The sounds she heard from that room rolled her stomach. She never imagined she would ever want to do anything behind closed doors with a boy. But now, his arm against hers, their skin to skin contact, she felt tingling and warmth in new places. It was too dark for him to see her blush, for that she was relieved.

He rose slightly from his low crouch. He told her that he was going first. He wanted to break his record. He was going to prove to himself that he could stand up to his father. No more would he hide in his room as he heard his mother plead and scream in agony. Time and time again he'd covered his ears to his mother's pain, silent tears marking is cowardice. He knew now his father would never change, it was only a matter of time before he hit his mother one too many times and she wouldn't get back up. The crushing heartache and despair was over for him. Now he was ready to be his mother's protector. Like the gallant knight, he would slay the beast and ride away into endless glory.

He looked at his best friend. The girl who had sat beside him on every lonely night. The little girl who he had watched slowly transform into a near woman. The small, soft lumps on her chest excited him in ways he felt both thrilled and guilty about. Alone in his small shower stall he would think of his father's pornography movies and watch himself grow. But always, as he neared climax, it was her face he saw.

He knew his mother loved him. And he loved his mother. As a concept he understood what love was. But only with her was he able to actually fully feel love. It was only recently that it had hit him like a ton of bricks. He loved her. He was going to save her—save them all. Then they were going to leave this hellhole in which they lived. They were going to find a little apartment in California and they were going to be normal. Nobody would drink. Nobody would curse. And nobody would hit anybody ever again.

A car came into view. Its lights tearing into the darkness, the engine noise ripping into the silence. He was dressed in all black. His favorite. Many times over the years cars swerved. Occasionally some stopped. Twice someone backed up, got out of the car, and searched for them. They were never discovered. They often wondered about the stories the drivers would tell to others when they reached their destination.

Still looking at her, he surprised her and himself by saying, "Ya really are beautiful. I'ma gonna to get us outta here, and I'ma gonna marry ya. And together we'll have that happily ever after our mommas wanted fer us." Then he leaned in and kissed her. It was gentle, maybe even a little timid, as it was his first kiss, but he was also sure in his decision. When his lips met hers, blood pooled in his groin and he felt the familiar arousal begin. Hyper aware that the car was fast approaching, he ended the kiss much sooner than he wanted.

He crawled up the bank to his favorite position. They had markers on the road they used for their contest; telephone poles, pot holes in the road, and road signs. There wasn't much out this way. But there was an exit sign. Neither of them had ever waited that long, it was far too close to where they sat.

His lunge was disrupted. His sneaker caught a wait-a-minute vine. He fell to his hands. Finally untangled, he began to sprint. She watched him go. Her mind screamed for him, grabbed for him, and continued kissing him, but her body did nothing. She reached up and touched her lips, they felt full and tingly. She noticed her nipples had hardened and it sent a chill up her spine. He had just told her he was going to marry her, and they would move away. He would be there, everyday, for the rest of her life, to kiss.

Her eyes scanned slightly left to the on-coming vehicle. Something inexplicable made warning bells go off in her head. The lights were tracking strange, not quite in a straight line. It wasn't until he was up on the road that she realized the car was swerving. She could see a cell phone's tell-tale glow illuminating the face of the driver. Even as she sucked in her breath to scream, "No!" the sound of the impact punched it out of her again.

The large, dark SUV slowed, the brake lights glowing like the angry eyes of a childhood monster. Holding her breath, she pressed herself low against the bank, still waiting for him to return to her.

The car door opened and the dome light spilled out onto the road. She could hear the woman on her phone. "Damnit! I don't know, a deer or something." The woman's voice was screechy and highly irritated. Instead of walking back to the impact area, she went directly to the front of her beloved vehicle.

"Oh, Christ! Yeah, there's a dent! Stupid animals! Stupid state! I hate this Godforsaken place. Why did this have to happen to me?" The woman on the phone continued to lament her sad situation as she climbed back into the driver's seat. She slammed the door forcefully, put the SUV into drive, and sped off. The night slowly engulfing it once again.

She exhaled, the smell of dead nutria rat wafting up once more. She waited. She waited for him to come running back across the street. She waited for him to explain what the horrible, hollow, thumping, squelching noise was. She waited as the mosquitoes buzzed in her ears. Sweat rolled down between her breasts and absorbed into her bra. Finally, slowly, she stood.

She saw a form on the road lying in a heap. The mass was too large to be a dog, and it hadn't been in the road when they arrived. She supposed it could've been a deer. Numbly, she walked to the body. Even in the deep darkness, she could see the black liquid pooling under his head. His arms and legs were twisted unnaturally at almost comic angles. Bones were protruding through his skin and reflecting what little light the night sky gave off. The perverse angle of his neck was too much to bear. But it was his shoes on the road—the shoes he had been hit right out of—that were the most difficult to see.

They had never made plans for this. Once, during her suicidal times, they discussed what to do with her body. But in the years since, they had come to feel immortal. Actually getting hit was never part of the game.

She stood frozen over his body. Turning around, she gazed across the road, opposite to where they would sit, and studied the lake. It was too large to see the far side. Southern bodies of water were notorious for gators. She knew there would be hordes of them out there. Turning back around, the first thing she did was pick up his sneakers and throw them into the water with all her might. She couldn't see them, but heard the faint splash. Facing him again, she leaned forward to grab his hands. As she began to pull, his right arm felt normal but his left arm sprang back like fresh baked bread, his shattered bones held in the loose sack of skin. She shuddered, but kept pulling. Stepping off the road and down the far bank, her shoes slid in mud and the liquidy noise was not unlike that of his head impacting the concrete.

The cold water crept up her legs. First through her sneakers, then her bare legs, then soaking her shorts. Once she was chest deep, she used the buoyancy of the water to maneuver his body. She looped her arms around him holding his back against her chest, his head lolling back on her shoulder. The bottom of the lake finally gave way and she began slowly swimming out to the center. Her mind held no thoughts. Her body propelled them further into the inky water, as if on autopilot.

It wasn't until her teeth began to chatter that she realized how cold she was. At first she told herself that once she was far enough out, she would release his body and swim home. But the longer she swam, the horror of going home alone without him terrified her. So she just kept swimming. For almost twenty minutes she propelled them out to the center.

Her body finally exhausted, she stopped to catch her breath. She turned in a slow circle, still holding his body firmly against her. She couldn't see the shore in any direction. Her heart felt like a lump of mercury in her chest, heavy and weighted. Treading water, her arms and legs ached. She couldn't make it to shore now even if she wanted to. But she knew she didn't want to.

She turned his body toward her, wrapping her legs around his waist and holding the back of his head. She was fairly certain, through his shattered skull, that she was touching his brain. Very deliberately she exhaled. As the air was released, their bodies began to sink. She kissed him as they sank. Their bodies continued to drop, her lips held fast against his. They performed a slow, morbid rumba in their decent.

Her body screamed for air. Her searing lungs willed her to kick free and swim to the top. But he had always been her lifeline, and she wouldn't let him go now. The water cooled the further they sank. Finally her body's reflexes overcame her desire to keep kissing him. Her mouth separated from his and her lips parted. Water rushed into her. As her mind became dark and murky like the water that surrounded her, she thought, *He finally got us out of here. I'm free.*

And a smile appeared on her dying face.

Michelle Jillian Bailey served eight years as a US Army helicopter pilot, an experience that gives her a unique perspective on the world, and informs her fiction and non-fiction writing. She recently completed her autobiographical book, *Pulling Pitch*, and is currently writing an adventure romance based on her years in the cockpit. Inspired by the well-constructed order of language to devise a dark tale that a reader can feel, Michelle wrote "Roadkill," her first published short story. She is the mother of three amazing children, an avid martial artist, NASCAR fan, and considers herself blessed beyond words.

The World From Below
Richard Lopez Salgado

To view people from above … it is an exhilarating experience. You look down from the thirtieth floor in your sky rise apartment overlooking the city. You see nothing but little ants—or should I say *sheep*—walking in herds toward their quotidian destinations. The Master of these sheep: money. Always watching what's ahead of them, sometimes looking back, just to make sure. *Hey buddy, no surprises.* In this city everybody sticks out like a sore thumb, wearing colorful outfits that once might have belonged to a circus. Now it is the trend; highly fashionable. And everyone is exposed to a threat, not knowing what this threat to civilization really is. Is it the lack of empathy which is consuming the world in single bites? And I, one of its victims?

On the thirtieth floor balcony; that is where I've been ever since I lost my job. Living on the thirtieth floor in downtown Miami, I thought I was a king. Now I know of my single truth: *I am also a sheep.* I used to watch the people below with my nose upturned, living my little illusions of grandeur, of superiority. Now I know the only superiority one really sees is that of material superiority, and I can make this claim on this rainy day from my balcony while the sheep run to their jobs to see who can make more money. Maybe that is why I took tremendous pleasure when I visited the Empire State Building. Observing from above, the Mecca of a rush of people in a hurry to go to work.

I remember just the walk being stressful enough; knowing I was heading to the office, knowing when I drive to work it will be rush hour, and when work is over, rush hour again. My spirit drains of all superiority by the return to the streets, to the level below, as I become a sheep amongst the sheep. The worst is going through an inner city. *Why can't everyone live in high rises?* I thought. *Why can't we just get rid of this filth? Of this poverty?* Mainly because of people like me.

But then again, everyone is guilty. Everyone, a hindrance to the evolution of his fellow man. Every person feeds off of the next, trying to survive in this combative atmosphere. Greed consumes us. I knew I had no brothers, all were enemies, even the ones I hadn't yet met. Shakespeare said, *"All the world's a stage, and all the men and women merely players."* We all deceive each other in the grand stage of life. Nietzsche called this the *Will to Power.* I call it the essence of life: greed. It is the very human desire that goes completely unrepressed. To want it all, and once you have it all, to want more. It never ends!

When things don't go one's way, there is always the need for compensation, the desire for undoing a wrong, and how are sheep to learn if not by teaching them a lesson? What I have learned from all this is that not everyone can learn. People have become complacent, conformist machines. Certain people simply cannot possess the capacity to learn from experience, that is, unless pain is involved. Pain is the mnemonic device here to impose behavioral change. In this case, a social movement was on my mind, and my capacity to inflict pain as of late has been astounding.

What is it about the rain that romanticizes things? Even dead flowers are beautiful in the rain. My first feel for administering punishment came after the failed promotion. I worked hard for six years of giving it my all just to have my ideas stolen in an instant by my own boss. A few months later, they laid me off during the recession of 2008. The following week, I bought a revolver. Not knowing exactly what to do with it, just the feel of it gave me great power. I touched it, felt the weight, inserted the bullets—it was all ecstatic.

An endless and formless flame began to ascend and spread throughout my body. I could undo any injustice with the pull of a trigger. I stopped driving my car. The gas prices were ridiculous. It rained every day, and I did not mind. I went for long walks around the banks on Brickell Avenue, seeing if anyone noticed the gun on my side.

To strike fear is not merely enough, but to punish—to punish is just. At thirty-three years old, I felt it was my duty to punish. The social ladder has punished me enough, and retribution was necessary.

After I lost the promotion I became terribly ill, and after the layoff, well, I was ready to punish. I went months without sleep. I started smoking cigarettes again. All I could think about was justice. My idea of justice. I bought some little white pills off the streets. I took one, two, three in a row. I slept for days. No one called me during all this time. What a surprise.

I decided to go to the office, and I saw the look of shock and annoyance as I entered. Someone had already replaced me. Was I always that expendable? The answer my ex-boss gave me: "Yes."

I was poisoning the bed with my dreams. I assume some

would call it nightmares. I was a loner, a vagabond in a bed of poison dreams. All became clear to me in an instant, and when I saw the big picture on my wall, it read in big neon letters: DESTRUCTION!

I figured some intimidation would go a long way. It was a Friday afternoon, the hour when all the bankers go to lunch. I took the revolver. I saw the busy faces of many ex-coworkers. They didn't even notice me there. I was a being without presence. I did not exist, and as I watched these busy sheep, they did not exist either. I walked around the populated Mary Brickell Village and no one, not even police officers passing by, looked at me. I did not exist.

That night I went back home and vomited fiercely. That night I woke up from my nightmare, and felt nothing but regret. I should have shot the lot of them. I went back to sleep with the only comfort dreaming that I pulled the trigger many times. As a direct result of this, I never left home without my gun.

I decided to go for some Cuban coffee. I ran into Gonzalo, an old acquaintance. Remembering we discussed the rise and fall of the Roman Empire, I recalled the story of Emperor Nero over an empanada.

"If history tends to repeat itself," Gonzalo said, while taking a bite, "and we are witnessing the degradation of culture, of family values, of political ethics, and this country is now owned by multinational corporations ... if the military industrial complex continues spreading its imperialism across the globe, and people sit and do nothing—more worried about going to work the next day—then yes, we are witnessing the rise and fall of the American Empire."

"But if this were true, wouldn't it be necessary for a type

of cleansing? What we need is an army of Nero's, ready to set fire to this shit hole. Let it burn and commence anew. Finally rid the world of this truth caused by the *Will to Power*, and our new religion—massive consumerism."

"The *Will to Power* is inevitable, my friend. Only a greater *will* can stop another."

I went home more cheerful and optimistic than I had been in years. I knew that my life would have some meaning as soon as I gave it meaning. I still carried the gun, but I no longer needed it for that feeling of power. I knew the gun was a necessary tool, yet the force came from ideas. My power comes from within. My purpose was to clean this city of the decadence which rules the people.

The cure: end decadence with decadence. Bring it as low as it can go until it can go no further. I am now a ticking bomb waiting any second. My being is a gun waiting to fire upon the ruling class. I slept tranquil every night, waiting for the day I was sure to carry out my plan.

The day came when I had no money for rent. It was time. My apartment overlooked the financial district. I thought about shooting from the balcony, but I would need a rifle and I was already in my last pennies. I decided to walk with the herd while they all rush to work. The previous weeks had been quiet dreams. I observed myself. My face had transformed. My unshaven face sparkled with madness. My eyes were big and heavy like two moons. I no longer carried that air of sanity which I once thought I possessed. I headed downstairs not knowing exactly how to feel, and I did not know if I would ever feel again.

As I got to South Miami Avenue, passing through all the bistros and fancy restaurants, the smell of food and coffee overwhelmed me. I was starving. My hands numbed, and the vein in my forehead began to tick. I headed toward the nearest bank. It was worse than summer as the sun scorched this winter day in Miami. It must have been ninety-five degrees. I was sweating profusely. Below fantastic sky scrapers, bums slept covered with filthy clothes and cardboard boxes. Suddenly I thought, *Will the sheep stop being sheep after this is over?* I laughed with rage. It was worth a try.

I opened the glass door of the shiny building. I figured I would start with the management. They were probably all there by taking credit for other people's work anyway. It was like the fairy tale that every immigrant is told; that if you work hard and save enough money scrubbing toilets, you too will become part of the privileged class. The reality is that those few who rule *took* their wealth, took it from someone else. I ask, did Europe become the most powerful continent because of their hard work, or was it by the looting and pillaging of the gold and resources in the Americas? They came, they conquered, and they *took* their wealth doing whatever it took, spilling innocent blood wherever they go. History always repeats itself, without a doubt. Hell, how do you think slavery began? The evolution of slavery has gone from physical shackles to mental ones that are now imbedded in our psyche. We are all slaves.

If I were lucky enough, maybe I would find some executives, a CEO or some other type that was high up the food chain. I told the receptionist I needed to speak to the manager of the financial institution. "What is this concerning, sir?" I looked at her blonde hair, her clueless smile, and said I had to speak to him of an urgent matter. She looked at me wary, or just plain stupid. How could I tell? I began to walk away slowly as I heard an effeminate voice say, "You asked to speak to me sir?" He had a big smile in his face.

I looked at him. "I just wanted to ask you something …" I said.

He looked at me in instant fear. His mouth distorted and he remained silent. I saw the security guard coming closer, approaching me, touching his side. Was he reaching for his walkie-talkie, a gun, a Taser, or did he just need to scratch? I wanted to yell, I wanted to … but I couldn't think. I shot the guard once in the chest, then the manager twice in the stomach. They both fell instantly. Everyone screamed. Everyone ran. HELP! PANIC.

I ran. My mind was numb, but I ran. I saw another man in a suit and I shot again. I had three shots left, but one was enough for me. When consciousness hit me, it was too late. I was with the herd again, women were shouting, everyone was frightened. I heard a man say, "Don't shoot!" Then I heard police sirens. Everybody scattered. I went inside the first place I saw. Running through the doors, people made way and yelled, "Oh, my god!"

Seconds seemed like minutes. I couldn't breathe. I had run a marathon. Someone yelled, "He's in there!" I quickly pulled out the gun. I still had a few bullets left. I should just end this right now. I put the gun in my mouth. I couldn't pull the trigger. I heard the police outside yelling for everyone to evacuate. Yet I still heard a mob of people, breathing, panting, screaming. I wanted to open and shoot but I only had a few bullets left.

Why don't they talk to me? I thought. *Are they toying with me?* Let them open the door and they'll see.

Five eternal minutes passed, and someone shouted,

"Come out with your hands up! We will shoot if necessary."
Then silence.

That recurring silence was killing me more than anything else. I didn't answer. I knew if I didn't kill myself, they probably would. Shoot first, ask questions later. That's all I knew from watching the stories in the news. But what if I surrender? Maybe I can still make it out alive. *Maybe those men are still alive*, I thought.

I took the gun and stuck it in my mouth. I crunched on the barrel as hard as I could. I thought I heard some teeth crack. A centimeter from pulling the trigger, I still couldn't do it. Silence was my death. What had I been looking for in a world of continual *becoming* and never *being*, as Plato said?

With my last breath, I grabbed a paper and pen from my coat pocket, and I began to write a note.

Saturday Night
Stephanie Rogish

The Sailor

"C'mon man, we're starting another game!"

"What? You've been playin' volleyball all day! Nah, I've already played and I haven't slept yet from my all-nighter … 'sides, I gotta call my wife. I missed a call and she's gonna be pissed."

The twenty-six-year-old walked back to his barracks alone, sweaty, and with sand stuck to his flip-flopped feet. While walking, he began listening to the messages from his wife.

"Hey, babe! I miss you! I'm getting ready to go out with the girls but I wanted to say hi and I love you!"

"Hey, babe! It's me again! Just wondering what you're doing. Hope you're being a good boy. Call me soon!"

He half-grinned to himself as he unlocked the door to his room. He kicked off his shoes, grabbed a towel, and went into the bathroom. All he wanted right now was a hot shower and a nap. He was tired from last night's long duty; hot, sweaty, and slightly dehydrated from spending all morning in the sun and drinking beer.

He stepped into the white tile shower, pulled the thick vinyl curtain closed, and let the hot water pour over his back.

He began to relax as he became engulfed in the steam. He rubbed his hands over his buzzed head. *PING!*

Another voicemail. If that was his wife again, he knew she'd be ticked. Her last message: *Hope you're being a good boy*, sounded more like a threat than a joke.

Not wanting to deal with her irateness, he didn't rush his shower. Once he felt human again, he turned off the water, stepped out onto the plain white hospital-looking tile, and dried off. His tiny room had a mini fridge, bed, and a closet that looked more like a locker. He took a bottle of Gatorade from the fridge, sat down on the corner of the bed, and checked his phone again.

Damn, it was his wife. He knew he needed to call her so he skipped listening to the voicemail and Skyped her instead.

The Sailor's Wife

"Hey, babe! I miss you! I'm getting ready to go out with the girls but I wanted to say hi and I love you!"

She set down her phone on the bathroom counter and picked up her mascara. With mouth open, eyes wide, she began brushing her lashes. The doorbell rang. She jogged over to let her girlfriends in. "Come on in, grab some drinks. I'm just finishing up." She waved her mascara tube over her shoulder as she headed back to the bathroom mirror.

From the living room she heard Gina, "Oh, I love this song!" The music got louder. A second later she could hear bottles clanking as they were being pulled from the fridge. "When's Brad going to be here?" called an overly loud voice from the kitchen.

"I dunno, he texted me a little while ago, should be here

soon." She picked up her phone and dialed her husband's number again. Long distance relationships were hard enough, but a fourteen hour time difference was really beginning to be a strain. A year apart with another year to go.

"Hey, babe! It's me again! Just wondering what you're doing. Hope you're being a good boy. Call me soon!"

She tried to sound like she was joking but it was hard to hide her annoyance at him for not answering. She set down the phone again and picked up her brush. She quickly ran it through her long hair and then decided she was good to go.

On her way back to the kitchen to join the girls, the doorbell rang again. "It's open!" she yelled. She reached across the counter for the bottle opener. Her long-time friend, Brad, entered the kitchen.

"Hey!" He greeted her with a six pack and a peck on the cheek.

"Hey, so what time does this place open?" She took one of the cold beers he offered.

"Not till eleven, so we've got time to have a drink and then head out to find a cab."

"Ok, good. I'm going to try to call my husband again. He must be busy. I've already left a couple of messages." She really wanted to say hi, and hear his voice before going out for the night. She knew it was already tomorrow-his-time.

"Hey hon, it's me again. Sorry we missed each other, but I'm going out soon and I might not hear my phone in the club. If you don't get this and call me back in the next fifteen or twenty minutes, then I'll just talk to you tomorrow. Bye, love you!"

The Sailor

The familiar jingle played briefly before she answered. The sound came on before her image—but what was all that noise? The sound of music, bottles clanking, and people talking and laughing came through his iPhone speaker. It took a few seconds for the picture to appear, but it seemed like minutes.

"Hey babe!" His wife appeared, smiling, holding a beer. Her hair and make-up were done and she was wearing that red shirt that he liked so much.

He swore he could smell her perfume.

"What's up?" he asked. "Sorry I missed you." He could see their framed wedding photo on the wall behind her. She was in the hallway of their apartment. "What's all that noise? You got people over?"

"Yeah, just a few girls. We're having a pre-club beverage before we go out." A hearty booming laugh came from some other part of their apartment.

"Who the hell is that? I thought you said it was just the girls!" When he made this call he was expecting her to be angry with him, that he was going to have to soothe her worries. She worries a lot these days. A fourteen hour time difference is rough on a marriage, especially one that is only a few years old.

She smiled and rolled her eyes. "Oh, that's just Brad. It's no big deal."

"Yeah, it is a big deal. I don't like it when guys are in *my* apartment while I'm not there."

He could tell she was trying to lighten the moment when she laughed it off. "Oh, he's totally harmless. He's going out with us because I think he likes Gina."

"No he doesn't! He likes *you*, and now that I'm all the way over here, he thinks I'm out of the picture. You let that son-of-a-bitch know that I'm very much still *in* the picture!"

As if on cue with very bad timing, Brad appeared on screen. Beer in one hand, his arm thrown around her shoulder, all smiles.

"Hey dude! Long time no see! How's the …"

"Get your arm off my wife," he growled through gritted teeth.

Brad's right arm lifted off her shoulders. His hand, palm facing forward in a *no harm done* gesture.

"Sorry, dude! I didn't mean to intrude. We were just havin' fun."

"Have fun with someone else's wife, NOT mine!"

By now, the other guests in his apartment sensed a decline in the jovial environment, and came over to see what was going on.

"Honey, come on. You're overreacting. Nothing is going on here. We've all been friends for a long time. You should know he'd never try anything …"

"Yeah, we've been friends a long time, but I've always been there. Now that I'm gone, he's gonna try to get in your pants."

She feigned humbleness. "No, he isn't."

From off screen, he heard, "Dude! You know me better than that!"

Her background was changing, she had walked into the kitchen and sat down at the counter.

— · · —

The Sailor's Wife

The friends stood around in the kitchen, catching up from their work week, telling stories. Laughing. The phone on the counter started playing the familiar Skype music. The tune caused a reflex in her hand to immediately shoot out and grab for the phone. She went into the hall where it was quieter, but not completely removed from the impromptu party.

"Hey babe!" she smiled, relieved to be able to talk to him.

"What's up? Sorry I missed you." She could tell he just got out of the shower. He still had water droplets on his shoulders and she thought she could smell his clean, fresh body-wash.

"What's all that noise? You got people over?" He looked tired. Was he annoyed that she had company?

"Yeah, just a few girls. We're having a pre-club beverage before we go out."

Her friends in the kitchen were laughing at one of their funny stories. As badly as she wanted to talk to her husband, she couldn't help but feel like she was missing the fun.

"Who the hell is that? I thought you said it was just the girls!"

"Oh, that's just Brad. It's no big deal." Even though they've all been friends for several years, she knew her husband was not a fan of Brad's. She needed to change the subject.

"Yeah, it is a big deal. I don't like it when guys are in *my* apartment while I'm not there."

She could tell he was getting upset. She tried to lighten the moment by laughing it off. She waved her beer hand to the kitchen and rolled her eyes. "Oh, he's totally harmless. He's going out with us because I think he likes Gina." She wasn't sure if Brad had any interest at all in Gina, she just knew she needed to divert Brad's supposed interest onto anyone except herself.

"No he doesn't! He likes *you,* and now that I'm all the way over here, he thinks I'm out of the picture. You let that son-of-a-bitch know that I'm very much still *in* the picture!"

She noticed Brad on his way down the hall to the bathroom. Hearing his buddy's voice, he stopped, put his arm around her so he could be in the camera's eye.

"Hey dude! Long time no see! How's the ..."

His pleasantries were not equally returned. "Get your arm off my wife."

Brad backed his hand off her shoulder, giving an *I surrender* expression. "Sorry dude! I didn't mean to intrude. We were just havin' fun."

"Have fun with someone else's wife, NOT mine!"

Brad's serious expression and tense shoulders changed the mood in the apartment. Laughter stopped. Bottles silenced. The other girls eased into the hallway, stood in front of their friend while the iPhone had its back to them. They threw her *what's going on?* expressions.

"Honey, come on. You're overreacting. Nothing is going on here. We've all been friends for a long time. You should know he'd never try anything ..."

Brad, clearly uncomfortable, made his way back into the kitchen for another beer. He stood, leaning against the sink as he popped the top.

"Yeah, we've been friends a long time, but I've always been there. Now that I'm gone, he's gonna try to get in your pants."

She moved off camera for a split second to wave her friends away.

"No, he isn't," she replied with downcast eyes.

"Dude! You know me better than that!" Brad projected his defense down the hallway.

Why was her husband acting this way?

She needed to sit down. She walked into the kitchen and sat on one of the wooden stools at the counter.

— · · —

The Sailor

"Honey, I think you're overreacting. Can we talk about this later? When you haven't been drinking?" Her tone was accusatory, which was the match on the gasoline.

"I'm not over reacting because I had a couple-a beers!" he shouted. "I'm pissed because my wife has another man in OUR apartment!"

He was pacing around the room now in his boxers. He was furious. Desperate. He knew this would not be happening if he were there. The Navy sent him away, but his wife wasn't ready to resign from a job she loved. They were trying to keep their marriage intact from opposite sides of the world, but he felt it crumbling at this very moment.

"So you wanna hang up? Literally, get me out of the picture?"

"No honey, that's not it. I just think you … I mean *we*, both need to cool off. Wait till we can have a private conversation."

"I don't want to wait to talk. I don't want to have privacy. I want all of them to know how much I love you … I can't live without you! And I can't live with the thought that you might be with some other guy."

"I love you too, but I'm not 'with some other guy.' I keep telling you that. Why won't you believe me? Don't you trust me?"

He replied with an unconvincing, "Yes. I trust *you*, but I don't trust *him*." He paused for a moment, staring at the floor. "You know, fine. If you want to be with that motherfucker, I'll bow out."

Keeping his phone in his hand, he pulled out his laptop

and opened it. He set the phone down and adjusted it so he was still on camera.

"What are you doing?" his wife asked. Her tone sounded worried, but also conveyed annoyance. This only fueled him further.

"I'm writing a letter."

"Okay, good. Write a letter, get your thoughts down, and we can talk about all of this tomorrow."

—— · · ——

The Sailor's Wife

"Honey, I think you're overreacting. Can we talk about this later? When you haven't been drinking?" It was difficult to hide the irritation in her voice because this wasn't the first time they have had a conversation like this.

"I'm not overreacting because I had a couple-a beers! I'm pissed because my wife has another man in OUR apartment!"

Brad set his beer down on the counter and mouthed, *I'm just gonna go.* She shook her head and gave him an apologetic look. She couldn't see her husband's face on camera. She knew he was pacing the room, a sure sign that he was agitated. When he reappeared, he had a wildly desperate look in his eyes.

"So you wanna hang up? Literally get me out of the picture?"

She was trying desperately to calm him. "No honey, that's not it. I just think you … I mean *we*, both need to cool off. Wait till we can have a private conversation."

"I don't want to wait to talk. I don't want to have privacy. I want all of them to know how much I love you … I can't live without you! And I can't live with the thought that you might be with some other guy."

She couldn't believe this. All she wanted to do was say a quick "hello" and "I love you" and suddenly she felt like her marriage was ending. How did things escalate so quickly?

"I love you too, but I'm not 'with some other guy.' I keep telling you that. Why won't you believe me? Don't you trust me?" She wasn't sure she really wanted to hear his response to the last question. She knew, deep down, that he didn't. He never really did. Strangely enough though, she never really gave him a reason to be suspicious.

"Yes. I trust *you*, but I don't trust *him*."

She watched him as he stared at the floor. Her mind was racing, desperate for the right things to say.

"You know, fine," he said. "If you want to be with that motherfucker, I'll bow out."

She felt dizzy. She could not believe what she was hearing. The man she promised her life to was suddenly backing out? She could see he was sitting at his little desk, opening his laptop.

"What are you doing?" she asked.

"I'm writing a letter."

"Okay, good." Feeling a little relieved that this might be the beginning of his cool-down, she said, "Write a letter, get your thoughts down, and we can talk about all of this tomorrow."

— · · —

The Sailor

Tears pooled in his eyes as he pecked away on the keyboard. He wanted the letter to be effective, get a reaction from her. She kept talking to him, "Honey, it's going to be all right. I do love you. You're going to be fine. *We're* going to be fine …"

He glanced away from the computer to look at the camera. "No, it's not going to be fine. This is too much! I can't watch you and some other guy—" He cut himself off. "I can't live like this. Picturing the two of you …"

"Seriously?" she responded indignantly.

Why was she *getting angry?* he wondered. She was the one being unfaithful. He heard her email alert.

"There. I just emailed you," he said as he pushed away from his computer and disappeared from the camera's view. Through his anger and hurt he rationalized that scaring his wife would set her straight. Show her how deeply he loved her.

He hoped that this idea might even convince her to move across the world to be with him.

━ ・ ・ ━

The Sailor's Wife

As she watched her husband type, she became filled with dread. She knew this was not going to be a good letter. His eyes were filling with tears. What on earth could he have to say to her to cause such a strong emotional response? She tried, once more, to convince him how much she loved him.

"Honey, it's going to be all right. I do love you. You're going to be fine. We're going to be fine …"

He glared at her for a brief moment and resumed his typing. "No, it's not going to be fine. This is too much! I can't watch you and some other guy—I can't live like this. Picturing the two of you …"

"Seriously?" She wondered how his mind could have fabricated this affair and gotten him so upset. The more she tried to convince him otherwise, the more he accused her. She sat, gaping at the camera, when her email alerted her to an incoming message.

"There. I just emailed you."

She watched him push away from his computer and disappear from view. Could she hear him digging through his closet? His backpack? What was he doing? She wanted him to come back into view, but she also wanted to read his tear-filled letter.

With one hand holding her phone, she used the other hand to open her laptop that was sitting on the counter next to her. She logged in, and opened her email.

Subject: *Goodbye*

Dear Jo,

I love you so much. I'd rather be dead than see you with anyone else. I knew this long distance had been hard on you, but it's been hard on me too. You're still there in our old life, with friends, and a job you love. The loneliness I feel here strangles me some days. I only want you to be happy. I can't explain it or say it enough, so I'm just going to show you.

Remember, I'm doing this for you.

Love,
Josh

— · · —

The Sailor

A desperate, but fake suicide letter should get her attention. If nothing else could show her how serious he was, this would be it. He knew she wouldn't be able to live with herself if she caused him to take his own life. This act would make her realize that she needed to leave that place, those people, and move with him. He gathered a few belts and buckled them end-to-end. He tossed them over the steel radiator pipes that ran along the ceiling of the fifty-year-old room. As she screamed at him through the phone, he set up the scene.

"I'm just going to make this easy on everyone and remove myself from the situation. I love you so damn much. I want you to be happy, and that's obviously not with me."

He drug a heavy wooden chair under the hanging belts and propped his iPhone camera on the desk. He leaned it against the Gatorade bottle so the belts and chair would be in view.

He was getting the reaction he had hoped from her.

— · · —

The Sailor's Wife

She was in disbelief of what she just read—confused by it. Could this be what she thought it was?

"No! Oh my god! Oh my god! No! What are you doing?"

She had forgotten she wasn't alone in her apartment until her friends came to read the email. His phone, still propped beside his computer, was not showing her much. She wished desperately that she could make it turn to view the room.

"Pick up the phone! I want to see what you're doing!" She held her phone close to her mouth as if her command would be better understood on the other end. As if her willing him worked, he picked up the phone and looked at her with tearful eyes.

"I'm just going to make this easy on everyone and remove

myself from the situation. I love you so damn much. I want you to be happy, and that's obviously not with me."

She heard a horrible hollow scraping as he drug a chair across the room. The image on her phone changed again; he was readjusting the position. It came to rest somewhere on his desk. All she could see was the opposite wall, the dark wooden chair, and … what was that hanging down? A belt? Several belts? It suddenly clicked into her mind what he was about to do.

"What are you doing? Stop! Help!" she screamed into her phone. Complete helplessness and panic washed over her. She knew her cries for help would not be heard by anyone other than her friends in her kitchen and the lonely man who didn't care.

Her friends gathered behind her, desperation rang from their voices as they tried to talk him out of this.

"What are you doing? Why are you doing this to me? You're killing me!" she screamed, hoping guilt, of all things, would work. Her thoughts were racing. *This is a dream, right? He's just trying to scare me and he's going to get down now.* Many times before, during video chats, she wished she could reach through the screen to touch or hug a loved one. At this moment though, she was incapacitated by fear. If only she could be there to keep him from stepping onto that chair, but she could do nothing except watch. If only she had someone to call who could rush in and stop him.

— · · —

The Sailor

His face reappeared on screen. "No dear, I'm killing *me*." He stepped onto the chair, and worked the loop of belts over his head. His chest rose and fell, took in, and then released a breath. He tightened them just enough to look effective; make it look convincing. He didn't step off the chair though, only bent his knees enough to look as though he were struggling.

With his knees bent, he leaned into the snare. He coughed a little, feeling slightly choked. All he wanted was to hear her say that she would come. That she would move to be with him. He would stand up, remove the belts, and get off the chair. But she didn't say it.

"Stand up!" she screamed. "Stand up! Stand up!"

Her panicked cry was not what he was longing to hear. He kept his knees bent a little longer, hoping her words would come. What did come were starbursts in the corners of his eyes. He stared at the camera, waiting. Then the blackness of accidental unconsciousness overtook him.

Those gathered in the kitchen just stared as his body went limp, feet still on the chair. He couldn't stand up now if he wanted to. His neck, now supporting all of his body's weight, began to stretch grotesquely. They watched as his face began to turn blue, and as he hung there, purple. Almost instantly his lips began to swell and his tongue hung loosely out of his mouth. He stared back at them through half-mast eyelids.

His widow dropped her phone, fell off the stool, and collapsed onto the cold floor. "Nooo!" she cried.

She will never know that his death was just a horrible accident; she will live with a lifetime of guilt.

Stephanie Rogish is a former elementary school teacher who has been a stay at home mom for ten years now. During this time, she has spent many hours volunteering at her children's schools, substitute teaching, and writing. Her first book in a children's book series, *Sheepdogs: Meet Our Nation's Warriors*, was co-written with Pulitzer Prize nominated author LTC Dave Grossman. Stephanie has an unnaturally large collection of cookbooks—which she reads cover to cover—and also enjoys scrapbooking and firearms training. To purchase *Sheepdogs: Meet Our Nation's Warriors*, please visit: www.usconcealedcarry.com/sheepdogs.

Consumed

Lee Diogeneia

Weeks. It had been weeks. William traced the narrow path that staggered down the hillside like an ancient, eroding staircase to the overgrown lakeshore. Trees marched from the forest to the water's edge for twenty feet on either side of him, leaning their weeping boughs forward as if to wash them in the lake. In the corner of the clearing, only a square of scorched stone and the fragile, blackened ribs of two walls betrayed that anyone had once dwelled there.

A root grasped at the toe of his leather boot, reminding him he had no right to cross the threshold of that sacred place. The sun bled through the sky at the horizon, casting twilight over his thoughts. Why was he here? Laurell was dead. It was his fault the others had come for her.

William looked down at his hands, newly-released from bandages. Even as he had challenged the flames to reach her, the memory of her soft, ivory skin was burned away. That they never found her body was a false redemption for his betrayal. He never should have revealed her. She had warned him that they wouldn't understand.

"She has bewitched you!" Hilde had said when he announced his intention to marry Laurell. Others followed suit, insisting that the woman he met in the woods had enchanted him and would devour his heart. The only way to save him was to destroy her.

His chest ached as he remembered her dancing at the water's edge on the day they came for her, spinning and disturbing the water so that it flew up and danced with her. Her screams when they took her still echoed in his dreams.

The present dimmed before William's memory. The first time he saw her, she was gathering firewood in a dress that was barely more than a shift. He had announced himself with averted eyes, but she was not demure and approached him straight away, filling his arms with the wood she had gathered. The sun gleamed like fire in her long auburn hair as it played in the breeze, and her pale eyes were as pure as a cloudless sky. She had bid him to follow, and William had done as she asked that day and for many to follow.

He remembered the first time he made love to her. Afterward, his soul resided in her body, and hers in his. Laurell *had* enchanted him, but not with magic.

"Please forgive me." William whispered the words as he had each of the dozen times he'd returned to her glade, now shunned by those who'd wrought his fate.

A sigh that should have been the wind drew him back to himself and he blinked against the darkness.

Tangled strands of auburn hair obscured her face, but he could see the glint of pale blue eyes. The dress she had worn that day clung to her as if she'd risen up from the very lake itself. He jammed the heels of his palms into his eyes until light erupted from the nerves as he stumbled backward. He looked toward the lake again. Laurell was still there.

He knew he was out of his mind, seeing phantoms, wisps. But the desire was too strong. Stepping carefully over the rocks and tree roots, he approached her, the scent of burning wood filling his nose.

She spoke not a word, her eyes fixed on his as he stood before her, the lake water lapping at his boots. He reached for her, but stopped abruptly, his corpse-like hands now instruments of defilement. Before he could withdraw them, she took both of them in her own.

He should have felt nothing, his hands dead things, but suddenly they were aflame again. Every finger, both palms, and up through his wrists agonized. His mind whirled, and his body screamed for him to pull away, but this was his forgiveness.

He opened his mind to the raging heat and kissed her.

The fever scorched its way into his chest and burst through his flesh. He threw is head back, and his shrieks echoed all around.

The lake, the trees, and his pain disappeared, consumed.

Lee. What a terrible name for a girl. On some level even the parents that named her must have thought so, because they called her by her first and middle names together—Lee Ann— which she endured inextricably until she escaped them and introduced herself to everyone in the daylight world as just *Lee*. Still a terrible name, but in the portions of the world that allowed for opportunistic anonymity, it got her things. Why? Because she was convinced her father wanted a son. What he got was a delicate, helpless, and *weird* little girl. Pennsylvania was where Lee was born, but Cleveland was where mom and dad and grandparents were from so that's where the grandparents were. Most specially, the gypsy grandfather with the best stories, the costumes and magic tricks. These things made her weirdness seem less weird and more like a special sort of normal that was lost to everyone else because they were blind and deaf to it. Her magical grandfather encouraged her creativity and writing. Grandfather, who could call wild robins and blue jays to his shoulder, entice earthworms from the ground without digging and who could twirl a silver dollar between his fingers until it evaporated into the air... grandfather who loved her stories. Lee. Forty-something years old now and still living in Northeast Ohio with her muse, her family, and a few cats, writing about vampires and fairies. www.diogeneia.com facebook.com/lee.diogeneia

The Uncanny Mr. Bones
Jacob Prytherch

The chill that seeped through the air outside was nothing compared to the biting cold that seemed to permeate every square inch of the storage facility. It drove William Crouch to distraction. He rubbed his hands, blew his tobacco laced breath into his palms, and even started to do slow laps around the dark concrete corridors, passing by the hundreds and hundreds of numbingly plain incrementally numbered doors before his lungs finally gave out at around lap three. He pulled his sleeve back and checked his reliable, if socially laughable, watch/calculator. It was still barely ten, meaning there was still eleven hours to go. Eleven long, lonely hours.

He tried to consider himself a security guard, but the job centre hadn't even been kind enough to give this role that title. Facility Watchman was how they had termed it, a role that was apparently perfect for his skill set. This was, of course, according to Susanne, the bright eyed and flaxen haired youth a third of his age who had sat behind the counter, and had tried to present it as a glorious opportunity for someone of his advancing years, where opportunities were few and far between.

Flitting between jobs at a whim—as he had done for the last thirty or so years—apparently hadn't been beneficial to his long term career prospects. The last ten years had been a carefully orchestrated dance with the benefits crows as he had tried in vain to keep the disability allowance for his trick hip. It was as straight a life as he was ever going to lead. It couldn't last forever though, so when the money had run out, and the flat had begun to visibly develop a light frosting due to a lack of heating, he knew it was time to get a job, at least until he could find a way to develop a new and incredibly hard to disprove ailment again.

It wasn't all bad if you knew how to make your own entertainment though, and Crouch certainly did. Once he had resurrected his old housebreaking skills and started to pick the padlocks on the storage units. The world had become his oyster. Well, not the world, but certainly a large selection of its unguarded goods, as long as he made sure that he had everything he wanted secreted away before the morning shift rolled in at nine.

He lit a roll-up and was on his third drag when he heard a distinctly purposeful cough to his left. He peered down the corridor to see the large form of Mr Keller, the site manager, waddling toward him. The man's winter jacket was done up tight over his huge belly, the zip virtually sweating with the effort of keeping his girth in check.

"No smoking, William," Keller said as he manoeuvred past, rubbing his stomach across Crouch despite his best efforts to avoid contact.

"Right you are, sir. Sorry, sir. I'll just smoke it to the good bit …" Crouch said, grinning to show mottled brown teeth.

"Don't play smart with me, Willy," Keller said, his face glowing in the light of the halogen lamps overhead. His trousers were bunched around his ankles as he had to buy large pairs just to accommodate his waist, but he never bothered about the leg size for some reason.

The man annoyed Crouch. In ordinary circumstances, he would have just shat on his desk and left, except the thought of that freezing house again … *no, not this winter.*

"Not Willy, sir. Nor William. Crouch," he said, prepared to let the other man's faults go if he at least called him by his preferred moniker.

He begrudgingly rubbed the end of the roll-up against the wall to put it out, leaving a small black smudge. Keller frowned at the mark, then looked back at Crouch's drawn features.

"This isn't secondary school man, this is a business. My business. You call me Mr. Keller. I call you William. No last names, no more ciggies, and keep your eyes peeled. I expect the same level of work from everyone employed here." Keller turned as quickly as his body would allow and waddling off toward the car park.

"Everyone except yourself, you bloody whale," muttered Crouch, secreting the cigarette in his palm until the fat man had left, before relighting it with a smirk.

He rubbed his hands together hungrily. He'd get to work all right.

⸻ • • ⸻

"This is more like it," Crouch said to himself. The freshly picked lock came away in his hand, and he pulled the door wide to reveal a mass of shamefully neglected items wrapped in shadows. He flicked the switch just beside the door, spreading a halo of white across old television sets, LPs, books, CDs, and videos.

"Living in the past a little are we? Bad thing to do, gotta move with the times. Don't want to be a relic," he said to himself as he picked up a couple of the cassettes, turning them over in puzzlement before realisation dawned on him. "Beta-Max! Bloody hell. Probably a Laser Disc somewhere in here too." Still, at least it was a better selection than that last container had held. Who would hire out storage for three tons of old newspapers?

He continued to rummage before eventually fishing out one or two smaller choice items of porcelain that he knew he'd be able to flog to Sidney Slater down on Cable Street. He was good on the details, old Sidney. He always told Crouch what to look out for, and he had no qualms about taking less-than-kosher stock.

Tap, tap.

Crouch stood up quickly, his reactions still sharp from the old days. He craned his neck to listen, though he didn't give in to the urge to panic. He had locked the doors himself after Keller had left, so unless someone had broken in, there shouldn't be another soul in the building, or at the very least not one who could reprimand him. Had someone else had the same idea, wanting to try their luck on the self-storage roulette?

He shuffled back to the entrance of the unit and poked his head out, scanning the warehouse from left to right. The only sound was a distant dripping. Another leak—the place was falling apart. He was surprised that Keller was able to keep it going. Maybe that was all it had been, a splashing of water …

Tap, tap.

His eyes flicked toward where the sound had come from, which lay around a corner to his right. The strip light flickered briefly before coming back on again, resuming its job of bathing the corridor in its bleached glow.

It was definitely not water. There was too much of a gap in between the double tap. It would surely be a sequence of single taps if it was …

Tap, tap.

This one had come more quickly, though it hadn't sounded any nearer. Crouch slipped out of the container and clipped the padlock back on, giving it a quick wrench to check it was secure before moving off and around the corner, pulling his torch out as he went.

The rhythmic tapping was low and almost inaudible, but still demanded attention. Two staccato beats close together, followed by a gap, then two more. Again. The sound seemed to rattle his skull, pulling his gaze around the building like a dog on a leash before his eyes finally rested on the partially rusted lock. There was a sticker underneath that had once given the name of the content's owner but now had yellowed and was illegible. Crouch skirted around a puddle that had formed from a crack in the glass of the ceiling far above him, and approached the door in a series of loping strides. He bent forward slowly, eyes wide, before pressing his ear against the bone chilling metal.

Even though he was far closer now, the sound seemed no louder than before, though it was just as insistent and driving.

Tap, tap … tap, tap.

Again.

Again.

His hand had pulled the lock picks from his pocket before he had even thought about it. He placed them carefully in the lock, twisting the metal rods and probing the mechanism as little flakes of rust fell away onto his boots, which were shuffling with the familiar nervous energy that always coursed through him before a break-in. With a final deft movement of his wrist, the padlock sprang open.

His hand paused for a second before he entered, as if there should be a fanfare to accompany the act, but there was no sound in the long darkness of the facility, nothing except the rhythm.

Tap, tap.

Crouch pushed open the door. His birdlike features twitched as he adjusted to the gloom. It was dark inside— as they all were—but this container was as black as pitch. It was more than faded colours, it was its own colour, deeper than shadow. The container gave the impression of a depth that was impossible given its outer dimensions, a vastness that promised limitless, hideous possibilities.

He hesitantly reached for the light switch, his hand running with tremors, before flicking it on.

The gold painted skull grinned at him, its polished teeth winking in the light.

Crouch couldn't help himself, yelping uncontrollably as he skipped out of the container, rubbing his hands across the back of his neck as his nerves jangled.

"Come on! What is that … what *is* that? Is this Halloween?" he cackled to himself, half laughing and half shouting as the tension was released.

The skeleton was majestic and terrible, a strange mix of the macabre and the gaudy, resplendent in a rainbow silk costume that was wrapped around it as if it were a travelling mystic. Its skull was painted with intricate whorls in black and purple across its gold painted brow, bringing to mind calligraphy, a deep respect for learning an art of words. Such a love was noble, Crouch considered, but also mind-numbingly dull, although there was still something fascinating about the patterns, as if they were some sort of devilish fingerprint.

It was around six feet tall and sat upon a pedestal within a velvet lined red and black case, its right arm held up by unseen clockwork or some other form of automation, tapping out its slow and steady rhythm on the glass in front of it. Its left arm was folded into the cloth across its chest like Napoleon. Stacks of large heavy ledgers had been piled on top of the case, which seemed a little disrespectful given how magnificent the skeleton was.

There was a small coin slot in the front of the box made of inlaid brass, which sat just above another larger slot. There was no indication of what currency it would accept, but the skeleton was obviously some sort of fairground attraction or novelty, probably dispensing cash-on-delivery advice for a pittance. Crouch wondered if whoever the skeleton had once been had wanted to be preserved as a strange gilded sideshow. Well, even if they hadn't, they surely couldn't complain about their new identity, as whatever their name had once been had now been replaced with a neatly painted moniker above the glass: *The Uncanny Mr. Bones.*

The rest of the container was considerably less interesting than the boxed skeleton, holding nothing more than piles of books, wrapped research papers, and artwork. Some of them may have been valuable but Crouch was wary about the traceability of paintings. Besides, next to Mr. Bones they were nothing. This thing was a true find. If only there was a way he could take it home, it would be quite the talking piece among him and the boys.

Tap, tap.

"You can stop now. I heard you. I'm here," Crouch murmured to himself as he moved closer to the glass, seeing his own reflection laid out across the grinning skull.

Tap.

The finger bone stayed pressed against the glass, pointing straight forward with a statuesque rigidity. Crouch looked down at the digit that was angled directly toward his heart.

"Well, that's unexpected," he said, biting his lip with grimy teeth. He scrutinised the skull more closely, watching the light reflect off its contours. "That's not paint, I'll stake my life on it. Gold leaf. That's gold leaf as sure as anything …"

He moved closer, feeling around the edges of the box with his spidery fingers as he searched for some sort of latch to get inside and find out a little more about how it worked. Somehow the back of the box was solid, with not even a single panel line. It was as if the contraption had been hollowed out of a single piece of wood.

"If it's one piece," Crouch said, wondering aloud as he moved down toward the floor and ran his finger around the bottom of the case, "how did they get the glass in?"

He stood up again, unfolding like a piece of crooked origami, and registered a considerable amount of surprise on his weathered features when he saw that the arm was now sitting at the skeleton's side. The skull's mouth was wide open. The darkness inside the shining teeth was strangely impenetrable, not even revealing the clockwork that had made the jaw stretch so wide.

"Mystical bugger, aren't you," Crouch said, backing away a little. He felt strangely compelled not to show his back to the thing, somehow dreading it moving again unseen. He shuffled out of the unit and pulled the door shut, leaving the padlock off for the moment.

He turned and leaned against the door, breathing deeply as he stared up at the skylights above. The night was clear with several stars sparking fitfully above him. There was no sound of traffic, probably due to the storage unit's location on a retail park, set away from the motorway and surrounded by land plotted for future development. The night was huge, empty, and silent. It was as if no one else existed, except Mr. Crouch and Mr. Bones.

He turned back toward the container and opened the door.

The skeleton's mouth was still open, giving the impression of a fish gasping for air. Either that or a prisoner screaming.

"Or singing," Crouch said. "A show tune or something. Jolson. Come on Crouchy, don't be so morbid."

He walked back to the skeleton, giving it his meanest swagger whilst pulling out his tobacco and papers from his greasy shirt. He started to roll a cigarette whilst keeping as much eye contact with the skull as possible. It was a strange act to perform in front of a dead object, he knew that, but it was one that he had used many times in his past to gain confidence and get the upper hand in a confrontation. The practice was no different here. Cool and calm, that was the key. This would be played out on Crouch's time. His nerves had been tweaked and he didn't appreciate that. He needed to find his footing again.

He looked at his watch. It was ten past one; still a long while to go.

"Just you and me Bonesy. Do you mind if I call you Bonesy?"

The skull gaped.

"Of course not, it's affectionate. We're kin, you and me."

A distant drip of water splashed onto the concrete floor.

"Both trapped."

He pulled out a pack of matches and selected one, striking it on the pack and letting the flame settle for a second before lighting up his cigarette. He took a couple of deep drags and pinched the cigarette into its usual position between the stained index and middle fingers of his right hand.

"Difference is, *I* can get out—just need to wait a couple of months until I find something better. Might see if I can sort out a tidy amount of loot first, then shoot off. Keep moving. It's why I never got a tattoo; they can trace you."

Another drag. Mr. Bones watched him through the spirals of smoke.

Crouch grinned back at the skull. "Heh, sorry. I know that's bollocks. Just never wanted the pain. Bloody needles. I never even got a TB jab."

He looked down at the coin slot. Something shone in the light, the hint of a curve. He bent down and flicked a fingernail in the slot, managing to dislodge a small coin that was so old that it lost all definition, save its circular shape. Green rust was spread across its copper surface.

"Well, look at that. My lucky day."

He rammed it into the coin slot, keeping his eyes on Mr. Bones to see if there was any reaction.

"Come on, show me what you can do."

The skeleton's jaw snapped shut with a click. There was a hint of movement in front of the skeleton's chest and its left arm was pulled from the robes, holding a fanned out selection of cards all bearing brightly coloured backs of the same design: a silhouette of a head and shoulders underneath a black sun. They were surprisingly well preserved, as was the whole contraption considering it looked to have been designed many decades ago. The skeleton's right hand reached across its body, and with a robotic assurance it snapped its index finger and thumb over a card and pulled it from the others before flicking it at the glass in front of it, leaving it to tumble into the shadowy recesses of the case.

Crouch craned his neck and pressed his head against the glass to see where it had gone but there was no sign of it.

"Well, that was useless …"

As his words trailed off, there was a rattling sound of hidden mechanisms, and a small square of stiff yellowing paper was pushed out of the opening under the coin slot before fluttering down to the floor. Crouch bent down to retrieve it whilst keeping one eye on the gleaming dead man. It was printed by an automated typewriter from the looks of it, with a few letters missing. Every word that needed an *E, I* or *D* simply had a space.

"W lcom trav ll r! am th Uncanny Mr. Bon s, t ll r of unwant d truths. Ar you r ady to b g n?"

"I think that says 'teller of truths'. Had a sense of the dramatic back then, didn't they, Bonesy?" Crouch said. He licked his lips, tasting the loose strands of tobacco that had fallen from the cigarette. "All right, I'm game."

Mr. Bones stared, gaudy and immobile.

"This is daft," Crouch said, scratching his nose. "I'm talking to a clock with bones attached."

Mr. Bones seemed to react to that, though it must have only been coincidental timing. The right arm once again moved up, grasped a card from the selection, and flicked it at the glass, whereupon it tapped against the surface and fell into darkness once again.

Crouch waited, his mouth working as if he were chewing a fly before the sound of the gears inside the machine started up again. Crouch fixed his eyes on the skull until the little card was presented in the slot. He reached down and pulled it out, flicking it over in the container's stark light.

"You w sh to b a r ch man."

"You wish to … barchman … be a … be a rich man, oh well, bravo," Crouch said, clapping the card between his bony fingers sarcastically. "Such insight."

The bony automaton simply sat there, the fan of cards still clutched in its fingers.

"Who doesn't wish to be a rich man, eh? Only a lefty, and they're just lying."

Nothing moved. Nothing stirred. He waited, flesh and blood waiting for the bones.

"This is old, too old. See you," he said angrily, flicking the card into the recesses of the container and turning on his heel. He turned right out of the container, moving forward quickly as he felt a seething anger grip him, though he was angry more at himself than the skeleton—after all, he was the mug who had talked to it like it could hear him.

"Here we are, this'll do," he said, lifting another padlock on an unopened storage unit, feeling relieved to be doing something else apart from conversing with himself, though he realised he was still muttering words aloud as if afraid he would drown in the silence of the warehouse. "I'll bring some music next time, buy a little CD player or something."

Tap, tap.

He dropped the lock picks in surprise before quickly

stooping to gather them up. He turned his neck to look back the way he had come. The sound had surely been too loud for such a distance, but then, in absolute silence, surely any sound carried?

He heard another drip from somewhere to his left, which was surprisingly audible and seemed to confirm his theory. He relaxed a little. Let the skeleton tap. He was in no rush.

Tap, tap.

"Fine, that's fine. Do what you have to. I'm not fussed," Crouch said, his fingers shaking a little as he tried to angle the lock pick. It was a simple padlock, no match for his years of experience, so why …

Tap, tap.

"Shut up," he said through gritted teeth before dropping the lock picks again. They fell into a puddle so he had to wipe them on his shirt before starting afresh. He closed his eyes and took a deep breath, feeling himself relax a little.

Tap, tap.

"All right. How, how is it able to do … how are you able to do that?" he shouted, looking back down the empty corridor.

"Maybe it was fitted with a movement sensor to try and draw people in," he muttered to himself as he unconsciously slipped his lock picks away.

His body already knew what his mind hadn't decided as he started to take a few steps back toward Mr. Bones. *But why make it so bloody fantastic and then shove it in a box?* There was also the knowledge at the back of his mind that the padlock on Mr. Bones' prison had clearly not been opened for a long time—decades maybe. *Did they have the technology back then?*

He was back at the unit before he realised what was happening.

Mr. Bones was pointing, solid and silent.

As Crouch moved into the container, the skeleton suddenly sprang back into life, reaching over and pulling another card out and flicking it against the glass once again.

"You'll run out of those eventually," Crouch said. "How are you supposed to get more?"

There had to be a way in. That must be how the cards were refilled. If only he could find it and prise that incessantly smiling skull from the skeleton's shoulders.

He shuffled forward, keeping one eye on Mr. Bones as he started to scoop and tug at the piles of books that skirted the case, dragging them to the floor where they fell open and became crumpled under his heavy steel toe-capped boots. Volumes and volumes of natural history, archaeology, physiology, theology; facts about everything and anything, trodden to a mess under wet rubber.

Eventually he had cleared a space around the case large enough for him to walk around. He ran a hand over the case's surface, feeling for a latch or some other mechanism that might open it. He found nothing. It was not until he had moved around to the back of the skeleton that it finally dawned on him that he hadn't even seen a power cable.

"Battery?" he said to himself weakly as he moved back to the front of the case.

The skeleton tipped its head to one side, as if pitying him.

"Go to Hell," Crouch said, giving the box a kick. The mechanism whirred back into life, grating and screeching as it slowly printed out another card. Of course! He'd forgotten about the card, though evidently Mr. Bones hadn't.

Crouch reached down and turned the card over with shivering fingers, his grey eyes scanning the letters quickly.

"You hav don what v r was n c ssary to b r ch."

"Whatever was necessary to be rich …" Crouch said quietly, his hand reaching instinctively for the breast pocket of his shirt, hanging over his heart before he pulled it away again. He started to seethe with indignation.

"Damn right, damn right. It's the only way to be, sunshine. You wouldn't know or you'd be buried right now. I bet you were a poor bastard, selling your bones to a carny just so your family would have a bit more bread for the winter months."

Crouch's mouth twisted into a sneer. The skull suddenly snapped up straight and the right hand reached over, picking three cards in quick succession and flicking them at the glass: one, two, three.

"Hit a nerve have we?" Crouch said, laughing through his nose.

The internal typewriter whirled into life, spewing out the resulting messages as quickly as they could be written. Crouch shook his head as he picked them up off the floor, trying to arrange them in the order they had flown out of the slot.

"D sp te your gr d, r ch s fall through your hands."
"You dr ft from plac to plac , w lling yours lf to b long."
"You hid ."

Upon reading the last card, Crouch creased his nose up and ripped it in two, throwing the pieces at the glass like confetti.

"Hid? Or is that hide? Doesn't matter. You don't lecture me, understand? You know nothing about me! And I see your *D* is working now, very convenient. Fixed yourself, did you?"

He stood, breathing heavily, before looking around himself as if seeing his location for the first time.

"Bloody Hell, what am I doing?"

He glanced back at the gold skull, its black patterns seeming to shimmer in the light.

"It's a corpse in a machine. I'm treating it like my dad."

He moved close to the glass, his breath creating a smudge of condensation. He ran a couple of fingers through it, watching as the gold bones peeked through.

"I'm taking back that nickname, Bonesy. Too good for you, you smirking bastard. Rot in your glass prison. I'm done here."

The skull jerked forward quickly, teeth snapping. Crouch staggered and fell backward over the pages of the books that he had scattered, kicking his legs at the shifting mass of paper as he scrambled away and out of the door, slamming it shut behind him. He leaned back against the unit, his breath frosting in front of his face. The cold was increasing with every hour. It was the least of his worries though. All he could think about was that skull; the empty sockets, the biting jaw, the needle dig of those words.

"It's clockwork—a sick toy. Come on," he said to himself. "You've dealt with worse things than this before, and you've kept a smile on your face. That Fergus was a meaty bastard but you—"

Tap, tap.

"Fuck this," he yelled, turning and pulling open the door before striding up to Mr. Bones.

The skeleton's arm was up again, pressed against the glass. The skull's mouth was closed, rows of shining teeth smiling wide. The storage unit was silent, save for Crouch's rattling breath.

"What do you want, eh?" Crouch said, clicking his teeth together in a way he hadn't done since his twenties, when he used to get into brawls down at the Dog and Collar. "You want to get me angry, eh? Get me riled up, ready to do something stupid? Well not this time."

Crouch backed away, his hand once again on his breast pocket. The skeleton raised a finger and placed it on the glass, pointing toward Crouch's heart, the hand, the pocket, and what was hidden.

Crouch spat out words at the corpse. "I'm leaving, and I'm quitting tomorrow. Get used to the silence, 'cos from the looks of it, this is the last you'll see of anyone for a long time. Your owner must be long dead by now." His eyes were wide and sweat was being squeezed from his brow.

The thing *had* to be machinery; a mass of wires, bones and cogs, electricity or clockwork. There cannot have been any life there. Such a logical assertion made sense, of course, but all the same it was hard to ignore the very human way that Mr. Bones began to nod, slowly and deliberately.

Crouch swung the door shut and started to run, not wanting to look behind him as he sprinted past unit after unit. His lanky legs and awkward gait making his knees ache as he made his way to the other side of the warehouse, finally slowing to a stop at the main entrance.

The area was little more than a large delivery bay with a rolling shutter that was firmly locked up, next to a lit up green emergency fire escape. His fingers twitched as he desperately scrabbled the key ring out of his pocket and tried to find the right ones to unlock the padlock before he gave a scream of annoyance, and simply charged at the fire escape, pushing the bar and almost falling into the freezing night air.

He hopped and skipped awkwardly down a slope of wet grass and started to walk into the wide expanse of bare land that ran into the distance before meeting up with a large road that zipped with occasional cars, their lights flaring white and red.

"Safe, safe," he said to himself, patting his chest pocket. It was still there, his constant reminders, his maps to the past. So small, so important.

"I'll quit. That's it. That's all. I can get another job, maybe even something closer to home. That's it. That's the one. The travelling; too much. Can't expect a body to make it all the way over here every night. I'm getting on—"

He screwed his eyes up tight, a tear pushing itself out of the corner of his eye.

Tap, tap.

He didn't scream. He didn't cry out. The only sound was the distant fizz of a lorry passing by. He looked up at the clear sky, ice cold, black and white. It was a picture, nothing more. There was no more reality out here than in his own head. There was nothing as tangible as the skeleton, and he knew it.

"I never even locked it."

He sighed long and hard—the exhalation of a thousand nightmares—before turning slowly and trudging back toward the warehouse.

"I'll just lock it up, that's all. Lock it up and walk away. I won't even go in," he said to himself. He moved without even remembering the route, slipping from corridor to corridor until he could see the small sliver of light that shone out from the old storage unit.

His hand paused on the padlock for what must have been minutes before moving away and up, pulling the door open.

Mr. Bones sat steady, patient, golden in the silk; a beautiful-terrible vision of the after-death.

"I ..." started Crouch, before words failed him. His mouth moved, soft murmurs of childlike submission.

The skeleton reached across its own body and slowly plucked another card, simply letting it fall this time. It was typed almost immediately, the card slipping into the slot. Crouch reached forward and read the words with itching, tired eyes.

"*K ll r.*"

Crouch tilted his head to one side, reading it again.

"*K ll r.*"

"Keller?" he asked, looking up at the skeleton. The shining skull followed his every move, blackened sockets following his body. "You think I'm Keller?"

Another card selection—this one quick—the card fluttering into the darkness like a flake of skin. Typing, dispensing, retrieval.

"You ar k ll r."

"Getting careless, should have used a capital letter there, old fella," Crouch said, relief starting to flow through his body. This was some practical joke set up by one of Keller's rich drinking buddies. It had to be. Maybe it had been meant to go off in the day, and had activated late.

Mr. Bones stared at him before moving its arm down behind the glass and pushing its fingers into the dark so that Crouch couldn't see them. There was a low scraping, like wood on metal, before the bony hand was brought up covered in straggling strands of dust.

"What are you up to?" Crouch asked, feeling a darkness at the edge of his vision. There was a palpable sense of threat in the way Mr. Bones reached over, grasping one of only two cards left in its dusty fingers before discarding it with what could almost be described as a gesture of disgust.

The sound of the typewriter was different, smoother …

The card was printed perfectly, each letter as it was meant to be.

"You are a killer."

Crouch stood, his mouth open and twitching like a fish. His hand was there, clutched so tightly over his chest that he could feel the fingernails drawing blood from his own flesh. His fingertips surrounded the folded papers that were in his pocket before he started to grin, teeth wide, lips stretched, eyes narrowing. Finally the truth of the matter. It was a challenge and Mr. Bones had bitten off more than he could chew with those painted corpse teeth.

"You're right, I am. I'm a bloody killer. To tell you the truth, I can't believe you spooked me. Can't believe I forgot myself."

Crouch pulled the photographs from his pocket, letting them fall from his fingers to land amongst the books—dead images amongst the dead trees.

"Keep them close, that's my way. May not be smart, been found out once or twice, but then …"

He looked down at a picture of a thin man with drawn features, his eyes wide in a death mask.

"… that's when I add to the collection."

Crouch reached down and picked up an image of a woman in her teens, lying awkwardly at the foot of a set of stairs.

"That was the first. She started it. Enid Morrison. Enid, ugly name for an ugly cow. Oh, she looked all pretty and that, but she wouldn't give you the time of day. Wouldn't give *me* the time of day anyway. Pushed her down the stairs. Not very skilful but it was my first attempt, and my first success. Had to stamp on her neck to finish it though. Sold her jewellery for ninety quid—"

Mr. Bones sat impassive. The gears had gone silent. There was not a sound except for Crouch's voice, throwing out his past in glee as he felt his confidence returning.

"Bastards like you—there were *always* bastards like you—trying to tell me what to do, how to live. I robbed the best, killed the worst."

The skeleton grinned. Crouch started to jab his finger at the various images that surrounded him.

A heavy set man with a red streaked face.

"This one, Joe Alsop, stabbed in the neck with a bottle in an alley behind the pub, drowned in his own blood."

A grey haired man with pale blue lips.

"That one, rich as anything, more gold than Solomon's mines. Took every bit of jewellery in his flat, lived for a year off the proceeds. Garrotted him with my belt when I was working as security in his own building. High profile, that one."

A large man, covered in sweat and vomit.

"My own dad, fed rat poison. Inheritance kept me for three and a half years. I always had more in common with the rats—"

The skeleton sprang to life, selecting and flicking the last card at the glass. The message was printed crisply on the yellowed card, the last words from Mr. Bones.

"*Such a pity.*"

"Pity?" Crouch yelled, kicking the case hard.

The skull clicked its teeth together a few times in reply.

"I don't want pity, I hate it! Don't you *dare* feel sorry for me. I've led a great life. I've spent more cash in the last twenty years than most people have in a lifetime! I don't regret anything I've done, any of it."

The skull lowered both arms to its side and stared ahead, silent and still.

"So you think you've got the last word, eh? Think we're going to leave it at that? No. No way, sunshine. You're done. Like all the others."

Crouch looked around his feet, kicking through the broken and torn books as he tried to find something big, something heavy. Eventually his eyes fell on the huge pile of almanacs on the top of the case.

"One of those should do, smash that grin off your face. Murdered by books, a new one for me," Crouch said, reaching up in front of Mr. Bones. The bottom ledger was weighed down by the others, but perhaps if he reached a little higher and picked a different one …

One glance, just a flick of the eyes and he saw it, the light in Mr. Bones' eyes. Red fires burned in those dead skeletal sockets, far away but infinitely detailed with figures crawling and writhing as desperately as shadows in the light. A crevasse spread far into the distance, skirted on either side by faces carved into the rock: Enid, Joe Alsop, his own father … and deep below the pull of a final and very real Hell.

He screamed. He couldn't help it or stop it, the air being wrenched from his lungs by a fear that he had never felt before, though it soon rose in its intensity as Mr. Bones' hand thrust its way through the glass—not breaking it, but simply passing through it as if it were insubstantial—and grabbed his wrist.

Cold fire burned as the skeleton's jaw rocked open and shut, the teeth glowing in the light oozing from its eyes. A low rumble filled the unit, a stuttering, groaning sound that could only be demonic, impossible laughter.

Crouch stretched and screeched and tugged and rocked, yanking his hand as the bony fingers bit into his flesh, blood running down his wrist. With a last wrench he fell to the floor and looked up in terror at the teetering case, only to see the last thing he would ever see: the pile of ledgers rocking themselves loose and tumbling down toward his head, ready to fill and spread his brain with their words.

—··—

"What is that thing?" Nathalie asked, reaching out toward the dark wooden case. A gilded skull grinned back at her behind the glass.

"Don't touch it, you always—look, just leave it," Carl said, breathing onto a cloth to wipe the fingerprints away. Even the delivery men had groped it. No respect. "It was found in a storage unit at the scene of a suicide, or accident, or something. Apparently Keller didn't even know there was anything in there. No record of an owner. I got it from him for a pittance. I think he just wanted to be rid of the thing."

"I can see why," Nathalie said, rubbing her eye with the heel of her hand.

"Don't mess with it, it'll bruise. If you bruise, I'll make it worse for you, you know that," Carl said, baring his teeth at his wife.

"I just—"

"Don't talk back!" Carl yelled, inadvertently knocking the case as he turned. The skull pivoted forward a little, its eye sockets resting on the scene. "Get upstairs, I'll be up soon."

Nathalie obeyed, as he knew she would. Stupid bitch, he

had no idea why he ever put up with her. She'd regret standing up to him later, he'd make sure of it.

He ran the cloth one last time over the glass and stood back, nodding in satisfaction.

"Good as new."

He turned and stomped up the stairs, already starting to remove his belt. He stopped at the top of the stairs and turned, craning his neck. There was a sound, quite indistinct over the noise of traffic outside, but definitely there …

Tap.

Tap.

Jacob Prytherch is an author of science fiction, horror and weird fiction. He started writing due to a love of Bradbury, Tolkien and Gaiman, and carries on writing due to restlessness. He currently lives in Birmingham with his wife and two daughters. Coffee is both his friend and his enemy. His first novel, *The Binary Man*, published in 2012, has since gone on to be the #1 cyberpunk bestseller on amazon.co.uk on two occasions. For updates visit https://www.facebook.com/jakeprytherch and 'like'. Main website - jakeprytherch.wix.com/main

Twin Lanes
A. Lee Ajang

Rick Bode had just snapped into conscious reality when he noticed that his car had skipped the guardrail after colliding with another, and was now plummeting into the valley. The utter quiet of his dream, despite being terrifying, was definitely pure fantasy compared to the quaking reality of death.

As the winds howled into the cracked driver's window, he could only think of the last few minutes of his travel leading him to this point. Maybe he could unwind the mystery and unlock some universal truth, and, in doing so, he would awaken in bed alive and well, rewarded for being so clever:

He sat patiently at the steering wheel, peevishly sighing at the motionless car jam that stretched out on the road before him. Somewhere in the distance, the winding road swiveled into a valley and disappeared. It was strange that such a seemingly isolated mountain area would be backed up in heavy traffic, but, nevertheless, both lanes, marked by imperfect white lines, were congested with waiting vehicles.

Flicking his wrist in frustration, he pushed the ignition back, and after a short rumble and groan, the car fell silent save the buzz of a local radio station. A voice blustered about demons and hell. It grumbled in and out of heavy static.

He gazed across the bordering line of cars to his left,

catching an unwanted glimpse at the elderly couple parked in a white car beside him. When met with an odious stare, he averted his eyes and shifted his gaze upward at the rising mountain slope winding around the narrow valley through which the road ran.

"I bet those pensioners are listening to the same station," Rick thought.

He tapped off the radio and cracked open the car window. He could hear the wind; it scratched chilled nails of frost at his windows. He could also hear the occasional flits of children laughing, but beneath the inconsequential sound, there was nothing, just tense quiet.

Rick twisted the ignition back on and slowly dazed in and out of consciousness until the sound all together stopped, and that is what jarred him; the sudden fright of absolute silence.

His head wrenched up violently. A heavy emptiness filled his belly.

The road was still blocked. Nothing had changed except the chilling sense of hollowness. Rick shook his head, trying to quake sound into the dizzying quietude. Maybe the other vehicles had shut off their engines as well; that was why it was so eerily quiet.

"Come on, people!" he said crisply. "Can't we get four lanes of traffic moving?"

His intent look sharpened as he panned across the congested mountain highway. *Four lanes?* he asked himself. He thought there had only been two. Had he been too tired to notice before?

Rick paled when he again looked to the white car beside him. The miserable old couple glared back with contorted faces. Their eyes were large and orange like autumn leaves. They snarled, earthy sludge spewing from their gaping mouths. In the review mirror, he could see the car behind him; the family, including the four children in the back seat, scowled forward with the same anomalous stare. In the car in front of him, heads turned on swivels, glaring back ravenously.

The man glanced to his right and was suddenly more confused; another white car and the same elderlies. Rick peered over the bordering row into the mysterious, duplicate lane. He was certain that he had caught a glimpse of a car that resembled his also bordering the white vehicle except on the opposite side.

A latch clicked as a white car door swung open, and a haggish, white mane rose into the blue sky. The elderly couple were exiting their vehicle, their wicked gaze fixed upon him. As they approached, their mangled fingers prodded out toward him. There was no time to piece together the mystery, and there seemed to be no sense to be made of it. In moments, they would be upon him.

Rick hurried himself awake, yanking the gear back desperately. His foot stomped hard on the pedal and the car swerved out, smacking the back bumper of the abutting car as it careened into the open.

The duplicate lanes had vanished, and only shoulder and mountain remained. He could see the now astonished gape of the elderly couple in his periphery as he drove forward. They remained in their white car, faces eroded by time not devilry.

The icy wind spilled through the window crack and tickled his cheeks. The car plunged helplessly into the dark valley.

Dead Drop

Steven Hartov

Jean René Dubois drove down Front Street in a fairly new Renault Touring Van, the kind that has big windows all around and seats twelve with the extra fold-down buckets. The single main thoroughfare of Philipsburg, capital of the Dutch side of the island of St. Maarten, glistened with a light wash of morning rain. The tall palms that shaded the small hotels and cafés on the beach side leaned over the narrow street, vaguely resisting a stiff breeze blowing in from Great Bay.

It had been blowing like that for three straight days. The big Catamarans that usually ran the tourists on a daily basis to St. Barts, Anguilla, and Saaba lay sail-less in their moorings, their small crews kicking aimlessly at the idle lines and stays.

It was too early for the tourist shops to open, and there were only a few very black Antillens in the street. Two of them were fisherman and one was a heavy woman pushing a shopping cart full of green bananas. Three small children in tan uniforms ran down Front Street, late for school at the big white church in the center of town.

Dubois parked the van in front of a small building on the north side of the street away from the beach front. There was a blue and white plastic sign that said *Epstein's Guest House*, rocking back and forth over the street. With all the beautiful beach resorts scattered around the island, Epstein's was clearly not for the well-heeled tourist.

Dubois got out and pushed his straw fedora back on his head. He walked around to the front of the Renault and frowned at the mud that had spattered his license plate. He spit on his brown fingers and then he bent over and carefully cleaned the orange-yellow plate so the words could be clearly seen:

ST. MAARTEN – THE FRIENDLY ISLAND.

A bell tinkled and the door to Epstein's opened, and Dubois stood up and smiled. He had an endearing grin, made more so by the fact that the soft flesh of the inside of his thick upper lip always stuck to his big white teeth.

"Good mornin' Meester Harris," Dubois sang in the deep French accent of his native Martinique.

"Morning, Jean."

J.D. Harris stood in the open doorway. He was a big man, pushing forty, with a full head of course brown hair and a lot of muscle left on his college ballplayer's body. His upper lip was mottled red where he had just shaved away a full moustache.

"Give me a hand, will ya?"

They slid back the side door of the Renault and carefully deposited Harris' diving gear; a seventy-two cubic foot tank with the old style rubber backpack, a buoyancy compensator vest with CO_2 inflator, and his regulator, fins, mask and snorkel. Harris made sure that his tank wouldn't roll around and he and Dubois slid into the front.

They drove down Front Street until they got to the Little Pier and took a left down Wilhelmina Hendrik, a narrow lane next to the post office where all the brass mail boxes for the whole town were outside along one wall. They took another left, past the police station, and headed west on Back Street and out of town.

They skirted the big inland Salt Pond, as large as a New England lake, and Harris stared at the spindly white cranes picking at the bugs in the shallow marshes. It didn't take much brains to figure that he was not in a talky mood, but Dubois wasn't going to let that stop him from trying to cheer up his "boss."

"Hope you had a *goood* breakfast today, Meester Harris." Dubois grinned at the American.

"It's J.D.," Harris corrected.

"Oh no, sir. Nooo. I work for *you* now, so I am Jean and you are Meester Harris. When you work for *me* then you will be J.D. and I will be Meester Dubois."

Harris smiled despite his mood. He still couldn't get used to the friendly and sometimes servantile nature of St. Maartens' black natives. He liked Jean, but he was vaguely uncomfortable around him. He wondered if there might be a volcano beneath that surface of ebony calm.

"Well," said Harris, "I didn't overdo it this morning. Just a couple eggs and coffee. I'm not too good out at sea. At least not on the surface."

Dubois frowned. "But I think you were once in navy, *n'est ce pas?*"

"Yeah. That's where I learned to puke. That's also why I got into the diving, real fast. Nice and calm down below, no matter what hell's blowing up top."

Dubois didn't quite understand all of the fast English, but he kept up the chatter.

"Well, weather has been real too bad these few days now. Make the tourists very sad. Tourists sad, we sad too."

They made a left after the Salt Pond and headed over the mountains toward the western side of the island and Mullet Bay. Harris was still too quiet for Dubois, who only enjoyed his work for the contact with people.

"I know it real hard on you, Meester Harris, you losing your partner and all. But maybe we find him today yet. Maybe he just went someplace nobody knows."

Harris pulled a pack of Camels from his shirt pocket and lit up with a match. He rolled down his window, leaned his thick elbow on it, and looked down at the sea and some distant white caps.

"Yeah, Jean. That's what I'm afraid of. He went someplace nobody knows."

—••—

J.D. Harris and Arthur Chester went way back, as far back as the U.S. Navy in the early seventies. They had started out in the service together, but neither of them much liked straight sea duty, so they got themselves transferred to diving school and hull maintenance. That was interesting enough for Harris, but Chester wanted more action. He got it with an Underwater Demolition Team and one last tour in Vietnam before they shut down the war.

After Nam, the two New Yorkers hooked back up again and opened a private investigations business in the City, putting their diving expertise to use on cases involving boats, salvage, and general maritime. Business was slow at first, but they started making real money when the recession hit and desperate vessel owners began sinking their own boats to collect on the insurance. The big property and casualty firms took note of Harris & Chester, Inc., and the partners dove on wrecks from Hoboken to Long Island, providing evidence as to whether the losses were acts of God or acts of Greed.

Their most recent case was a big one, but it was really outside their jurisdiction. Three employees of a waterfront supply outfit in Newark, New Jersey had been murdered in a parking garage in Manhattan. Everybody knew the outfit was Mob-owned, so the NYPD had shrugged at the case. But the families of the dead wouldn't let it lie. They hired Harris & Chester. Four months into the case, the two P.I.'s had plenty of leads, no hard proof, and lots of suspicions.

J.D. Harris and Art Chester figured out pretty quickly that the Newark outfit sold a few anchor chains and wheelhouse instruments, but made its real money smuggling cocaine. The waterproof canisters were picked up by air at night, probably from Colombia, and dumped with a marker not far off St. Barts. One of the faster tourist Cats out of St. Maarten (Harris still didn't know which one) was dropping its load of passengers at the smaller island in the morning, then sailing back into open water while the tourists shopped and sunned on the beaches. Divers went over the side, picked up the canisters and affixed them to the insides of the twin hulls. The Cat would then pick up its tourists on St. Barts, head back to Great Bay in St. Maarten, and at night the divers did their work once more.

By collecting rumors and plying loose local lips with whiskey, that was as clear a sketch as Harris and Chester were able to draw. They still didn't know how the coke got to Newark from Great Bay, but they were getting warmer. So warm, in fact, that they'd been warned off by a threatening phone call. But they'd made a lot of enemies in fifteen years in the business, and other such warnings had never scared them off. Arthur Chester was a tough combat veteran and J.D. Harris had quick reflexes and brains. They could handle themselves.

Then they made the big mistake. They got a tip. An anonymous tip. The most dangerous kind. It was a quickly-whispered phone call to their New York office, a guy with an Antillen lilt.

There was a sunken wreck of an old British Man'O'War about half a mile off the southern coast of St. Maarten in about fifty feet of water. It was a wooden hulled four-master that went down in 1801, so nothing was left but the iron: cannons, portholes, and one huge anchor. The Coke Cat, so the caller claimed, used the wreck for a dead drop. Someplace on the body of that sunken anchor was a small container, and if its contents could be intercepted between the times of the drop and the pickup, all the loose ends would fall neatly into place. It wasn't a stash for drugs, just an information drop, like which plane or boat would be used to make the final run to New York.

Harris and Chester didn't usually bite blind, but this time they could taste it. Harris didn't want to risk it, but Chester insisted. So Harris stayed in New York to beat back the work pileup and Arthur Chester went down to St. Maarten to dive on the wreck.

It was a popular dive spot, and to stay inconspicuous, Chester decided to go out there with a group of tourist divers. He had called J.D. the morning of the dive, three days previous, before the weather kicked up.

And then he was gone. He never came back to the boat.

The dive operators had gone crazy looking for him, but with the strong Atlantic currents he might have gone anywhere. There wasn't much hope, and for three days the whitecaps made the search impossible.

Diving accidents do happen. Amateurs run out of air and panic; sometimes they cramp up; sometimes a big fish scares them and they hold their breath and shoot for the surface, blowing out their lungs; and sometimes they just plain drown. But J.D. Harris knew too well that none of those things could have happened to Arthur Chester.

———

The Renault Minibus entered the sprawling resort complex at the Sheraton Mullet Bay. Harris snapped out of his dark thoughts and realized that Jean René Dubois had been talking.

"What'd you say, Jean?"

"I say golf course looks nice and green after few days shower, eh?"

"Yeah. Looks good."

The Sheraton complex was like an island unto itself. The guest houses, restaurants, casinos, and beaches were spread out so far that the customers used courtesy buses to get around.

Jean drove down to the water sports center and dive school. It looked pretty closed up. All lessons and dives had been cancelled due to the weather, and the story of a missing diver probably hadn't helped much. The small concrete dive building huddled near the deserted beach in a grove of high palms. A big red *Diver Down* flag with a white diagonal stripe through the middle whipped in the wind above the roof. The gates were locked up tight.

Dubois parked the Renault in the sand and Harris hauled his equipment to the ground. Dubois got out and stood there staring at the big American. The Antillen's eyes glistened.

"I wait for you here, Meester Harris."

"No, Jean. I don't know how long it'll be."

The black man seemed rooted to the spot. He curled his toes in the sand as if to hang on.

"I think I wait for you."

Harris took him by the arm and guided him back into the driver's seat. He spoke gently.

"Listen, mon ami. I'll be fine. Now go drum up some other business till tonight. You meet me at Epstein's at seven. I'll take care of you then and we'll go out for some food, okay?"

Dubois seemed somewhat appeased and he forced a gummy smile.

"Okay, boss." He started the engine.

"And Jean," Harris added as if in afterthought. "You need some cash, tell Willie at the desk I said to let you into my room. There's a few bucks in the toe of the left boat shoe in the closet."

He didn't want to say, 'If I'm dead you can have the five hundred bucks in my room,' but Dubois' lip turned down at the implication anyway. He pulled on his sunglasses, said, "Bon chance, mon frere," and drove away.

It was not J.D. Harris' first trip to St. Maarten. He and Chester had been to the Friendly Island before, mostly to escape the dreary diving in the murky waters of New England and rest their eyes on the girls in bikinis. They had come to know the owner of the dive shop at Mullet Bay, a Viet Nam vet named Chick O'Connor, who had a shrapnel-scarred body and a nice life in the Caribbean. They liked O'Connor's quiet demeanor and trusted his professionalism, which was why Chester had used Chick's excursion as cover for his dive on the dead drop.

But Harris felt bad about having used O'Connor this way without clueing him in beforehand. As Chick now appeared in his pickup, it was clear that *he* felt even worse for having been unable to save Arthur Chester. He parked the truck in the sand, his shoulders bent as he descended from the cab. God knew he had enough corpses in his past and hadn't needed this one too.

Harris and O'Connor exchanged handshakes and grunted greetings.

"J.D."

"Chick."

The muscular dive master scratched his blond beard and looked at his bare brown feet.

"I lost him, J.D. I lost Chester."

Harris poked a hard finger into O'Connor's chest and left it there.

"You didn't lose shit, O'Connor. *I* lost him."

They looked at each other for a moment and Harris said, "Gimme a weight belt and twelve pounds and let's go."

They put the gear in the truck and drove over to Simpson Bay Lagoon, where O'Connor had a twenty-four-foot Renegade dive boat gassed up and ready to go. Harris had called Chick the day before and they'd set up the dive for 9:30 am. They hadn't said much on the phone, and now they both knew that each was only angry at himself and no one else. But still there was an edge on it.

Even in the Lagoon the wind had whipped up a pretty good chop and the air tanks banged in the racks at the back of the boat. The two men stood behind the windscreen and squinted with the intermittent sun. Finally, O'Connor spoke. He had to yell above the engine and the wash.

"I wish Chester'd cut me in on it. Then I coulda watched him."

"Yeah. I wish *somebody'd* watched him." Harris regretted that quickly. "Well fuck me, Chick, and my piss poor mouth."

"Forget it." O'Connor said nothing else for a minute, then he continued. "I don't let nobody dive without a buddy. That's why I've got a good business. Arthur had a buddy, but I guess his buddy was no damn good."

Harris was pulled from his brooding by this new information.

"What buddy? Who was he?"

"Not he, pal. She. Just some tourist on her first open-water. Good lookin' girl. Redhead. Boat was all tourists that day except for Art. I didn't know he needed any protection so I paired them up. I still don't know shit." O'Connor looked at Harris. "Did he need protection, J.D.?"

"Yeah, he needed it."

"Shoulda known. I never did figure Art for a drowner."

They cut under a low bridge through the channel into Simpson Bay proper and out toward open water where immediately the swell grew into whitecaps and troughs. Harris had to hang on hard to the rim of the bridge as the boat danced on the peaks and smashed down into the valleys. They were both soaking wet.

"So who was this ditsy broad?" asked Harris. He really had to shout now.

"I dunno. Actually, I didn't pair them up. She did. She seemed to take a liking to Art."

Harris' mind churned, along with his stomach. Years in the business had made him a very suspicious man. A *buddy* to a SCUBA diver meant much more than some other kid with you in the pool at summer camp. A SCUBA buddy was supposed to watch your every move, get you out of trouble, save your life if he had to. Or in this case, if *she* had to. But a first-time diver wouldn't have known what to do in a real emergency. The sight of her buddy drowning would have sent her to the surface in a panic.

O'Connor was shouting again.

"Ya know, these fucking resort courses are for shit, but we do the best we can. Three hours instruction and a little beach diving one day, and then an easy open water dive another day. That's how we make our money. We do it nice and easy and folks get hooked, and then they wanna take the full course, ya know?"

The boat was really crashing now as they rounded the point near Billy Folly and headed straight out toward the wreck site.

"Take is easy," Harris shouted. "I'm a puker."

"It's bad slow, and it's bad fast," said O'Connor. "You wanna get out there and get in the water or ya wanna wallow for awhile?"

"Okay. Step on it." Harris clenched his teeth and O'Connor put it at full throttle and it was actually better because the Renegade flew over the waves.

"Tell me more," Harris yelled. "The girl and the dive."

"Well, this broad was slick. She took the resort course last week and picked it up real nice. Ya know how lotsa folks panic the first time under with a tank? Not this girl. Couple a guys couldn't hack it in the rough water off the beach, but she hung in there. Real gutsy."

The sun was out and the clouds were gone, but Harris left his T-shirt on because his New York skin would burn real fast in the Caribbean heat. O'Connor's scarred body was brown as a pipe bowl. The winds and waves did not diminish.

"So, the other day," O'Connor went on, "she shows up for the dive and so did Art. They were the last ones over the side and they stayed at the back of the group. We did the usual tour of the wreck. You know, feed the fish, take pictures, all that crap. Art was a pro, didn't use up much air, and she had typical girl's lungs so all the rest ran out of air first and I took 'em back up. Didn't figure Art much needed me to babysit so I let the two of 'em stay under."

Harris was gripping the bridge rail and trying to focus on one spot on the horizon, but he was hearing every word and picturing it.

"Few minutes later, she pops up all panicky like. Can't find her buddy. So I went over with a fresh tank, looked in every hole I know, and Christ I know *every* hole down there. Nothin'. When I came back up everybody was real shaky and the girl was sittin' in the boat cryin'. Then I called it in on the radio."

"Ya know," O'Connor said, "Chester ain't the first diver lost in these waters. Last year Spit Williams—guy runs a dive shop on the French side—had a tourist drown and he got swept out to sea in five minutes flat."

Harris still said nothing. O'Connor looked at him hard.

"Was this some hairy operation, J.D.? You ain't told me nothin' yet."

"Yeah, Chick. It's bad news now."

"You're gonna have to tell me a story later."

"I will."

Something had ahold of J.D.'s heart, surrounding it like a fist, squeezing. He didn't want to jump to conclusions, but he was a man who played his hunches and they were usually on the money. O'Connor watched J.D. just staring out ahead.

"You're thinkin' what I just got myself to thinkin', ain't ya," he said.

"Let's just get down there, Chick."

O'Connor found his spot by quick triangulation off of points on shore. He cut the engine, dropped a bow anchor and the now silent boat pitched, yawed, and rolled in the swell. They had on their gear and were in the water in less than a minute.

The transition from waves, wind, and gravity to the silent weightlessness of the undersea had always been a joy to J.D. Harris, but now he didn't care for it. He hadn't been down for a few months and today he'd shaved off his moustache to get a tight mask fit. The rubber irritated the raw skin, but he hardly noticed it. He hovered below the white hull for moment, checked the pull on his regulator and his air pressure gauge, and felt for his buckles and straps to insure all was in order. He glanced at the knife strapped to his leg. He had taken it from the boat.

O'Connor was already out front and below leading the way, a stream of bubbles rising from his head. The dive master held a 450 triple-sling spear gun in both hands, like he was carrying his M-16 through the jungles of Nam. Ordinarily he would never carry the weapon on a pleasure dive, but he didn't need Harris to tell him to take insurance.

They did not *descend into the gloom*. The light was strong and the water color was sapphire with a hundred-foot visibility. The sea floor was sixty feet below and the water was only slightly darker there. Big yellowtails, used to being fed scraps of bread by the tourists, crowded around Harris, but he moved through them and followed O'Connor's black swim fins. Large outcroppings of coral reef appeared. Brightly-striped clown fish darted in and out of the cattail fans, and big blue parrotfish with sharp beaks cruised in pairs. A reed-thin trumpetfish poked at some purple fan coral with his mouthpiece, and a large stingray fluttered along the sandy bottom. It was like a rich man's aquarium, but today Harris didn't care.

The first sign of the wreck appeared on the shelf of a reef. It was a large cannon, encrusted with rust and coral. J.D. hung there for a moment and equalized the pressure in his ears, pinching his nostrils through the dents in his mask and forcing air into his Eustachian tubes. His ears popped and the discomfort was gone.

O'Connor doubled back to him and made a palm-up gesture. *What now?*

Harris took the lead. Past the cannon, a pair of high coral reefs formed a long winding canyon, and he kicked slowly over a trail of encrusted wreckage—more cannons, the irons of a hatchway, a heavy chain, a porthole. His breathing was slow and steady until he saw the ancient anchor. Suddenly his pulse quickened, and the air from his tank came in quicker rasps. He rolled onto his back and spotted O'Connor above him, gripping the spear gun and turning his head from side to side like a fighter pilot. O'Connor looked down and gave him the *okay* sign.

Harris slowed his breathing and carried on. The anchor was a giant, its rusty shaft the length of a telephone pole and the curved cross-spar at the far end about twelve feet long from point to point. It was in deep shadow, leaning against a coral cliff like a *T* that had toppled over. The anchor's ring at the bottom of the *T* was buried in the sand, and one blade of the cross-spar jutted toward the surface.

Harris exhaled a long breath, letting his weight belt take him down. A small cloud of black and yellow Angels burst open and flitted away from the iron monster. He began at the buried end of the shaft, touching nothing, just looking. Even if the story about the dead drop was a phony lead, he figured the site might be rigged somehow to take him out too. But except for the barnacles and rust blisters, the shaft looked clean, and he rose along its angled length for fifteen feet, finding nothing.

Where the shaft intersected with the cross-spar, the underside was in deep shadow. There was a dark smudge where the heavy irons joined and smaller fish seemed to be feeding on something. He swam in closer, but he still couldn't see what they were pulling at. He reached out a hand and waved them away.

His eyes bugged and he grunted into his regulator and he back-peddled so hard that his tank clanged against the reef. Salt from his tear ducts stung his eyes and he sank to the sea bed and just sat there, his heart pounding against his chest straps and the air from his tank tasting like kerosene. He looked up through his spew of bubbles and saw O'Connor swimming toward him. He waved him off. He forced himself back to the spot.

For a long minute, Harris just stared and blinked. There on the underside of the anchor shaft, a green metallic cylinder was arc-welded to the iron. Just inside its mouth was a small animal trap—the type used to decapitate rabbits and badgers.

The trap had been sprung, its steel teeth like a set of grinning dentures. Clenched between them were two human fingers.

They were white, almost translucent with the effects of the sea water, and they'd been nipped and torn by the feeding fish. Harris tasted bile. He was going to vomit into his regulator. He had heard of many a diver who'd drowned that way after diving—sea-sick off of wave-tossed boats—and only his fear of it kept his stomach in check. If he lost it, O'Connor wouldn't be able to save him.

It was only his rage that gave him the strength to do what he had to do next. With his hands shaking, he pulled the knife from his leg scabbard and pried open the steel teeth. The two white digits floated down to the sand. He pulled the knife out, and the spring clanged. He dropped down to the sea floor. No one had to tell him whose fingers lay at his feet, yet something glinted near one of the white knuckles.

It was Arthur Chester's high school football ring.

Harris screamed into his mouthpiece as he lunged at the fingers, scooped them up, and shot for the surface. He rocketed past O'Connor, who was shocked into action and swam after him at full tilt, exhaling hard from his lungs. Harris raced for the Renegade's anchor line and spotted the slamming hull above. He didn't stop screaming until he broke the surface, spit out his regulator, grabbed the rim of the boat with his free hand, and hurled what was left of his partner into the bridge.

O'Connor burst up beside him like a porpoise, tearing his mask off his face, and spitting out his regulator.

"What the fuck, J.D.!"

"Get in the boat, Chick," Harris rasped.

"Did you exhale for Christ's sake? You coulda blown a lung!"

"Just get in the *goddamn* boat and take my tank."

O'Connor pulled off his own tank and heaved it into the Renegade. He scrambled up the aluminum ladder, and reached back to take J.D.'s tank and his weight belt.

Harris clung to a guy rope on the hull. The waves tossed the boat. The hull banged his head and he gasped for air.

"Chick," he grunted. "Pull anchor and rev her up."

O'Connor moved fast inside the boat. He pulled up the anchor and started the engine, and for a moment he looked down at the deck and froze behind the wheel and hissed, "Mother *fuckers.*"

Harris let the waves bounce him around. He didn't want to get into the boat. He felt it coming; waves of nausea roiling up from deep in his gut and he vomited into the water, over and over, retching hard as the brown cloud spread around him and was quickly taken away by the current. When it was gone he let the cold seawater wash over his head and sluice through his mouth until he felt clean again.

He hauled himself up the ladder, pulled it over the side, and let it bang down on the deck. He collapsed on his back and looked at the rolling sky as O'Connor opened up the throttles, swung about, and headed for home.

—— · · ——

"How'd she pay, Chrissy?"

"Cash."

O'Connor and Harris stood outside the dive shack talking to O'Connor's office manager and long-time dive buddy, a friendly and capable woman long ago from San Francisco. They were doing everything they could to jog their memories about the day of Arthur Chester's *accident.*

The sun was full up and the day was already hot despite the stiff breeze, but J.D. Harris stood there shivering in his wet T-shirt and swim trunks. The circular bar on the beach front had just raised its shutters for the day, and O'Connor's other assistant, a native named Tony, appeared with a plastic tumbler full of Jack Daniels. He handed it to J.D., who thanked him with a nod and tossed back the liquid fire in one gulp. Harris scraped off his T-shirt and tossed it onto the hood of the pickup, which was parked in the sun.

Chrissy held the daily log open in her palms. It was a large loose-leaf with the dive manifests, medical questionnaires, and waivers that would-be divers had to fill out, date, and sign. Her long blond hair brushed the pages as she ran a short fingernail over the listings for the date of the fatal dive.

"Yep, this's gotta be her 'cause the only other girl that day was dark, and had this Italian name here, Guliano."

"Lemme see." O'Connor took the notebook and Harris and Tony looked over his shoulder. "Veronica Barber."

"Yeah, that's right," Chrissy said. "'Cause she called herself Ronnie."

O'Connor looked at the waiver where she'd given her local and home addresses. "La Samana. That's the ritzy hotel just over the French side near Long Beach. Gave her address in the States as 620 East 84th Street in Manhattan."

No one spoke for a moment, and then Harris said, "Cute. Real sweet girl."

"What do you mean?" asked Chrissy.

"There *is* no 620 East 84th Street." Harris was looking up at the Diver Down flag where it rippled and snapped in the wind. "Unless she lives under the East River."

"Chick, I think maybe we should call in the police, man," said Tony.

"Yeah, maybe we should," Chrissy agreed.

"No." Harris was quick to it. "No cops."

"Why not, Mr. Harris?" asked Tony.

O'Connor did not ask why not.

"Cause we only have suspicions, Tony," Harris said. "No corpse equals no foul play." Harris caught O'Connor's eye and gave an imperceptible twitch of his head. Chester's fingers were still their secret.

"Anyway," said O'Connor, "You think if this girl did something shitty, she's gonna wait around for the heat?"

"What would *you* do, Chick?" Harris asked.

Tony jumped in. "I would be long away, Mr. Harris. I would be far away and very fast."

Harris was still looking at O'Connor. "Chick?"

The dive master scratched his beard. "That's what anybody would do. Any amateur. But a pro, a real hard ass … she'd stick around."

"That's right." Harris picked up his Camels from the stone ledge where he'd left them before the dive. He lit up.

O'Connor turned to Chrissy. "Call La Samana and give 'em this name. It's probably phony. Bet they never heard of her."

Chrissy disappeared into the shop.

"Tony," O'Connor said, "If anybody shows up for a lesson this afternoon, you and Chrissy can take 'em. But only beach work. No boat. Go work over your gear."

Tony wasn't happy, but he nodded and went into the dive shop, leaving his boss and Mr. Harris alone.

"We'll check out the taxi stands at Mullet first," Harris said.

"Right. If anybody saw her, they'll remember," O'Connor said. "She had a knockout body and a nothing bikini."

Chrissy came back out.

"Like you said, Chick, never heard of her. But I just remembered one more thing. When everybody broke up, they all went over to the courtesy bus stop and she was with them. Even with that downer day I remember 'cause I was jealous of those tight cheeks. That bus only runs in one direction from our stop toward Maho."

"That's why I keep you around," O'Connor said.

— • • —

O'Connor and Harris didn't have to go very far. They took the truck over to the Maho Beach Hotel and Casino, part of the Mullet Bay complex, where a number of taxi drivers always hung out waiting for fares. On the way, Harris filled in O'Connor on the case. During the return trip aboard the Renegade, he had been too weak and sick at heart to speak.

O'Connor had been at Mullet Bay for seven years. He knew every driver who worked the resort and probably most drivers on the island. He talked to a cabbie named Georges, gave him the info, and they waited while Georges polled the other drivers in their native Antillen patois; a musical mixture of French, Dutch, English, and local vocabulary. Almost immediately, Georges returned with another cab driver, a little man with short white curls on his walnut brown scalp.

"Yes, yes, Mr. O'Connor. I remember her." The other driver grinned and almost danced from foot to foot. "She was beautiful girl, long red hair like beak of the Sugar Thief bird. But no, I did not take her to La Samana. She want to go to Little Bay. I remember that was day it rained all afternoon and blowed all night. She did not speak much but very, very pretty."

"Thanks, Hector." O'Connor grabbed the little man's shoulders. "I owe you a drink."

Harris and O'Connor quick-marched to the truck. Harris' nostrils were flaring like a bull's.

"Don't get yourself all worked up," O'Connor said as he started up the truck. "Eighty-twenty the girl's long gone."

"You don't know these people, Chick. They wasted three wharf rats in Manhattan. Eighty-twenty this broad's sunning herself on the beach."

They pulled the pickup onto the main thoroughfare of the Mullet complex and Harris told O'Connor to stop the truck.

"Wait a minute. You got a piece, or maybe a powerhead?"

O'Connor looked at Harris and cut the engine.

"Now look, pal. You calm yourself. What ya gonna do, waste this broad and drag me under with ya?"

"No, I'm not gonna waste her. But we don't know what she's got, or if she's alone. You wanna go naked?"

O'Connor thought for a moment. Then he sighed, started the engine, mumbled, "I thought I was done with all this shit," and headed back for the dive shop.

— · · —

A powerhead is a special anti-shark device. Mechanically, it's simple. A short gun barrel fits inside a metal sleeve where it can slide freely and the barrel chambers either a shotgun shell or a large-caliber round. There is a fixed firing pin at the base of the sleeve and the whole mechanism is affixed to the end of a long metal pole.

If a shark approaches within striking distance, the diver yanks a safety pin from the sleeve and drives the end of the barrel against the shark's head, slamming the base of the shell against the firing pin. The shell fires and kills the shark instantly.

Harris and O'Connor drove over the mountains back toward Philipsburg. They both smoked. Harris held a long canvas gear bag on his lap. The three foot shaft of the powerhead almost fit into the bag, but the end of the handle, with its black plastic bicycle grip, poked out through the zipper.

Instead of going into Philipsburg proper, they followed Long Wall Road to the head of town, ran down Armenhuisstaeeg Kerkofstrat, and turned right at the head of Front Street, heading south toward the Little Bay Beach Hotel. They topped a hill, where to the left, all of Great Bay and its colorful boats lay spread out under the afternoon sun. Below and to the right, the Little Bay resort lay under rows of palms encircling a secluded beach. It was a special little spot, popular with honeymooners, combining a pristine beach front with open air cafes, a small night club, and an old fashioned casino. It was the perfect place for lovers, but love was the last thing on J.D. Harris' mind.

They parked the truck and O'Connor told Harris to wait for him. He knew most of the folks at Little Bay, and they threw him a lot of business but he wouldn't get much cooperation if his friends got a look at the expression on J.D.'s face.

O'Connor walked into the small lobby of the resort.

Young couples, some of them burned crimson from the tropical sun, lounged around low wooden tables and sipped tall Pina Coladas. A beautiful Antillen woman sat behind the tourist information desk and smiled broadly when she saw O'Connor. She had gold fillings framing her front teeth and luminous green eyes. O'Connor flirted with her.

"Sylvia, you gorgeous thing."

"Oh, Mr. O'Connor!" She blushed, but with her nut brown cheeks it wasn't visible.

"Listen, babe, I'm looking for one of my students."

O'Connor began to describe the girl but he didn't get far.

"Oh, you must be talking about Miss Red. I do not know her last name, but she is very beautiful."

"Yeah, that's her, hon. Red."

"She lives down at the end, a beach room. It is 129 I think. Oh, but I am sorry for you, Mr. O'Connor." Sylvia placed her chin on her palm and raised an eyebrow. "I think she is leaving today."

"Well, maybe I'll catch her. I'll catch you too, but later."

"Oh, you," Sylvia said, but O'Connor was out the door.

— • • —

Harris and O'Connor walked carefully along the cement boardwalk that led to the beach-front rooms. They scanned the sand and all the lounge chairs, and examined the water for a mane of red hair, but no one fit the image of "Red."

They entered a long corridor, arriving at the last of the attached rooms at the farthest end of the resort. The left side of the hallway was walled with latticework and half open to the Atlantic breezes from Great Bay. The beach-side was lined with doors. They found room 129.

Harris clutched the gear bag and stood off to the right of the door. O'Connor took the left and pointed to his own chest. Harris nodded. O'Connor rapped a knuckle on the door.

A voice answered, somehow not the voice Harris expected. It was a sweet female voice, drowsy with the sun and the sea.

"Yes? Who is it?"

O'Connor's voice dropped to a syrupy hum, taking on the accent of a native Antillen. Harris raised an eyebrow, impressed.

"Tow-ells, miss. I bring clean tow-ells."

There was a short pause.

"Thanks, but I have towels."

Sweat beaded on O'Connor's forehead. He stared at Harris who quickly looked around, and then rapped his own knuckles on the wooden door.

"Oh, for Christ's sake," they heard her mumble, and suddenly the door knob turned. Like twin machines fired by the same electrical charge, Harris and O'Connor burst into the room.

The girl jumped back and O'Connor quickly slammed the door.

Images flashed through Harris' brain. The big glass French doors to the beach were closed and gauzy white curtains filtered the light into a shady gloom. An air conditioner was blowing hard and the room was cold. The girl was stunning, even with her mouth open in stupid surprise. Her dark red hair was wet and slicked back from her forehead and down her back. Her hands had come away from where they held a white cover-up closed over her body. Her breasts still held the wrap mostly in place.

A huge dark figure leaped up from the sheets of a rumpled bed, and Harris inhaled the musty smell of sex.

O'Connor recognized the naked man. It was Tom-Tom, a pit boss in the Great Bay Casino known for his toughness and the pleasure he derived from dispatching rowdy customers. Suddenly all of O'Connor's doubts about the girl's culpability flew away. Tom-Tom drove a fancy French sports car and flashed a lot of cash for a casino goon. O'Connor had always wondered where the big man got his money.

Harris was taking in something else, a pile of sophisticated SCUBA gear in one corner of the room. There was a single tank and a double rig, plus an assortment of masks, regulators, and pressure gauges—not the stuff of a beginner.

J.D. Harris was not the polite investigator. He believed that surprise was his element and often the first verbal exchange could reveal a suspect's guilt or innocence. He could read eyes like the FBI read polygraphs. He fought to control his voice.

"I'm the other half, lady."

The redhead just stood there, gaping.

"You watched my partner, didn't ya? Watched his moves, his hotel. Then you followed him out to Mullet and signed up for the dive. Your *first* dive, my ass. Buddied up to him. Ol' Art was a sucker for a body like that. He liked women. He also liked his life."

Tom-Tom stood on the other side of the bed. His huge shoulders were bunched and he was clenching his big fists. He grunted and started moving around the bed. O'Connor put out a palm.

"Now you be cool, Tom-Tom. You just be *real* cool."

Harris seemed to only see the girl.

"And then what, Red? Or whatever your name is. Art was

no fool. He wouldn't have just stuck his hand in that rig, so you shoved his elbow. Got his hand in a real tight jam, didn't he? Then what'd ya do? Help him lose his regulator?"

Harris was hissing now through clenched teeth, but the girl had composed herself and managed to speak.

"You're nuts, mister."

"Yeah? And then what? When his lungs were full of seawater and he got nice and quiet, you ripped him free and let the current take him. Right?"

"You're out of your fucking mind," she said.

"Ya think so?" Harris slowly reached into the gear bag and came out with a clenched fist. "Then what's this?"

He opened his hand quickly, and there in his trembling palm was Arthur Chester's finger with the ruby of his class ring gleaming.

The girl screamed. Tom-Tom scooped up something from the floor and suddenly he had a weight belt with ten pounds of iron arcing over his head. O'Connor yelled and launched himself at Tom-Tom's wrist, but Harris already had the powerhead out, and the pin pulled.

Harris charged the girl, elbowing her face and knocking her to the bed. Then like an Olympic fencer, he lunged at the pit boss, driving forward two-fisted with the powerhead, and slamming the barrel into Tom-Tom's thigh bone just above his left knee. The explosion banged in the small room and the big man's legs flew out from under him. He slammed to the floor on his face and squealed like a wounded animal, his hands scrabbling to grip one of the bed legs. There was blood on the wall behind him. The stench of scorched powder filled the room.

O'Connor steadied himself where he'd fallen against a

mirrored dresser. The weight belt had shattered the mirror. Harris just stood where he was, breathing. The girl was curled up at one corner of the bed, clutching her robe. But she did not cry. She stared at Harris.

Harris reached into the gear bag and pulled out another shotgun shell. He cleared the barrel of the powerhead and reset the chamber with the fresh shell. O'Connor was staring at him.

"Don't, J.D … Don't."

Then the girl began to plead.

"No, please, my God. I didn't want to do it to him. I had to. I had to. You don't know these people. I *had* to."

"Don't, J.D." O'Connor was frozen against the dresser. "*Jay Dee* don't *do* it."

Harris took another moment to breathe. He had what he wanted, and a witness.

"Lady, you goddamn …" He struggled for the words. "You better hope there's an extradition treaty with the States. Cause if there isn't, I'm gonna kill you right here on this friendly island. Maybe not today, or even this week. But soon. *Real* soon."

He handed the powerhead to O'Connor, and then he bent and gently picked up Arthur Chester's finger from the floor. He opened his shirt pocket, took out his Camels, and buttoned the finger inside. He lit up, but he had a hard time striking the match. He ignored the big man crying on the floor.

"Watch 'em, Chick," he said to O'Connor. "Watch 'em real good. I'm gonna go outside and throw up. And then I'm gonna call the cops, if they're not already here."

J.D. Harris walked out of the hotel room. He slammed the door behind him and the girl finally started to cry.

O'Connor gripped the powerhead in both hands. He turned to the two figures in the gloom of the room, and he watched them real good.

❧

Steven Hartov is a New York Times bestselling author of fiction and non-fiction works. He co-authored *In the Company of Heroes* and *The Night Stalkers*, and contributed to *Great Raids in History* and *American Warrior*. He is also the author of the highly-acclaimed espionage trilogy, *The Heat of Ramadan*, *The Nylon Hand of God*, and *The Devil's Shepherd*. His most recent publication is *Afghanistan on the Bounce*. For six years he served as Editor-in-Chief of Special Operations Report and has written for the Journal of International Security, Gear magazine, Maxim, Playboy, Readers Digest, and K-9 Cop magazine. His works are recommended readings by the US Army War College. He is currently completing a novel about Afghanistan. Web site: www.stevenhartov.com. Facebook: Steven Hartov - Author.

Aurora
Faith Cooper

I've never belonged here. The thing is, I've never been sure why. The water softly graces my legs, back and forth with the tide. The darkness crowds my mind and fills my eyes. Am I the only one to question the way things have always been? For some reason I have never felt right about this life. Everything is so artificial; I have nothing to hold onto. The sandy shore of Ebony Beach is the only place I feel somewhat alive. When this life haunts too much and jabs too deeply (which it often does), this is where I run to.

Suddenly I feel the urge to take a dive into the cool, black waters. This is something nobody dares to do since we can't actually see what is down there. Our eyes have only adapted to the darkness of the land, not of the vast seas. My thoughts have me alarmed. *Why would I do that?* I ask myself. But the feeling won't shake, and before I can change my mind, I take the plunge.

At first, nothing seemed out of place. Under the water was dark just like the land, only more opaque; denser. My arms glided through the depths, propelling me forward. My old instincts returning to my body as I aimlessly wandered in the waves of the Shadow Sea.

At a very young age, we are all taught to swim in pools.

Some people continued to swim throughout their life if they had a pool at home. Nothing mysterious about one's own pool, but the sea was always a forbidden place. Fears of the unknown have always taken reign over the people of this world.

I came back up for air and I smiled. A real smile was hard to come by, so I went back under. What happened next changed my whole world.

The familiar darkness exploded and was no more. This brightness filled my eyes and I had to close them. I slowly eased my lids open a little at a time. I began to swim forward, possibly out of curiosity, or maybe something deeper. I swam into this brightness and noticed little swimming creatures all around me. I could actually see things! Deeper and deeper I pushed myself until I could feel my need for air cry inside of me. Just when I thought I had found my grave, I found myself falling and then landing in sand.

My eyes had been clenched shut in fear, but I opened them after I desperately gasped for the air that was suddenly present. Shock sprinted through my body as I drank in my surroundings. I could see everything! What odd sand, it wasn't grey or black. And the water, oh the water was beautiful. I decided this must be "color". Something in story books and silly tales; something believed to be a myth. I looked up and there I found the source of what I believed is the fabled "light". A big ball of exploding brightness, too intense to look at for long as my eyes began to feel burning.

As I was sitting on the shore and marveling at my new surroundings, I heard soft footsteps. I turned and saw a man walking toward me. His hair was the color of the bright orb in the sky and his skin had life. The clothing he donned was a party of these colors. I had never seen anyone like this before. It was all so beautiful.

"Hello there, miss," the man greeted me as he continued to walk closer. "You look lost, can I be of help?"

I just stared at him with my mouth agape. The shock had apparently not left my body just yet. He laughed and I finally regained control.

"Sorry," I began, "I just … I'm just—"

"—not from around here?" he guessed for me.

I nodded yes.

"Well it's about time!" he exclaimed as he jumped up and extended his hand. "Come, I have much to show you."

A mischievous smile stretched across his face and I forgot how to speak again. I took his hand and stood to my feet. My feet! Oh, my whole body! It looks like his! So soft and full of life, not the dull grey I'm accustomed to seeing. I stood there examining my whole body and gasping in wonder, forgetting I wasn't alone. The man's hearty laughter interrupted my examination and I looked away awkwardly.

"I am so glad you are finally here!" he shouted, startling me. "Sorry, I will explain soon enough. Can you run?" he asked.

"Yeah …" I cautiously answered.

"Let's go then!" he said as he broke into the fastest run I had ever seen.

One minute he was there, and literally one second later he was a mile down the beach. I just stood there in disbelief. And then suddenly he was back at my side.

"Come on! Give it a try!"

His words caused me to leap in fright at his sudden presence. He bolted away again and I decided I didn't want to be left behind, plus he seemed to know things that I needed to know. So I began to run like I usually would, and soon it felt as though I was flying, only my feet were on the ground still. Moving incredibly fast, but still grounded. Soon I was right next to the man and he smiled.

"Now that's more like it!" he yelled.

We ran for a while longer, and then I noticed I was alone in my run. I stopped and looked around. Behind me, I could barely see a dot waving at me. I knew it must be the man. I had kept on running when he had stopped and I didn't know it. I returned to his side and let out an outburst of excitement, "Oh, my gosh!" and I broke into laughter. The man joined my laughter and I could have sworn we laughed for hours.

After we both regained composure, he led me into this big and elaborately decorated building. I was still getting used to all this *color*, and I stared at everything with the innocence of a newborn baby. We went into a small room with chairs lined up like a classroom. He instructed me to sit down, and as I did, a moving image appeared in front of me on a large screen. I gasped and my eyes grew wide with wonder. The picture was alive! It was as if I were looking out a window, watching real life. Moving and talking pictures!

"This is what we call a video," the man started, "And this video will explain all you need to know about this world you have happened upon. Watch closely."

I nodded in agreement and shifted my focus back to the "video".

An hour later I found myself picking up my jaw from the floor and unpeeling my eyes from the screen. This was a completely different world I had stumbled upon. This world is called Aurora, and it is a place of peace, and a place of color.

Aurora is a place completely opposite of my old home, Quietus. Quietus was a world void of color. Everything was set in blacks and grays. This new world is a world founded by those brave enough to do what I did, and plunge into the murky depths; people in search for something more, or the people looking for an end to their misery. This place was born out of people like me. I was meant to find this place, and immediately I knew I was never going back to my old home.

Finally I remembered where I was, and I remembered the man who brought me here. I quickly swiveled my head and looked behind me. There he was just standing by the door with his arms folded across his chest and a smirk etched into his face.

"Don't worry, take your time. I know it's a lot to absorb. It was pretty hard for me to grasp when I first got here."

Wordlessly I stared at him, or rather through him, as my thoughts were churning like vicious waves on what I had just discovered. I faintly heard his laughter and came back to reality.

"You weren't born here?" I managed to ask softly.

"Nope. I was one of those crazy kids sick of my life back in the dark lands. Actually, I was one of those in search for an end. I'm not sure about your home life, but mine was pretty bad," he began.

"Well," I swallowed a lump in my throat at the sudden memories flooding into my mind of my life back home. "I don't know how bad you had it, but I can't see how life could have been much worse than what I've dealt with." I wasn't going to say more but the genuine concern in this man's face let me know he understood. I felt strangely comforted and decided to continue. "I too was in search for an end, or at least that is what my body decided as I sat along the grey shores of Ebony Beach. Maybe I didn't necessarily want an end, but I knew I didn't want what I had. I should have been more afraid of the darkness as I glided through the black abyss of water. I should have been concerned that I was going deeper, instead of coming back up when I felt my lungs start screaming for air. But I didn't care. Either I was going to find something else or I was going to die. But strangely I didn't think of it that way. My mind was surrounded by such a peace that even the cry of my crumbling lungs didn't concern me. It was like I somehow knew there was something and I had to keep swimming toward it. I didn't even think about death, I just knew I wasn't about to come back up and into the world I escaped from. Little did I know, I would truly end up in a different world."

I smiled as I realized the truth of the matter. I was somewhere else. My old life truly is gone and I am never going back. I looked at the man and he just stood there looking at me and nodding. He understood.

"Well, there is no more looking back. That is what I told myself upon my arrival here. That old life is dead and gone now! Welcome to your new existence!"

His smile expanded like a rubber band and shone as bright as my newfound hope. I couldn't help but replicate his smile as I began to dance around the room. I felt like a new person, like a baby discovering life for the first time. *What have I been missing?* I thought to myself.

Soon I was joined in my dance by the man, and we jumped and danced and ran around the room and then into the hallways of the building. Pure happiness and clean joy exploded out of us as we celebrated a new life. My new life.

"You know what?" the man suddenly began as we both slowed down, panting and collapsing on the shimmering floor. "I never told you my name. It's Alex, short for Alexavier. What shall I call you? I don't want your old name, I want you to choose a new name for yourself. A new identity for your new life."

"Umm … I don't know any good names," I began.

"Ah, that's right, of course you don't know any good names from this world. Here, let me help," he said as he ran down the hall away from me. He came out a minute later carrying a large book. "Okay, here is a name book. Our founders put this list together after researching the history of this world, and looking at word origins and their meanings. Just find the one that speaks to your heart. That's what I did."

I took the heavy book and scoured the pages, thinking deeply as I read through many lists of names categorized by similar meanings. Finally, I found the one that grabbed my attention.

"Call me Nova," I said aloud. "It means new."

"I like it!" Alex shouted "Nova!"

I felt my heart melt peacefully at the sound of my new name; the sound of my new life.

L'ultima Raccolta Dei Rifuti

The Ultimate Garbage Collection

Alfred Balcon

The Human City

The city is human and we feel the extension of its arms in its innermost recesses, like giant alien-like tentacles creeping up on us. Its skeleton is the playground of our daily endeavours. Its skin: our sidewalks. Every day we make our way through its streets like blood coursing through arteries, its organic fuel being regenerated by the second. Countless memories are blown up on the cities' billboards like Saturday-night blue movies. Hardcore.

We take the pulse of this city through the lens of a kaleidoscope, transforming, editing, enhancing the way the images are returned back to us. Our vision: your eyes …

Our target: an apartment building on Melancholy Road. Ten stories tall. The roof of the dark red brick building was redone a week ago. However, the contractor, more interested in planning his upcoming long week-end of wild debauchery than doing the job right, cut corners and botched the job. With heavy rains, the roof would certainly start leaking again very soon. Oh well!

And the way the November morning broke in Purla, that day was quite unusual. Nothing like that has ever been witnessed in that part of town—or in all of North America for that matter—as long as our social consciousness can remember. The tragic event was reported on CNN's Breaking News update and made the front pages of the world's papers and tabloids.

Let's go back a few hours before this human tragedy occurred. Four hours to be exact. At that time, it's 3:00 a.m. The moon is shining bright through the clouds. Our line of sight chooses the top floor of the apartment building in question. Apartment #9. An open window lets us in. Closer. A little bit closer. To the right. Watch the cat … Bingo. We are now in the kitchen of il Senior Marcello, an eighty-two-year-old Italian man. Born in Sicily, but lived in Purla since he was eighteen years old.

The kitchen is dark, cold, and damp. The room is lit solely by the soft glow of a set of candles purchased at Le Super Marché, Purla's most popular grocery store. The smell of eucalyptus permeates the air in an attempt to calm the senses, a necessity in today's stressful times.

Although the kitchen is small, its set-up is convenient, practical. The appliances are old, but in fine working condition. The Sicilian native has always refused to use a microwave oven, claiming that it was the worst invention of the century, and that it should be banned from every household in America because he believed it would eventually make us sick and kill us all. In his kitchen, everything has its place, and there is a place for everything. The dishes were recently cleaned and are drying up on a rack in the sink. Water is boiling in the kettle on the front burner of the gas stove. Tea will be ready soon. Marcello is standing between the cooking area and the dining area. For his age, he still stands unusually straight and tall, and his shoulders still seem solid despite bearing the heavy burden of the past. He is staring at the long corridor ahead of him, his eyes lost for a moment in the shadows of his solitude.

Outside the walls of Apartment #9, night-clubbers, reeking of alcohol and sweat from a night of partying, are invading the streets of Purla like in Romero's *Night of The Living Dead*. They are everywhere, high on crack and tweeting the night away on their stupid mobile phones; who kissed who, who got fingered by whom in the dirty washrooms of the Chemical Lounge. That sort of shit. They are embracing whatever is left of the night; kicking at garbage cans, screaming and yelling, sketching graffiti here and there, as proof that they were here, to show the world that they existed, and that this night will never be the same once they retreat in the silent comfort of their parents' homes, trading the coolness of their leather trench coats for the warmth of their cotton sheets. But as the night progresses, our imaginative camera catches them running like a mob of vampires, trying to reach their coffins before sunrise, before the light burns their flesh to dust ...

━ • • ━

Into Marcello's Mind

Lost in his thoughts, Marcello didn't even notice that the water had been boiling for a couple of minutes already. He walks to the stove, picks up the kettle, and pours the boiling water in his favourite mug—the one shaped like the Italian boot, his homeland. Sometimes he wishes he had never left there. Sometimes he wishes he never grew old. But sometimes, shit happens.

He then walks to the cupboard to choose his tea, hesitating between chamomile and earl grey. Chamomile it is. Once his hot, calm, soothing beverage has finished steeping, he returns to the living room. Sitting down, he takes extra care not to spill tea on his new trousers.

Jack, his best friend and living companion, rubs his furry head on his leg, purring away. The cat does not seem to understand why its master is awake and up at such an early hour again tonight. Does that mean he will get an earlier breakfast? In this cat's dreams … But tonight, Jack senses that something is different. There is something strange in the air. The mood of the room has somehow been altered. Something's definitely up. And it does not smell too good.

— · · —

4:00 a.m. The silence has returned to the streets of Purla. The turbulence of the youth has vanished, and the dark night is heading for the finish line before the break of dawn brings back all the Purliens to their daily routine like mechanical little robots: working, talking, sweating.

Marcello is sipping his tea in the living room, and apart from the couch on which he is sitting, the room is completely empty. No frames on the walls or even bookshelves to display his favourite stories. Surprisingly, no television can be found between the four walls of this very sad apartment. One thing is for sure, it has not always been like that. Something changed in recent years. In the last month, to be precise. There is music, though. There has always been music in Marcello's life, in happy times as well as in sad ones. The wonder of Miles Davis' trumpet fills the room with organic and sensual sounds, its vibrant notes coming from a portable CD player plugged on the floor next to the velvety piece of furniture.

Jack leaves the living room. The four-legged animal heads

for the long corridor, the one Marcello was staring at earlier. This corridor leads to four rooms. We know because our eyes have seen every parcel of this city, examined every inch of it, scrutinized every detail. Once the feline has reached the end of the *couloir*, it drops to the floor and starts grooming itself, staring directly at its Master. This gesture on the part of the cat seems to trigger something in Marcello because the Italian man gets up, leaves his empty cup of tea on the sofa, and exits the living room.

For a very short moment, the old man looks as though he's in a trance; eyes lost in dark memories, his body completely immobilized. Frozen. Paralyzed. He looks at the long corridor as though he is in front of a museum. His eyes move from one door to the next, trying to decide which one to focus on. They are all identical, except for their color: green, blue, yellow, and black. But what exactly could there be behind these wooden gateways? Beauty or horror? Let's find out.

The first room definitely has an outdoorsy feel to it. As soon as Marcello opens the door, we are transported outside. The green floor carpeting feels like grass on a soccer field. The effect is so realistic, that if we closed our eyes for a moment, we could almost feel the hot summer wind blowing on our face, and if we keep them closed for just a few seconds more, we could almost hear the beautiful sound coming from the birds' chirping. A fast scan of the surroundings tells us some important information about the room. First, there is a picture of a boy and Marcello on the night table. This father-and-son photography must have been taken during a soccer tournament as other teams are playing on a fairly large field in the background, and the boy, holding a soccer ball, has a medal around his neck. The kid looks very happy, and the father seems very proud of his son. The room is a shrine to the passion of this boy for soccer; trophies, posters of soccer celebrities and stars, team pictures, very first pair of cleats, as well as other memorabilia. There are no recent pictures of the two, nor of other siblings for that matter. They are a testament of better days, when the relationship between the two was good. Let's pursue our journey and see what the blue door holds for us.

While the green room was all about soccer, this one is all about arts and music. Different shades of blue give it a very calming effect. The bed cover is made of a cloud print fabric, adding to the imaginative feel of the room. Here too is a picture of a boy and Marcello on the night stand. While the boy in the green room had dark hair, this one has blond hair. This picture was taken at a piano recital. The two of them seem very happy together, and there is also a woman in the background looking toward the father and son. She is no passerby. She is undoubtedly a member of the family. Wife? Sister?

Our eyes move from the picture to glance over to the rest of the room. The walls display a great variety of drawings created by a child's hand. Trees stand tall through vibrant splashes of green. Dolphins meet up with dinosaurs in tennis courts. Halloween and Christmas are also very present in these artistic demonstrations. Before closing the door behind us, our eyes meet with the cat's, who is standing right next to the next room. The one with the yellow door. Marcello slowly walks over, takes a hard long look at all the other colored-doors before opening the sunny colored one.

It's summer in here. Everything is yellow; the walls, the bed cover, the furniture, the night lamps. There's that woman again from the blue room. Here, in one beautifully framed painting centered over the bed, is Marcello and his so very beautiful … wife. Her ocean blue eyes show her softness, intelligence, and kindness. She is a genuine person. But as we scan the rest of the room, two other shocking details call our attention. Although all the pieces of furniture seem to match and blend in here, it looks like the bed is the original one the two used to share. Used to …

If we were to touch the daisy print bed cover with the tip of just one finger, passionate images of long lovemaking sessions would surely appear in our minds, telling us that husband and wife shared a happy life; a long journey of love and respect filled with sensuality and happiness. At the other end of this life's spectrum are echoes of a much sadder ending to this beautiful love story, and those tragic details are portrayed on a small table next to the window. There stands a wooden black box containing her ashes, a hospital picture of a much older and dying Melody in what seems to be the last instants of her life, and a fresh bouquet of yellow roses arranged in a glass pot. Death and life sharing the same space next to a window of hope. Another set of lives ruined by cancer.

Before opening the black door, the *plat de résistance* on our journey through Marcello's life, let us review all the information that has been presented to us so far in this demonstration of desperation. We are in the presence of an old Italian man living by himself with his cat in an empty apartment. In this sad and lonely living space, there are four rooms kept like museums exhibiting the lives of the loved ones that he has cherished. But what has really happened to these people, and more precisely, to the interactions between them? Why are the living quarters apart from the four rooms so empty? And what about all of Marcello's belongings? What does Marcello have in store for us?

The door of the black room opens, making a creaking spooky sound. As soon as there is enough space, Jack runs inside. Marcello follows. It's 5 a.m. The floor is filled with scrapbooks full of handwritten notes, journal entries, poems, drawings, as well as letters addressed to his sons—letters that were never opened and simply returned to sender.

At this point in time, Jack is lying on the only piece of furniture in this small bedroom; an old mattress thrown in the middle. Empty walls. Empty life. Empty mind. Unlike the other rooms, this one does not have any pictures. It has no personality, no identity, no meaning. There is even a manuscript that Marcello has been trying to work on for the longest time, never being able to complete it since the passing of his wife. A novel just lying there, waiting to be finished. Waiting to be shared and published.

There is absolutely no trace of his family in this room, or should we say prison cell. A life sentence of misery and solitude. The kids never forgave their father for falling into a deep depression following their mother's death after a long battle with cancer. They should have been there for him. They should have dealt with the grief of losing that special person together. But instead, they abandoned him, dropping him like an old dirty smelly sock, like a bag full of dirt on garbage day.

Looking outside the bedroom window, Marcello stares at the life on the other side of these walls, scanning the deserted street with his vision. He is looking for something, waiting for some sort of awakening, a revelation in the making. But what exactly?

He then takes a long hard look at the black room, then at the yellow one, registering all of their details, copying them to his mental hard drive as if he never wants to forget them. He repeats the same process with the two other rooms.

Reaching the end of the corridor, he turns and takes one long last look at his half-empty apartment.

It's now time to make sure that all of Jack's needs are met. Marcello ensures that his beloved cat's two bowls are full of water and food.

He picks up Jack for one last time, giving him the most tender and beautiful hug. Jack closes his eyes and purrs away, feeling comfortable, loved and secure in his arms. Marcello then puts the cat on the floor right beside him. Jack does not move an inch and looks right up at his master. It feels as though something tragic is about to happen.

The end is near, and that feeling is getting stronger by the second.

Time to Go!

6:15 a.m. It seems like a switch just got flipped in Marcello's mind. Suddenly, there is something definitely different about him. The man previously so full of passion toward his cat, and the memories that he is leaving behind, is now acting as if he were some kind of robot, fully detached from reality. The next steps seemed to have been programmed. In a matter of speaking, rehearsed, for their execution is flawlessly precise.

6:30 a.m. In front of his front door, Marcello starts undressing himself, not just his pants and shirt, but his underwear as well, without turning to look behind him. He must go on with his plan, regardless of the past, regardless of what's in front of him. Naked.

Over the course of the last months, he had slowly started to give away all of his belongings to his friends, beginning with all the unnecessary stuff in order to keep only what really matters to him, so that, in the end, he would only leave behind the essential of what he used to be. Marcello's DNA. Nothing more. Nothing less.

6:35 a.m. Leaving everything behind, he exits his apartment. We watch him close the door behind him. Naked. The cat silently stays in the back of the wooden structure, waiting.

6:40 a.m. Marcello has already started his descent toward the *rez-de-chaussée* (some might call it Hell). Nothing seems so stop him. He is focused and determined. Not even the old pain in his knees could slow him down. Seventh floor.

As he passes through the staircase, the echo of the other tenants' lives reaches our attentive ears. Some sing, some fight, some laugh, some cry. Mrs. White has already started her daily house cleaning as we hear the sound of her vacuum cleaner rubbing against her living room carpet. A couple of newlyweds are having sex in their newly renovated bathroom. As far as Monsieur Personne is concerned, he is still contemplating his suicidal thoughts, and he is planning on leaving this world before the end of the month, leaving a handful of unpaid bills behind. Who the hell cares!

6:45 a.m. Second floor. Everything is going according to plan. Marcello will soon get to the ground floor. Purla is slowly waking up. The sun has risen. He has reached his destination.

6:50 a.m. Marcello pushes the building's door open. The second his naked foot touches the asphalt, he notices the coldness of the day. He then slowly walks to the street in front of the apartment tower. Although he is without clothes, and thus clashes in the background with his nudity, it seems that he has become invisible to his surroundings. It seems that the second he closed the door of his apartment, he has stopped existing in the eyes of society.

Mrs. White takes her black dog, Blackie, for a walk. As she passes next to the old man, she does not say a word, nor acts differently toward him. Blackie stops, lifts its leg, and pees on Marcello's feet.

7:00 a.m. Marcello is standing on the sidewalk looking toward the end of the street. At 7:00 a.m. sharp, a big black truck appears on Melancholy Road. Today is garbage day. The vehicle stops by every house, and two guys get off the truck and throw in the garbage left on the curb; boxes, black garbage bags, trimmed tree branches, and so on. All these unwanted, unneeded things make their way to the menacing insides of the four-wheeled ogre being pulverized and decapitated by its deadly mechanical teeth. *Tchak! Tchak! Tchak!*

The truck slowly approaches. Two houses left to go. Marcello is sitting on a garbage bag, his eyes lost into nothingness.

The back engine parks itself in front of the naked man. Joey and Tom get down. They start throwing in the mountain of garbage bags. As they get to Marcello, Joey asks his partner for help.

"Hey, Tom. Can you and give me a hand when you can? This thing is pretty fucking heavy!"

They both pick up Marcello as if he were an old sofa. Dirty. Smelly. Useless. And on the count of three, the old Italian naked man is thrown into the truck. Marcello does not say a word or move. He thanks God it's finally over, and then closes his eyes.

Once the two men are done picking up all the disposed items, they both jump back on the side of the truck, press the button to smash all the junk that was thrown in, and go on with their day as if nothing out of the ordinary has happened.

Mr. Curious coldly watched the scene from his front balcony on the eighth floor. He is so happy that his old broken down television was finally picked up. He hesitated for such a long time before throwing it away …

As the truck reaches its next stop for junk pick-up, we hear the heart of the machine smashing, destroying the content of its gut. It has something new to chew on today. A horrible mix of wine bottles, broken bones, and juicy leftovers echoes in the morning air … The excess liquid, mostly Marcello's bodily fluids, leak from under the truck, leaving a brownish trace on the pavement. This is his legacy, the remains of a poster boy for misery. Soon, the city's cleaning truck will come and clean all the streets of Purla. By then, Marcello will have vanished forever from the face of the Earth, joining his beautiful wife in the gardens of Heaven, finally finding an oasis of peace in a maelstrom of turbulence.

The other tenants of the apartment building in which Marcello lived in go on with their day. Madame Gusto is receiving some out-of-town guests and she has started preparing her famous mushroom risotto. Mrs. & Mr. Brown are fighting over their daughter who has a drug addiction; the wife wants to help her out even if this will bring her back on the streets while the father is willing to let her die there. As for Monsieur Personne, he is still contemplating more than ever his suicidal thoughts to finally exit this life. But we don't see that he will make it before month end.

In Apartment #9, Jack is still standing in front of the door. He plans not to eat nor drink anything until his master returns, or until they finally meet again in a much better place …

❧

Alfred Balcon has been writing forever. Freelance writer for various publications, blogger (www.uzinamo.blogspot.ca), and novelist. When he is not working to earn a living, or to take care of his family, he writes horror stories filled with weird landscapes and strange characters. So goes the creation of Alfred who lives in an alternate reality, surrounded by his books, his robotic music, and culinary, and literary fantasies.

If This Color Could Tell a Story
Cynthia Paone

Something happened that day that changed my life forever. I met a girl who thought I was perfect.

The first day she saw me, her eyes lit up and her smile grew larger than it ever had before. She told the man at the front counter of the store that she loved me the moment her eyes spotted me. She just knew I was the right color.

She skipped out of the store with a smile on her face and love in her heart.

When we finally made it home, she methodically coated every inch of her wall with me. She told me that I made her heart feel warm and the room feel cozy. When she looked at me, she thought only of love. She was so excited about bringing me home that she invited her best friend over to meet me.

Her friend stopped abruptly at the doorway of the room where I resided. This so-called friend expressed an unexpected sinister disliking of my dwelling. She spoke such words of hate and anger. She felt thoughts of death. She was scared of my color.

The friend kindly, and somewhat urgently, thanked her for inviting her over to the house to check me out. Then she stated that she could not stay any longer.

I heard her walk her friend to the front door to let her out. She sighed in disappointment as she locked the deadbolt.

I could hear the sound of defeat in the aimless shuffle of her feet as she walked toward the kitchen.

She called a second friend to come over. This friend just has to love the room as much as she does.

I heard the second friend ring the doorbell. There was so much optimism in both of their voices as she was let into the house. I could hear them get closer to the room where I inhabited. I braced myself and prepared for the worse, yet hoped for the best.

I watched the second friend's eyes grow big. She started to yell, demanding to know why I represented so much evil and hatred.

The second friend was cordially thanked for coming by, and ushered hastily toward the front door.

When the second friend was gone, my caretaker walked back into the room where I now lived. She sat in a chair and stared at me with confusion and morose.

I felt ashamed. I knew what she must be thinking, *How can a color that's supposed to make people feel warm and loved make someone feel such turmoil?*

This was my great dilemma. I was designed to represent Cupid's arrow going through fun-shaped hearts. Once every year lovers even exploit me to represent their love through chocolate hearts and cards. I can bring a smile to any girl's face. Yet all of the visitors have reacted negatively toward me.

My caretaker sat in her chair and reluctantly called a third friend.

When the third friend arrived and walked into the room, my caretaker asked her what she thought of me. The friend's eyes widened and she grinned from ear to ear.

I knew that smile all too well.

The friend exclaimed that I was beautiful and warm, spreading love all around. She said that I made her heart feel whole.

I realized then that people will only see what they want to see. I am only a color. That's all I will ever be. I never imagined that I could be a foe to one person, and a friend to another. I am only a color.

I am bright but can be dark.

I am loved by many but hated by most.

I can make some feel loved and others feel hate.

I am constantly judged and frequently misunderstood.

I am labeled.

I am what some bleed.

I am only what you see me as.

I can only be this color.

And this color is who I am.

Just Another Day in Hell
Stephen Rhodes

Sergeant Grath watched the sun rise as he finished his cigarette. He savoured the tobacco, the smell of scented leaves as they burnt.

"Just another day in hell," he said as he threw the butt of the cigarette away. He swung one leg over the barrel of Deliverance's main battle cannon and jumped down off the Sovereign Class Tank onto the dry, red earth of Caldia. "Rise and shine folks, our good lady needs prepping for the day's events."

Grath walked by and kicked the boots of the four figures sleeping under the tank. He was rewarded by grunts and moans as they were roused to action by the all too familiar voice of their commanding officer.

"We've only just put our heads down," said a voice dry as dust.

"You had four hours, that's good enough for a soldier," Grath said as he continued his inspection of the tank.

She still carried some scars from the previous night's fighting, but he knew Solia would have them fixed soon enough. He walked around the tank a few more times before forcing his crew out of their lethargy.

The civil war for Caldia had been raging now for three solar orbits, yet to the crew of Deliverance, it felt like an eternity.

This wasn't a conflict any of the 57th army wanted to fight. Putting down an insurgency was miserable work, but they were soldiers, and soldiers obeyed orders. Rebel cells opposed to Imperial rule had popped up across the planet but had been quickly scattered by the planet's standing army. It wasn't until the rebels stormed the Imperial Palace and assassinated the Governor, claiming independence, that the Imperial Army was called in to respond.

The rebels had plenty of time to fortify Irkell, the capital of Caldia, before the 57th fleet arrived in orbit. Two dreadnaught class capital ships were destroyed by planetary defense weapons before the fleet signaled for retreat and got out of range. The only option remaining was to make planetfall on the opposite side of Caldia and take it piece by piece. The Deliverance was part of the first wave.

"All systems are operational, sir. Takes more than a few scratches to silence our good lady," Solia said as she wiped oil and sweat from her forehead.

"How are we for munitions?" Grath asked, using a hand to help carry his voice over the thundering sound of Deliverance's engines.

"We're good on primary shells but I wouldn't mind some hell fires. Those things melt through armour faster than the spit of a Hakkuan Dragon," Luca said as he popped his head out from within the tank, a box of ammunition under each arm.

"You're always looking for a bigger explosion, like our girl doesn't do enough damage as is," Vasser said from the pilot's seat as he stroked the top of the drive console.

"Can't hurt to ask, I suppose," Grath said as he stroked the stubble on his chin. "Although Fulgar is still pissed at us for that incident during the assault on Aurek."

"I already apologised for that, but it's hardly my fault that the guy can't keep his tank in formation," Luca said. "I had a clear line of sight to the bunker before that idiot tried to steal our glory."

"Go easy on him Luca. It must be hard commanding the second best tank crew in the 57th."

They shared a laugh at Vasser's comment. Rivalry between the tank commanders kept them all on their toes, but no one could dispute the reputation of Deliverance's crew. Grath had trained them to be the best, and they all took great pride in it.

"Sir, command's on the line. They are starting the mission briefing," Eidadme said in her typical quick and concise manner.

"Tell them I will be right there." Grath climbed up to his command station within the turret and grabbed his officer's cap. "I want Deliverance ready by the time I get back." He jumped down and made the long walk to the central command bunker.

"Sergeant Grath, glad you could join us," Commander Deoner Jakar said with a nod. "How's Deliverance holding up?"

"Morning, sir. The old girl is doing fine. Ready to go as always," Grath said as he walked into the briefing room, saluted, and placed his cap under his arm.

The rest of the officers stood around, studying the central holographic terminal. A city with high walls marked with numerous red chevrons was displayed. Outside the city, Grath could see the unmistakable icons of armoured formations.

"Glad to hear it. Now that we're all here, let's discuss the plan to finally take back this planet from those cowards."

Grath slowly realised what the holographic display showed.

It was Irkell, the capital of Caldia. The city was a fortress, and the insurgents had rallied the people to their cause. The walls around the city were eighty feet high, and every ten metres along the perimeter, an enormous turret stood vigilant. This would not be an easy victory by any means.

"We're going to hit Irkell?"

"That's correct, Sergeant. I have grown tired of this planet, and these rebels. It's time they felt the full might of the 57th. We are going to attack the city just before noon." Jakar began walking around the holographic display, changing the image to show the army's placement. "I intend to commit one hundred percent of our armoured division to the assault. We will strike with our full force on a single section of the wall, overwhelming their defenses. Our primary objectives are the orbital defense installations and shield generators."

"Why are we taking out the shield generators sir? Our tanks will already be within the sphere of influence," said an officer Grath didn't recognise. He was young, probably earned himself a promotion when a lucky sniper shot took out his commanding officer.

"The shields need to be taken offline so the fleet can finish the job. Our objective is to disable the defenses and get out."

Grath swallowed a response. He had been part of missions like this before. Irkell was a city of millions, most of which were not insurgents. They were citizens of the Empire and Grath understood what he was about to do.

"What is the civilian evacuation plan?" Grath asked.

General Jakar cleared his throat. "There is no evacuation plan. We intend to send a message to the people of Caldia and every other outer rim planet that belongs to the Empire."

"These people are not all rebels, sir."

"These people let their planet be overthrown and are now assisting in its defense. They are just as responsible for this situation as Caldia's incompetent Governor," Jakar said, his voice louder, carrying around the room. "We are going to turn Irkell to dust and build a monument to remind others what it means to betray the Empire."

"This is their centre of power, sir. The insurgents will not give it up without a fight," Grath said, his mind trying to formulate a plan that could provide an alternate strategy.

"Cut the head off the beast and the body will die. We will end this rebellion today." Jakar paced away from the officers. He paused as he gazed at the rising sun through the door of the bunker, the tank's silhouettes shimmering in the morning heat. "Ready your vehicles, the attack commences in three hours. Dismissed."

Grath walked back from the briefing with his head slumped. His mind wandered as he passed rows of tanks, their crews busy repairing or rearming the metallic behemoths they served. They looked like ants to Grath; scurrying across the surface of enormous mounds of steel. It was a symbiotic relationship. The crews repaired and maintained the tanks, and the war machines protected them and destroyed their enemies.

It felt like superstition to Grath. The tanks were a tool, a weapon of war, but he didn't begrudge the soldiers their beliefs, so long as they did their job. That was the difference between the soldiers of the 57th and the insurgents. Grath and his men were trained for this. It was their job to defend the Empire. The insurgents were fighting for their beliefs.

"What's the plan, boss?" Luca asked Grath as he approached Deliverance.

"Get us ready to move out. We have a long drive ahead of us."

—··—

The army began the long march to Irkell, several hours after the briefing. Progress was slow in order to keep the possibility of detection down to a minimum, and to avoid creating too much dust. Two thousand battle tanks lumbered across the plains of Caldia with dozens of armoured personnel carriers, support vehicles, and artillery following closely behind. The column stretched behind the lead vehicles for miles, crawling toward the city like an enormous, mechanical centipede hunting its prey.

Grath sat in his command station on board Deliverance. His elevated position from within the turret granted him the best tactical view of the battlefield. He looked out across the red terrain at the Lani river running to the West of the column—the water racing the vehicles to the coast where Irkell and the ocean resided.

"How long until we are within visual range of the city?" Grath asked into his comm.

"A couple more hours yet, sir. We would be there much sooner if we were travelling at a decent speed," Vasser said as she adjusted Deliverance's course. "Honestly I could get out and walk faster."

"Well this is preferable to getting our collective asses blown to pieces before we get to the city. At this speed we won't be detected by long range motion scanners."

Luca grunted. "We don't need to sneak, just get them within my sights and I'll make sure our asses remain un-blown up."

"That's not a word, Luca, you dumb ass," Vasser said. "And I'm not sure our girl wants to put her well-being entirely in your hands."

"I've told you, the sponson was damaged. I couldn't turn it fast enough," Luca said, his voice taking on an apologetic tone.

"Don't blame Deliverance. If she wasn't cooperating, it's because you did something to upset her," Vasser said.

"I do nothing but ..."

"Sir, I'm hearing reports from the front. We have incoming," Eidadme said over the comm.

The crew looked at each other, concern etched on their faces. Grath snapped to full alert. He switched his attention to the command consoles at his station and began scanning the information.

The front of the advancing column was under attack by enemy aircraft. Rebel bombers streaked the convoy with bombs and armour piercing rounds. Explosives and high calibre munitions tore through the vulnerable top armour of the Sovereign-class tanks, as wave after wave of bombers dropped through the clouds that drifted high above the advancing army. They started at the head of the column and worked their way back, leaving nothing but wreckage and death in their wake.

"Threat assessment?" Grath asked as he tried to make sense of the chaotic information being fed to his console from the rest of the 57th.

"Seems like all aerial, sir," Eidadme said in between relaying other messages and listening to new reports.

Grath listened in horror. The attack had started only moments ago and already the losses were disastrous.

"Tell the convoy to break formation and spread out. Tell everyone to switch their turret control to anti-air. We're going to fill the sky with shells before they reach us. Also contact the 1st and tell them to get the hell out of there," Grath said to Eidadme as he began firing off his own command communications. If they were going to survive this, he needed to act fast.

Luca activated the side sponsons on Deliverance. There was one on each side, sticking out of the tank's main body like little bulbous appendages. Each sponson housed a pair of lancers; incredibly powerful machine guns that could fire a thousand rounds per minute. They weren't accurate, but what they lacked in precision they made up for in raw firepower. The turrets whirred to life at the command of the gunner, the sponsons twisting until the lancers were pointed skyward.

Grath could now see the smoke from the head of the column. He could hear the sound of weapons being fired, and could feel the ground shake from the explosives. The first of the insurgent bombers pierced through the smoke, flying towards the 2nd division, hunting for new prey. The craft was quite agile, its shape similar to that of an arrowhead. The pilot compartment was housed at the front with a quad-barreled cannon hanging below it. The wings did not stretch out from either side, but were positioned at an extreme angle where the tips ran parallel to the fuselage at the rear of the aircraft.

"All vehicles report synchronization, sir," Eidadme said, a smile starting on Grath's face as he stared at the approaching bomber.

"Open fire."

Grath clasped his hands to his ears as the sound of hundreds of lancer batteries threatened to deafen him. The entire 2nd division fired their Lancer batteries as one; the synchronization allowing the platoon to fill the sky with a deadly barrage of flak. The tanks had spread out and now covered a specific section of air space ahead of the column.

The bomber Grath watched emerge from the smoke was blown out of the sky. Secondary explosions erupted within its structure as the lancer rounds pierced its delicate armour in a dozen locations. As the aircraft fell to the ground in pieces, the rest of the bomber squadron erupted from the smoke cloud, their pilots eager to avenge their fallen comrade.

"Where are they coming from?" Grath asked.

"Reports say they are approaching from the east. We suspected the insurgents had a base of operations within the Shattered Mountains. I guess we can all but confirm that now," Eidadme said in response.

"Well I think it's safe to say they know we are coming. That's going to make taking Irkell much harder."

"That's if we survive to see it. These bombers are getting through," Vasser said as she drove Deliverance through the chaos.

The bombers were driving through the anti-air fire. Despite taking heavy losses, they continued launching volleys of cluster missiles into the scattered tanks below.

Grath ducked out of reflex as a missile flew overhead. He felt the explosion and turned to see The Prospector, now little more than a flaming wreck, drift off its path and crash into a nearby crater. No one crawled out of the shattered remains. The losses started to mount as more bombers breached through the smoke, now the only memory of the 1st division.

"Sir, the lancers are running dry," Luca said, the implication in his voice urging Grath to act.

"How long do we have?"

"Couple of minutes at most," Luca said.

Grath thought for a moment, assessing the situation, trying to think of a solution. The 57th couldn't afford to lose two entire divisions before reaching Irkell. He had to do something.

"Sound the retreat. We need to rendezvous with the 3rd and 4th before we lose too many men," Grath relayed to his crew.

"We haven't been given a retreat order, sir," Eidadme said.

"I don't give a shit. If we stay here, we are fucked! Signal the rest of the 2nd. Tell them to start a tactical withdrawal. I'll deal with Jakar if we survive this."

The tanks of the 2nd division began to retreat, pulling back into a tight formation to create a tighter screen of covering fire. The bombers gave pursuit, stalking the retreating tanks and picking off the slow, or out of formation, vehicles with lethal efficiency. The anti-air fire began to fade as many of the Sovereigns ran out of ammunition. The sponson weaponry was designed to be a secondary weapon system, used to suppress enemy positions whilst the main cannon reloads or finds a target. They were not meant to be used as dedicated anti-air support, and this fact was starting to show.

As if sensing this weakness, like predators stalking injured prey, a group of bombers changed course and angled toward the retreating tank formation. They were flying straight for the centre of the armoured mass, their counter measures providing enough safety to pass through the thinning amount of flak defending the tanks. One of the bombers took a hit that clipped its wings and forced it out of formation. The bomber broke off its pursuit and flew away from its wingmen, knowing it could no longer take part in the attack. The two remaining craft adjusted their position to maximize their coverage. They angled down toward the ground, flying low, their missile pods opening in preparation to fire.

"Brace for impact," Grath shouted as he closed the turret hatch and gripped his seat. He heard the explosions and felt the shockwave rock Deliverance. When it was over, he was still alive, his tank still in one piece.

A familiar sound washed over him as he heard the sound of engines above. Grath reached out and opened the turret hatch once again; his eyes adjusting to the light. He could make out the flaming wreckage of two bombers scattered across the earth in the distance. He looked up to see several squadrons of Raptors—fighter craft used by the Imperial Military—fly overhead. In the distance, he could see yet more Raptors engaged in a brutal dogfight with the enemy.

"Looks like the fleet is still up there watching over us," Luca said as he slumped back in his chair and sighed.

The aerial attack had taken a heavy toll on the 57th. The advance on Irkell was halted whilst they consolidated their position and calculated their losses. The insurgent aircraft were driven off by the Raptors intervention, but not all of them were destroyed. The surviving craft fled east and vanished from sensors once they reached the Shattered Mountains.

Jakar sent scouting parties to ensure the route to Irkell was clear whilst the officers met to discuss the best way to proceed. Grath was one of the first there, reaching Jakar's command vehicle as he still wiped the sweat and grime from his face.

"What's the word, Commander? What are the losses?" Grath asked as he saluted his superior. He knew the assessment would not be pretty.

Jakar looked up from the map he had perched on the hull of his command vehicle. "We lost the 1st in its entirety, and part of the 2nd."

The insurgents caught them completely unaware and the army paid the price. He clenched his fists, knowing that if the 57th had taken the time to seek out the rumoured airfields on the way to Irkell, this attack could have been avoided.

"These rebels are more organised than I gave them credit for. It would appear that elements of the planetary defense force joined their cause as well. These rogue elements need to be dealt with," Jakar continued.

"So we are going after the bases instead of Irkell?" Grath asked.

"No. The mission will continue as planned. You, however, will take a squad, find the hidden base within the Shattered Mountains, and neutralise their air force."

Grath eyes widened; his mind raced. "Sir, if you're pushing on the city, you need every vehicle at your disposal."

"What I need, Sergeant, is to ensure that we don't get flanked by enemy aircraft during a crucial moment during the siege. Five tanks taking out that threat will make more of a difference than five more at the gates of Irkell."

"I see your point, but the mountains cover a huge area. How are we meant to find the base before you attack the city?"

"We will set up a defensive position here and wait for your signal. Our scouts report that armoured convoys travel into the mountains, providing supplies and men for the base there. Tagging one and following it seems like your best chance of finding it," Jakar said as he beckoned Grath over to look at the map he was holding.

—·•—

"This sucks," Vasser said as he slumped in the driver's seat.

Deliverance sat in the undergrowth at the foot of the Shattered Mountains, powered down and hidden by camouflage nets. The rest of the tank squad was just behind Deliverance, silent and unmoving like the mountains and rocks around them.

The mountains formed the spine of the continent. Eons of tectonic activity has created a chaotic landscape covered in peaks, some tall and proud, others splintered and hunched; the results of a constant battle between the continental plates slamming together and pulling apart. The scar in Caldia's crust was so vast it could be seen from space, and this gave rise to the regions name.

The tank squad had spent several hours driving to the only visible entrance to the mountain range where they now waited for an enemy convoy to drive by.

"Beats getting shot at by enemy bombers," Luca said in response with a grunt.

"Well, if we do our job right, that won't happen again,"

"If the Jakar had done *his* job right, it would never have happened to begin with."

Grath was about to interject in the conversation when the side hatch of the tank creaked open. Solia entered Deliverance and sat down on the steel floor, her chest heaving with exertion.

"Tracking mine planted, sir. If anyone rolls up this way, we'll tag them," Solia said between breaths.

Grath nodded. "Good work, now get some sleep. We might need to move out fast, so best catch up on it now."

It was just past midnight when the indicator for the tracer

mine beeped. Eidadme jerked out of the light sleep she was in and began to track the vehicle Solia's mine had tagged.

"We got a live one."

"I can see them. Six vehicles with two heavy escorts," Vasser said from his vantage point at the front of the tank, the green glow of the night vision camera screen illuminating his face in the dark interior of Deliverance.

Grath looked at the image on his screen, the convoy currently driving past their position. They were entering the Shattered Mountains, moving slowly and with no lights on. The convoy was relatively small. The thing that worried Grath, however, was the convoy escort taking up the rear.

"Those tanks are Executioners," Grath said, his voice barely a whisper. He knew they couldn't hear him but he was strangely afraid that simply uttering their name might draw their attention.

The Executioners were enormous, almost twice the size of Deliverance. They out-classed them in both armour and fire power.

"I thought the Empire stopped using Executioners in favour of the Dauntless," Luca said.

"They did," Solia said before Grath could respond, "but worlds on the edge of the Empire haven't seen recent military action. They still rely on the older, heavier tanks."

If they sent two Executioners, whatever is in that convoy must be important, Grath thought as he weighed up his options.

"We need to take out those Executioners before they get to the base if we are to have any chance of success. Let's give them a bit of a lead, then follow and try to take them out from behind before they are aware of what hit them," Grath said to his crew as they watched the vehicles pass them by.

The convoy rolled past without incident, as did the first of the Executioner escorts. The final tank was about to pass by Deliverance when it stopped.

"What's it doing? Has it seen us?" Luca asked, his voice trembling.

Everyone froze, fearing that their movements might somehow be detected. Grath could feel himself holding his breath. The turret of the Executioner began to turn, the end of the barrel coming to rest facing Deliverance's hidden position. Realization dawned on Grath.

"Eidadme, order the squad to fully power down," he said in a hushed tone so only his communications officer could hear.

She nodded and turned to her comms.

Suddenly the serenity of the night was shattered as a flash of blinding incandescence and roar of thunder erupted from the barrel of the Executioner. The shell whistled over Deliverance and detonated with god-like force as it found its mark.

"Sir, Stryker is down," Eidadme said over the comm.

Dammit, they must have advanced sensors on those things, Grath thought as he formulated a plan. "Get us out of here, Vasser. Right now."

Deliverance hummed back to life as its systems were fed power once more. The engine roared and the great war machine shot out of hiding and into the clearing. Behind her came the three remaining members of the squad, firing shell after shell at the Executioner. Their shots deflected harmlessly off the larger tank's thick armour without causing so much as a few dents and scratches. The Executioner responded, adding its own voice to the howl of battle. The first shell punched straight through the lead sovereign and detonated whilst buried in the armour of the one behind it.

Grath could hear the sound of screaming over the squad comm channel until it abruptly stopped. Eidadme cut the feed knowing from personal experience what damage hearing such things could do.

"Fire! For fuck's sake, fire," Grath yelled into his headset over the deafening roar of a nearby explosion.

"What do you think I'm bloody doing? I can't see a thing through this smoke," Luca said as he attempted to seek the target.

The Executioner had deployed a smoke screen to increase the advantage it had over the smaller tanks. A full squadron of soldiers had also disembarked from its rear compartment and had taken positions on the other side of the clearing to lay down cover fire.

"Fire at the thing firing at us," Solia interjected, her voice tinged with panic as she tried to recalibrate the engine for battle.

The Deliverance rumbled forward, its main cannon unleashing a barrage of heavy ordnance whilst the side sponsons laid down a continuous stream of suppression fire. The impacts got the attention of the Executioner which began rotating its turret to bear on Deliverance.

"Vasser, we have its attention," Grath said as he watched the turret continue to turn.

Without warning, Deliverance lurched to a full stop, throwing Grath against the side of his compartment. The Executioner's main cannon barked forth once more, but this time the shot went wide as the gunner overcompensated for Deliverance's movement and position. The shell flew off into the distance and detonated harmlessly against the mountainside.

"Nice move but a little warning would be appreciated," Grath said as he rubbed his forehead.

"Sorry, sir, but I was a little busy. I'll be sure to send you a memo next time I plan to save your skin."

Grath decided to let that slide for now. They were being hunted by a heavy battle tank after all. They needed to act quickly or this brief advantage was going to mean nothing.

"Get us behind her and get us close. I reckon that turret isn't designed for close engagements," Grath said to Vasser who nodded in acknowledgement. "Luca, focus fire on the infantry until we can get into position."

Luca began turning the turret toward the soldiers who took up positions on the other side of the clearing, using large boulders and fallen trees as cover to pepper the tanks with small arms fire and grenades. The Deliverance's gunner turned all of her might on the infantry. Within a few salvos of fire from the main cannon and both sponsons, the area was decimated with nothing left but smoke and fire, the barrel glowing red in the dark.

"Good shooting, Luca," Grath said. "Eidadme, contact the remaining Sovereigns, tell them to—"

His words were interrupted as Deliverance shook with tremendous force. The tank continued to move forward and then slowly lurched to one side, a screeching noise issuing from the left of the tank.

"Our track's been hit. We can't move," Solia said.

"Shit, we can't stay here. That big bastard will be ready to fire again soon," Vasser said, her voice only just managing to contain her dread at the thought of being cooked alive within the tank.

Luca looked through his targeting visor and found the soldier who survived his attack. The man was already in the process of reloading the rocket launcher he carried when Luca gunned him down with the lancers. There was no satisfaction in the kill; the damage was done.

"Change of plan, ladies and gents. We're going to be commandeering that Executioner from our rebel friends," Grath said as he released the lock on his turret hatch. "Grab your guns and make for the rear entrance of the enemy vehicle. Eidadme, send a message to the other Sovereigns and tell them to attract their attention."

"Goodbye, old girl. We'll come back for you once the mission is done, I promise," Vasser said as he grabbed his machine gun and ran for the nearest exit hatch.

The crew all ran into the smoke surrounding the Executioner. Grath was the first to reach the rear. He dropped to one knee and put the rifle to his shoulder. He scanned around but could see very little.

Figures started to appear through the smoke as more of his crew reached him. Grath was about to ask if everyone was okay when the Executioner's cannon fired several times. The shockwave knocked the crew of Deliverance to the ground, the air ripped from their lungs and their ears rang. Heat washed over them as their precious war machine was hit by the full force of the shell. Debris flew high into the air and little remained of the tank they all once called home. Scraps of molten armour fell from the sky like rain drops of lava.

The light of the explosion pierced through the smoke and Grath could see a figure rising from near the wreckage of Deliverance.

Vasser was the last out of the tank as he had needed to say his final farewells. He survived the explosion by sheer luck more than anything.

As he rose from the ground, coughing and shaking from the explosion, Grath heard the sound of a hatch being released. He turned to see a dark figure appear on the top of the Executioner. The figure aimed a pistol at Vasser, and before Grath could shout a warning, he pulled the trigger. The smoke screen was quickly reclaiming the darkness, but Grath could see the body of his friend fall back down to the ground.

"For Deliverance and Vasser!" Grath yelled as he aimed his rifle at the figure and pulled the trigger several times.

The enemy collapsed and Grath began to climb up on top of the Executioner. He reached the turret hatch and pried it open. The man inside looked up in surprise. Grath dropped a grenade in his lap and closed the hatch once again. The rear ramp slammed down as three soldiers ran out only to be cut down by the surviving crew of Deliverance. They rushed up the ramp and began the gruesome work of clearing the vehicle of hostiles. After several minutes of fighting, the Executioner was now theirs.

The night grew calm and still once more. The fighting had lasted only a few minutes, but the weight of it felt much longer. The smoke cover finally cleared, the convoy was nowhere to be seen and all around the Executioner were the flaming remains of the Sovereign squad—debris and corpses littered the entire area.

"So what's our next move?" Solia asked as she began to rip open console panels and tinker with circuitry.

"We are going to fix this thing, catch up with the convoy, and drive straight into these bastard's base," Grath said, his face a mask of grim determination. "Then we are going to lay waste to everything."

It didn't take long for the Executioner to catch up with the convoy. Luca insisted they named it *Vasser*, not that it mattered. They weren't going to be using it for long. They transmitted a standard broken comms message to the insurgents which was accepted.

Grath thought they must have anticipated the Executioner being victorious, otherwise both tanks might have stayed for the fight. The convoy carried on its slow methodical advance through the shattered mountains. It took almost five hours before Grath—who was now driving the tank—spotted the hidden base.

The compound was nestled at the foot of a colossal mountain, tucked underneath a lip of rock. The path up to the front of the base was flanked by two large defense turrets and surrounded by concrete walls.

The convoy entered the insurgent base, the turrets paying them no attention as they passed. Grath could now make out the hidden runways carved deep into the side of the mountain itself.

There were two runways in total. At the far end of each, Grath could make out dozens of aircraft, parked for repair and rearmament. The convoy turned toward the left hand side of the base, the vehicles parking near the entrance to the first runway. The other Executioner continued past them and headed toward the rear of the base. As Grath drove past the trucks, he saw them beginning to unload the contents.

"What are they?" Grath asked as he looked on, confused.

Luca broke from his daydream and turned to look out of the Executioner at what Grath had noticed. His eyes widened as he realised what he was looking at.

"They are short range tactical nuclear warheads, Sarge, and that's a lot of them."

"How do you know that?" Solia asked, her voice full of doubt at Luca's words.

"Like Vasser used to say, I am all about the explosions, and those things make some of the biggest."

Grath couldn't work out why or how these insurgents had acquired weapons of that calibre. Then it dawned on him, the realisation punching him in the gut.

"They are going to drop them on the 57th," he said, still shocked at the thought.

The crew turned to look at him, their eyes widening with shock as they understood what this would mean.

"What about the radiation?" Eidadme asked. "If they drop that many nukes, they will condemn their entire planet to death."

"I guess they would rather see their world burn free, than live under Imperial rule."

"We have to stop them, Grath," Luca said.

"We will. It's about time we completed our mission. For Vasser."

"For Vasser," the crew of Deliverance said in solemnly.

The first sign the insurgents had that they were under attack was when one of the Executioner tanks exploded, showering the northern runway with debris and fire. Alarms rang out across the base as men scrambled to find who was attacking them. The Executioner class battle tank, Vasser, drove slowly along the runway, its sponsons blazing away at the stationary aircraft. It only took a few shots to cause a chain reaction that ripped its way along the ranks of parked aircraft, the resulting detonations causing the entire base to shake.

"Luca, turn those weapon caches to dust," Grath ordered as he focused on steering the Vasser and firing the sponsons.

"With pleasure."

The battle cannon mounted upon the Executioner roared in defiance; the deadly ordnance destroying the missiles without triggering the warheads they contained. The repurposed war machine continued to unleash death upon the rebels. Several enemy vehicles attempted to form a blockade but they were no match for the Executioner. Grath hammered down on the acceleration and smashed through.

"I could get used to this. These old Executioners are slow and clunky but not bad in a fight," Luca said as he reloaded and fired yet another devastating cannon shot.

Grath reached into his pocket and pulled out the device Jakar had given to him for the mission. He pressed the button and sent the confirmation signal. He did not hesitate despite his earlier concerns. These insurgents and this planet had cost him dearly. Not only had they destroyed his beloved Deliverance, but they also killed Vasser. For those crimes, he would gladly watch this world burn.

The Executioner rocked from several impacts. Grath returned his thoughts to the present and checked the sensors for enemy movement. He could make out several vehicles speeding through the compound entrance. Grath recognised the vehicles as a smirk grew upon his face. The insurgents only had a squad of Sovereigns left at the base and they were now forming a last ditch assault on the Executioner.

"Well, I guess now we have to return the favour," Grath said as he realigned the sponsons and cycled to armour piercing ammunition.

"Open fire, Luca. Give them hell."

The Executioner opened fire with all three weapons, the sponson turrets piercing the lead sovereign with a dozen rounds, the entry holes still glowing red when the tank veered off to the side and stopped. The main cannon barked in response to the shells impacting its front armour. The round tore the top off one of the enemy tanks. The remaining three began to retreat, but it was too late. The Executioner was amongst them, pouring shell after shell into the tanks trying to fall back.

It took the Executioner another thirty minutes to fully obliterate the rebel base and all of its occupants. By the time the sun began to rise, there was nothing but craters and smoke remaining of the hidden airfield.

Grath climbed out of the tank and looked out across the mountain range. On the horizon he could see the silhouette of a city barely visible in the distance. Grath pulled out a cigarette from his jacket and lit it. He took a long, exhausted drag and slowly exhaled, the serenity of the Shattered Mountains washing over him.

"Just another day in hell," he said as he watched the city in the distance become engulfed in bright, blue beams of light.

Stephen Rhodes is a video game developer and writer. He was born in England, and currently lives in Nottingham. Stephen is a Narrative Designer for Deep Silver Dambuster Studios where he is currently working on *Homefront: The Revolution.* When he isn't making or playing video games, he spends a lot of his time reading and writing, mainly fantasy and science fiction. He is a self-confessed film junkie and his favorite film is Ridley Scott's classic, *Blade Runner.*

It's Yours

Dan Golden

The city buzzes with excitement as we enter through the front gate. Trading booths are randomly placed about Main Street. People shuffle from destination to destination along their routes to the next thing that they have to do. I pause to look at one of these trading booths. It's small, it's quaint, and it's undoubtedly unique. There's an old sign hanging just over the table: *Antiques*. As a man smiles at me, a shiver runs through me at the sight of his grin, yet I still venture forward. There's just something about the things on his table that catches my attention.

Although my guide has wandered ahead of me, he motions to not waste any time with such petty traders. I pay no heed. This is my idea after all. If I have something in mind, I should do it. I see no reason at this moment not to. I smile back for politeness.

He asks me, then what am I looking for?

"Nothing in mind," I reply.

He smiles still and searches for something on his table. A moment later and there appears a lamp; old and gray with dust all over it. I ask him, "How much?"

He just smiles all the while. "It's yours, keep it."

I see no reason to argue. I shrug and place the lamp in my

pack that hangs from my right shoulder. "Thanks!" I say and turn to leave.

My guide shakes his head, yet I don't notice. I'm not sure whether I'm beaming from inside, or if maybe the sun has reflected off the lamp I had just acquired making me glow with a sort of delightful pride.

The sun beats down a warmth on my head and face as we continue to walk. Children chase one another and laughter fills the air with noise. People. I don't ever remember seeing this many on one street before. *Magnificent* and *pretty* are words that cannot even justify the appearance of what some of these folks wear. Yet more than a half of these people are dressed in clothes similar to that of me and my guide. I sigh. How nice would it would be to live in that castle over yonder? A palace, that of the gods.

In all this walking, I suddenly catch a glimpse of an angel coming to me as I pass yet another booth that sells food. My mind wanders as I turn from the many aromas in the air to the sight that hits me just as fast as a bullet train. I lose my footage from the tracks. Even my guide can't get my attention for a full minute. I just stare.

She's the most beautiful thing I have ever seen.

Long hair stretches down the middle of her back. Blue eyes shimmer from her face like the deep color of a cloudless sky. She wears a white dress. A unicorn in the form of a person. I jump away from the tracks as my guide speaks.

"She's not for you, Jake."

"Wh-who is she?"

He just smiles and keeps on walking. I continue on as well. I try to forget what I so desperately need to know about the girl whose unicorn form leaves her sea of vision from my heaven. People drift in and out of the crowd but nobody else is like her. My mind wanders to a distant sea of unicorns and imagery far beyond anyone's imagination. I can never forget.

I sigh a deep sigh that lets out in front of my breath. It's a sigh that bears the weight of thousands of men, slaves who endure pain to the billionth degree every night and day. My soul is vanquished without her. I don't even know why I care so much about someone who I know nothing about. Love is mysterious, is it not? My next sigh leave my mouth trembling. My brain also furiously challenges different reasons.

The woman who I caught a glimpse of today, I mean the unicorn, is all I can think of. There could be thousands of women surrounding me but none have what she has. My thoughts traverse time and space. Once submerged into the farthest galaxy, I am no longer me anymore.

I'm tired from so much walking. It's been a long day. I yawn. My mouth makes the *O* so huge I feel like my lips are going to burst and my tongue will be left hanging. Sleep overcomes me. I look around for my guide but he has already left. It's a good thing I have found my way home already.

So I lay me down to rest. And as I wonder about everything, I drift into a sleep that is so undisturbed that even the white mouse with tiny sharp teeth scampering along the floorboards doesn't wake me.

My dreams vary throughout the night. If I were to sleep forever, this night would be kind of like that. If I had died in my sleep, I probably wouldn't have minded so much. Because I would have died happy.

Unbeknownst to me, a dark shadow snatches my lamp—probably during one of my hot hellish dreams where even the fan next to me cannot cool anything. The shadow slips through my room just as silently as a leaf that floats from a tree branch. When I finally awake at the sound of my own consciousness nagging me to start the day, sunlight filters through the kitchen window. I look at myself in the mirror.

Jet black hair, a pointy nose, and a somewhat muscular body stares back at me. My skin peels from the sun. Somehow I remember having problems whenever I stay outside too long. My skin is almost as white as my teeth. Green eyes shimmer from their sockets like pretty emeralds. I put on my street clothes to begin the day. I don't even notice anything amiss.

Once outside, I blink to get accustomed to the bright light. The sun strikes me just as hard. Today isn't as crowded as it was before. As I look around for my guide, or for anyone at all for that matter, I see no one. The only familiar face is that of my camel tied to a post just outside the door.

I decide to leave him there as I figure the possibility of needing him today is pretty slim. Although the castle over yonder doesn't appear to be quite that distant, its immense size is overwhelming. I begin to walk north down the path of Main Street toward the palace. The few people that are up and about walk briskly past me, minding their own business. I mind my own business myself only because I don't exactly know anybody here.

After some time of walking, I see a sign on a door that says: *BREAKFAST HOT COLD ANY TIME OF DAY*. I glance up at the sun and realize that I don't even know what time it is, nor have I any real idea how to tell by the sun. Only by judging from the amount of sleep that I had last night and perhaps from the length of my shadow (or was that someone else's?) do I realize that the time of day is about noonish already. I walk into the restaurant, not even really thinking about money. This time it's my stomach that drives me toward my destination.

I fumble around the pockets of my monk's attire. I hadn't noticed pockets there earlier, perhaps because they're on the inside, or perhaps because I'm wearing my other set of clothes. In any case, I stumble upon a wallet thin and made of leather. I smile to myself as I find some money inside. Whenever travelling it's always a good idea to have money. I'm quite happy to have it with me now, especially in this place.

A short stout man with hair protruding from his chin in a long pointy mess comes up to my table. He asks me if I would like to see a menu.

"Yes, of course. That's why I entered this very establishment in the first place!"

My stomach answers me more than my mouth. Here I am in the middle of the desert with pizza and hamburgers on the menu. This is indeed a magical place! If some creature like the unicorn can live here, then anything is bound to happen.

What is love without magic anyway?

The desserts on the menu also catch my eyes. Desserts in a desert! Who'd have thought? My stomach roars with desire and I have to make a choice. I see all kinds of choices. It's all here. The list just goes on forever.

I order two blueberry pancakes with a tall glass of orange juice. I smile to myself again. In just a few moments the waiter will bring me my juice and I'll be able to quench my ever-so-nagging thirst. As I glance up and scrutinize the details of the restaurant, I notice that there is a bar at the other side of the room opposite where my table is located. Along the same side of my table are various other tables scattered about. None of them seem to be fully occupied. There are a few people at the bar and I glance back as I skim the vodka and tequila bottles. I remember how many times I have been drunk. Where had I ended up before?

My waiter shuffles forward as the orange juice seems to sparkle in the noon sunlit rays through the front window. He then places the juice on my table in front of me on the opposite side of my napkin which holds silverware. I sip the orange juice greedily but carefully as to not drink too much too fast. It swirls in my mouth like a gushing river of water being pulled through a cave bouncing upon walls and spouting up and out inside little crevices. It's possibly the smoothest orange juice I have ever tasted in my entire life.

Just as my stomach growls loudly like a beast snarling at its prey, my waiter has on his tray two overly sized pancakes. The plate seems too small for what I see on it. I commence my eating as fast as a speeding bullet would leave its rifle in a revolutionary war.

After my first few bites, two beaming eyes stare back at me from underneath the table. I stare back with curiosity and amazement. A small tiny mouse beams up at me like a white cotton ball with eyes, pink feet, and a pink tail swaying from its behind. I pause in the middle of my meal. What's it trying to tell me?

Then there is nobody left but me. I look around again and everyone else is gone, even the waiter. Then somehow, I can see the bartender. A ghost in the room. That's when she comes in without any warning at all, and to my utter amazement. White light fills the room, sparkling the walls with glitter as the room turns crystal, and I shield my eyes.

It's too much, although at the same time, I really can't get enough.

When I look up again she's gone. Something rattles in front of me on the floor. It looks vaguely familiar, like something I had bought in an antique store somehow.

When my soul lands will my body ever stop its tingling?

Vampire Coyote
Alex Lonchiadis

They sit uncomfortably close to each other; two children forced to sit on their mother's laps. For the younger child, it is comforting. She would have preferred to sit on her Mami's lap even though they were alone in the back of the van. Despite its ample cargo space, this van is not equipped to transport people, except for the two seats in the cockpit, which are separated by a protective cage.

For the migrants in the cargo area, comfort does not come as easily. For those who still have their coats or sweaters, they serve as seats on the rubber floor mat. But it does little to cushion against the jostling of the van over the desert landscape. Nineteen people seated along the floor of the nondescript, unmarked white cargo van barreling over untouched, desolate desert, all struggle just to maintain an upright, seated position. There is no conversation, no sounds except the shocks of the van and the humming of the young girl. She appears to be enjoying the ride.

Feeling safe in her mother's lap and seeing the world with a child's innocence, her nearly four-year-old mind finds humor in the bouncing of the transport. It's like a ride children beg their parents to take them on at the carnival. With the largest of bumps—when these tired and desperate people collide with each other in the momentary loss of gravity, causing the only conversation among them to be in the form of polite apology—the child laughs with glee. In any other surroundings, far from this dire circumstance they find themselves, a child's laughter would be a welcome and warming sound. Here, in the back of a cargo van being smuggled across the US border under the cover of darkness, it is an eerily somber sound.

Even Cesar, the nine-year-old boy that is quite upset to have to sit in his mother's lap, found it slightly disturbing. While he likely couldn't put it into words, he understood the nature of this journey, and could feel how inappropriate that laughter sounded.

Cesar did his best to hide his fear. *Men do not show fear*, he would tell himself, *men should not be afraid. Boys feel fear. Boys and women, but not men.* But he saw in the faces of the men in this van—those hardened from years of living difficult lives of long, laborious hours at multiple jobs for meager pay—that they felt that same horrible fear when they looked at the Dark Man. Felt it deep within their souls, felt that they may be being driven to hell by *el Diablo* himself.

The Dark Man drove along, indifferent to their thoughts and emotions. He could sense all of their fear, and could hear all of their thoughts as if they were speaking to him directly. But it was too late for them. There is no action they could now take to escape what they so rightly feared.

They were right to be afraid.

Without warning, the van skidded to an abrupt halt on the hardpan desert. The nineteen people in the back lurched forward. *Are we here?* Cesar thought to himself. *Have we made it to America?*

Yes. The Dark Man's voice filled Cesar's mind like thunder over the tin roof of his former home, shaking him. *Stay calm. Your journey is nearly complete.*

The Dark Man was getting out of the driver's seat. Hearing the door close and then the door locks snap, Cesar found the thought of being locked in oddly comforting. Looking around, he saw similar relief in the faces of his fellow travelers, as well. From outside, voices.

"Greetings, Nikolas. You're early."

"Lanius. Greetings to you, as well," Nikolas replied, pointing casually over his shoulder at the van. "This vehicle offered both comfort and adequate handling at higher speeds. I am pleased. We should use this type more often."

"And the cargo?" Lanius inquired with a raised eyebrow.

"Docile now, but their fear of me was amusing during the ride."

"You should be mindful of their numbers, Nikolas. While it is certain that we could track them all down out here if they should sprint for the sake of their lives, it is a far cry easier to keep them calm. And our clients would likely not be pleased with having to wait. Nor would they prefer to select from those in a panicked state." His tone was that of a scolding father or older brother. But they were neither to each other.

The words from Lanius' mouth wiped the cool smile from Nikolas' lips. His face hardened into an angry gaze, betraying the message of his next words. "Yes, my Lord. I see the wisdom in your logic."

Receiving both messages clearly, Lanius flashed a confident smirk. "All is well, then Nikolas." With a pause, his smirk turned to a fiery glare. His ice-blue eyes flashed of bright green lenses like those of a cat. "Prepare our product for market." He spoke now with a sneer, revealing his fangs in glimpses between his words. "Our first customers of the evening approach."

With a shallow bow and sweep of his arm, Nikolas turned toward the van once again. His long coat trailing to his right with the strong wind, his gait of liquid grace carried him swiftly to the rear doors of the van.

Behind him Lanius turned and sniffed at the wind. It was Diana, her scent unmistakable. *And she travels with a new escort, a young companion* Lanius was certain he had not yet made acquaintance. From the east, as the wind shifted, Lanius caught the scent of another old vampire. *Cinnin,* he thought. *It will indeed be a good night.*

Lanius stood tall, facing his customers as they arrived, wrapping his arms behind him and gripping his own wrists. The gusts wrapped his long oilskin coat around him like the membrane of an amoeba, continually moving and altering shape. The heels of his dark leather boots, scuffed and worn, made barely an impression in the hardpan ground.

With the same rush of air, Diana appeared before him with her companion. She stood in black knee-high boots shining with the starlight. Her crimson dress, like blood, cutting across her milky white thighs. A wide black leather belt cinched across her waist, contrasting her shape further with ample cleavage when the wind did not let her long, blonde hair rest across her chest. Her appearance was familiar to Lanius, but no less striking. That was, after all, the same manner in which she was dressed when the two of them had last shared a happy moment. When they last feasted together before parting.

Her companion was slight, and dressed in all black without

a coat. He appeared to be a stick figure against Lanius. He was shorter than Diana, standing in a slight hunch behind her. The position of a submissive servant. Her current plaything.

"Greetings, Diana," Lanius said, welcoming her, without so much as a glance toward her pet. "I see you have a new toy."

She opened her mouth to retort Lanius' statement, but another rush of wind blew as Cinnin appeared before them. A large vampire of brutish appearance, Cinnin still clung to the garments of old; a chainmail vest under the crude hide that served as an overcoat, his long hair splayed across his square chin and cheeks.

"Greetings, Diana!" he smiled broadly. "I thought that I sensed beauty in the area. It seemed so great as to surely be that of two women. I should have known it to be only you," he said with a wink.

"Greetings to you, Cinnin," Lanius interrupted. "Perhaps you sensed Diana's companion alongside her. I nearly confused him for a woman myself." His condescension was without a trace of veil as he stared down the stranger.

Upon hearing the insult, Julian sprang forward to attack. His reaction was so swift, Diana was unable to catch his arm as he passed her, and she could only watch as Julian took the bait. Diana knew he was lost already. Covering the ground between them in a blink of the eye, Julian attacked Lanius head on. Without moving but his right arm, Lanius caught Julian's neck and held him up for a moment to observe the snarling, salivating, and stupid vampire.

"You are a pathetic idiot not worthy of being a vampire. I doubt that you were worthy of being a man before Diana foolishly turned you. Be there any rhyme or reason to your next incarnation, you shall live as a brain-damaged sewer rat."

Lanius squeezed his hand into a fist. Julian's neck squished between his fingers like mashed potatoes through the tines of a fork. Julian's body fell from Lanius' grip, turning to ash in the air, and swept clean away by a new gust of wind.

Absently wiping his hand against his side, Lanius looked at Diana. "I question why you would turn such a man and why you would continue to keep his company. I fear your judgment slips, Diana."

"That is not for you to decide, Lanius," Diana hissed with restrained frustration. "You chose to leave. Your authority over those with whom I choose to spend my time vaporized the moment the door closed behind you when you left me crying for your comfort." Her voice wavered with a mixture of rage and hurt. Her eyes showing pain but her snarling lips and exposed fangs represented her extraordinary anger.

As Diana stood with fists clenched and trembling lips, Lanius stood stoic. "It matters not. It is done and cannot be undone. A creature such as he gives us all a bad name. This world is a better place without him," he said with a dismissive arrogance and then, without pausing to await reply, "ah, here is Nikolas with the evening menu. Perhaps you could find a more suitable companion, Diana? It is ill advised to be traveling without escort. What if a brute such as Cinnin were to happen upon you?"

With that, Cinnin laughed uproariously as only a brute can. Filling the night air with his deep laughter as Diana stood glaring at Lanius with hurt, hate, and love streaming from her eyes. And Lanius, studying Diana's face, showed no regret for either his actions or his words.

"Let's see what we have here!" bellowed Cinnin through his laughter. "Ah, this female looks like a fine specimen." He sniffed the air in the direction of an attractive Mexican woman standing in line with her fellow migrants—those seeking the opportunities and promise of America. "Yes, she is healthy. And strong."

Walking down the line of the nineteen humans on display, Cinnin looked sharply at Lanius. "I'll take her. And the largest male."

"I see you have not let any manners find their way into your life, Cinnin. I believe etiquette forces us to allow the lady first choice," he said with an eloquence designed for radio as he made an over pronounced sweeping bow toward Diana. "Please, my lady. For you only, a special tonight. Any male of your choice, at no charge, with any purchase."

Diana, unable to look at Lanius through her rage and embarrassment, managed to steady her voice. "The female Cinnin spoke of, and the male child."

"Of course," Lanius chided, "you do not have to choose the child simply to deprive me of the second highest priced item in my inventory. If you prefer a larger male, you may choose one and get the male child for free."

"I've made my choice. Standard rate for the adult female. The male child at no charge. Nikolas has my information. I will take my goods, and my leave, with your permission. As you said, it is unwise for me to travel without an adequate escort. I should like to return home with haste."

"I thought that this was first come, first served!" Cinnin's booming voice seemed to shake the very ground. "I'll not stand idly by Lanius. I chose that female."

Before the dust rose from the desert floor where his feet carried him, Lanius covered the several yards between himself and Cinnin and had his throat in his hand.

"You will do exactly that, Cinnin!" Lanius, now holding Cinnin's face just inches from his own and glaring into his eyes, raised his voice in anger. "And if you interrupt my discussion again, old friend or not, you shall share the same wind as Diana's former pet."

In an instant, Cinnin's face showed his immense fear and then unquestioning desire to comply. Upon Lanius releasing him, Cinnin quietly rubbed his neck as he slunk away to stand next to Nikolas.

Lanius, pausing just a moment to regain his composure, turned back toward Diana with a smile. "I should be most delighted to escort you myself, Diana, if you would be so patient as to await the completion of my tasks here. Certainly you could not find a more suitable escort than I, and particularly on such short notice."

"I am most flattered, my Lord, but must respectfully decline. I have pressing personal matters to attend to, and my schedule hasn't an allowance for patience this evening. Please accept my most humble apologies and grant me leave?"

Lanius stood silently, studying Diana's face. His own smile fading slowly as he waited for Diana to reconsider and accept his offer. His smile melted into the pressed lips of restrained anger, appearing no more than a scar below his nose.

"Perhaps you misunderstood, Diana. I have offered to be your personal escort for the remainder of this most pleasant evening. Provided it can remain pleasant."

His voice turned rough at the last of his reply, intending for the words to be a warning to Diana, Cinnin, Nikolas, and the other vampire customers cautiously approaching. The latter approached with the manner of any human heading to market, list in hand, and mind on matters beyond this errand.

But sensing the drama as they neared, now milled about observing a short distance away.

"I heard and understood you, Lanius. I am most grateful at your generous offer. However, as you stated yourself, it is unwise for me to travel without escort, and as I have stated, my schedule does not allow me adequate time to await the completion of your tasks here. If you will grant me leave, I will return to the safety of my home with great haste."

"Be gone then, woman," Lanius rebutted gruffly. "I haven't the forbearance for such as you tonight. I only offered because it was polite, considering that you had lost your previous escort by my hand. Your leave is granted, use it while you have it." He turned abruptly away from her and bellowed, "Nikolas! Gather the fools who wait idly a short distance from here, and tell them that if they wish to make a purchase, they should do so quickly. Go now, you useless dog. Before I treat you as such."

As Lanius addressed Nikolas, Diana took her two humans by their arms—Cesar and Abelina— who were still affected by the influence of Nikolas and Lanius. Diana swept away their commands from the minds of her humans, replacing them with her own influence, and speaking softly into their minds. Her intent to be comforting, but the solemnity of her voice was unmistakable. Come with me, she comforted them. Your joys in the freedom of America shall begin with me.

Are you sad, my Lady? The reply entered Diana's mind and she stopped as if being slapped. It was the boy. The boy had asked that question in her mind. It was the boy.

She glanced at Lanius, now cursing Nikolas, and knew he must not have sensed it in the boy. Shh ... she thought in the child's mind. If you wish to live another moment, clear your mind and do not try to communicate with anyone. If he senses you, we shall all die here by his hand.

She was holding the boy's chin between her thumb and forefinger, looking in his eyes. She saw his understanding. She cringed when he made the most imperceptible nod, thinking it would be noticed by the other vampires. Lanius was too angry, and too agitated to see. She gripped them each by their arms and with a rush of air, they were gone.

The lesser vampires now approaching, inspecting the remaining migrants, were wary of Lanius. Cinnin, shouldering his way past the others to show his own limited dominance, selected a male and female. Gripping them by their arms, he nodded at Nikolas and was gone with a rush of wind. The others quickly did the same.

Lanius recognized a woman vampire that selected the small female child. He also noticed that was her only selection. As he wondered silently why she did not pick an adult as well, a sudden realization came to him. A frightening truth filled his mind with imminent importance. He cursed himself a million times over for allowing his petty feelings for Diana mask his detection of such an imperative specimen. The child was descendant of a Carpathian—his bloodline was nearly extinct, and once fully grown, he would have the capacity to remove Lanius from his entitled position. Diana chose him and then was in a great rush to remove him from Lanius' presence. She knew what the child really was.

Lanius took to the sky with violent abandon. With the strike of his hands, he destroyed the lesser vampires and their purchases in rapid succession. Most had no chance to begin raising their defenses. Lanius radiated out from his position, leaving naught but ashes and the puddles of bloody gore that had been humans a moment ago in his wake. He destroyed them all, slaying them one by one.

Lanius caught Cinnin and his two humans in mid-flight. Seizing him by the scruff of his neck like a schoolteacher snatching a truant child, Lanius pulled Cinnin to the earth by one hand, and slew the two humans with the other.

Landing next to the puddles of human flesh, Cinnin stopped with shock. He had never been surprised by an adversary in all his hundreds of years. Superb senses had abound in him even before being turned. And now, before he had known there was someone near him, Lanius had seized him, slaughtered his new livestock, and was already screaming orders at him.

Cinnin struggled to gather his bearings in the whirlwind of activity that had all happened in a fraction of a moment. As his mind caught up, he began to make sense of the commands that Lanius was screaming.

"Cinnin, find Diana and bring her and the boy to me! If you do so, I will provide you with five females and five males upon delivery. If you do it not, I will pull you apart with my bare hands, so as to prolong the pain of your death for as long as it amuses me!"

Cinnin could not produce even one word from his clenched throat. He simply nodded and was gone, wanting to be away from Lanius before he decided to kill him to appease his rage.

Lanius stood in the desert. Alone now and far away from where Nikolas had left the blood spattered van, abandoning the site for the scavengers of the desert to clean.

He closed his eyes and stretched his arms out to his sides, concentrating and searching to find any trace of Diana or the child. Was he too late? Had Diana had time to sufficiently cover her tracks? If he could not find them, surely Cinnin would not either.

He decided that Diana would be too smart to just go home. He would start with the friends of hers that he knew, and see if she has hidden the boy with one of them.

— • • —

Diana sped across the desert with purpose. She must put as much distance as she can between her and Lanius before he senses the child, and follows. As she ran with the two humans in tow, she comforted them. *I will not harm you. Be still and do not try to talk with me until we are at a safe distance.* These words filled Cesar's mind and he felt at ease.

Diana arrived with her two passengers at Angela's house; a human whom she had befriended some time ago. Angela, a rich widow, was the beneficiary to the millions of dollars her late-husband had made in oil speculation.

Knowing that it was very late, Diana awoke Angela by knocking on her bedroom window. Angela signaled for her to go to the front door.

"Diana? For Christ's sake what are you doing here at this hour? And who are they?" Angela said sleepily, gesturing toward the woman and boy.

"I have a favor to ask of you. Do you still own that cabin in Maine way out in the woods?" Diana hurried Cesar and Abelina into the house.

"Why, yes," Angela replied, "but what could be so urgent about a vacation spot that you need to wake me?"

Diana sighed. "It is far too much to explain now. I must ask that you trust me for the moment and do as I ask. I assure you that when there is time, I will tell all you want to know. For now, all you need to know is that this boy, Cesar, is in grave danger and it is very important that he stays alive. I need you to take him to your cabin and stay there until I contact you. Can you do that for me?"

Angela was bewildered. Although she was uneasy about the request, she did trust Diana, and she agreed.

"You must leave immediately. Every moment that passes is a moment closer to his demise," Diana ordered.

"I have to call for the jet, and pack some things."

"Very well," Diana said with obvious frustration. "But do it as quickly as you can, and do not use your credit cards. Only cash. File your flight plan to a different city and change it mid-flight. Do not rent a car or use your ID anywhere. Nothing that can be traced."

Diana turned to Cesar and spoke. "If you do as I say, you will live. Go with this woman and stay at her cabin. I will contact you when it is safe. Until then, do not leave any trace of where you are going."

Cesar slowly nodded. He could sense the urgency in Diana's mind and knew that it was genuine fear.

Diana turned back to Angela. "Good luck. I hope to see you soon."

With that, Diana took Abelina by the arm and was gone.

Angela, trusting Diana's sense of urgency, snapped into action. She called her pilot from her landline and told him that he must ready the jet as soon as possible, and to register a flight plan for Charleston, South Carolina. The pilot, in a sleepy voice, said that he understood and was about to ask what was so urgent, but Angela hung up as he opened his mouth.

She turned to Cesar. "Have you eaten anything?"

Cesar calmly replied, "I am not hungry, but I have to go to the bathroom."

"Hurry," she said, "down the hall on the left."

She frantically threw clothes and toiletries into a suitcase and then, in the back of her closet, the most important thing. She pulled up the carpet in the back corner and there was a floor safe. She dialed the combination and it didn't open. She jerked the handle a few times and then, realizing the problem, she took a second to calm herself. She spun the dial a few times to clear the lock and then slowly entered the combination. This time the handle clicked.

My just-in-case money, she thought, gathering the stacks of bills. She tossed most of the cash into the suitcase and slid a small stack into her purse. She threw her purse on her shoulder, grabbed the handle of the suitcase, and headed downstairs.

"Are you ready?" Angela asked, trying not to sound as panicky as she felt.

Cesar calmly smiled and said, "Let's go."

The airport was nearly empty at this hour with only a few lonely business travelers stuck in a layover. She took her bags and Cesar through the private security screening, and was on the tarmac soon enough. She thought that they were doing well for time.

"We're nearly ready to depart, Mrs. Patrick," the pilot greeted her. "Who is your friend?"

"This is Cesar, Tom. Glad to see you were able to get here on such short notice."

"What's the big hurry, ma'am?"

"It's a long story, Tom. Let's leave it for another day. Shall we take off soon?"

Tom, sensing the secrecy in his passenger's voice and posture, decided it was best not to pry.

END